The man in g

from the table next to the one recently vacated by the two women. This had to be his contact. The man had watched Kurt on the sly since he arrived at the restaurant. Moreover, the guy matched the description right down to the red pocket square in his suit breast pocket and the thin, pale scar running along his left jawline. Making a quick decision, Kurt pushed his chair back and tossed some cash on the table.

"It's been interesting guys, but I'm calling it a night. Use this to cover my tab."

"What's the rush, Heinz? We haven't even ordered dinner."

"I guess my sins are catching up with me. It's return to quarters and bed for me."

"You headed back with us on the return flight tomorrow?"

"Nope, I'm here with the Old Man for the duration. You boys have a good trip."

The street was nearly deserted when Kurt stepped out onto its glistening concrete surface. Misty rain created halos around the sparse street lamps and obscured most objects more than a few feet distant. Only the two women, Sarah and Agnes, stood under an umbrella waiting for a taxi. Kurt watched them from the restaurant's portico. Focused on their conversation, they seemed oblivious to anyone behind them.

Glancing to his right, Kurt saw his man in gray scurrying toward the cross street. He stepped onto the sidewalk and crept along a good twenty paces behind. When his quarry slowed at the corner and looked back over his shoulder, Kurt stepped into the shadow of a doorway behind the taxi stand and waited.

Praise for Linda Bennett Pennell

Casablanca: Appointment at Dawn

by

Linda Bennett Pennell

This is a work of fiction. Names, characters, places, and incidents are either the product of the author's imagination or are used fictitiously, and any resemblance to actual persons living or dead, business establishments, events, or locales, is entirely coincidental.

Casablanca: Appointment at Dawn

COPYRIGHT © 2015 by Linda Bennett Pennell

Cover Art by *Tina Lynn Stout*

The Wild Rose Press, Inc.
PO Box 708
Adams Basin, NY 14410-0708
Visit us at www.thewildrosepress.com

Publishing History
First Vintage Rose Edition, 2015
Print ISBN 978-1-5092-0279-9
Digital ISBN 978-1-5092-0280-5

Published in the United States of America

Dedications

To my sweet husband John,
our much-loved sons Jake and Frank,
my extended family,
my critique partner Ronelda,
and my wonderful friends.
Your faith in me and support mean more than words
can adequately express.

Chapter 1

Casablanca
December 31, 1942

The muscles at the base of Sarah's skull knotted a little tighter as the wave of baritone noise washed over her. What a big ole snafu tonight turned out to be. This little sally into nighttime Casablanca went sour shortly after they walked into the place. Several minutes of watching couples dance cheek-to-cheek and Agnes's insistence on picking up the threads of a social life began to stink. *Therapeutic necessity she said. Therapy, my foot. More like ripping the bandage off a wound.*

Raucous laughter poured into the room from just outside the entry, sending a stab of pain through Sarah. Wincing, she closed her eyes and let out a low sigh. Why did these guys always have to be so blasted loud?

Sarah didn't recognize the voices, but knew what she would see when her eyes opened again. She massaged her temples while slowly lifting her lids, then cut her gaze toward the restaurant's arched entrance. From beneath her lashes, she counted four pairs of Army Air Corps issue russet brogues paused on the threshold. A moment's fidgety hesitation spent rocking back on their heels and the standard restaurant noise of conversation and dinner service clatter softened. If she cared to look around the room, all eyes would probably

1

be focused on the figures in the doorway. Another beat surveying their domain, then all of the air in the room suddenly got sucked up. They simply filled all the space wherever they happened to be.

It *never* failed.

As much as she willed herself not to, she couldn't quite tear her eyes away from the quartet being led toward the last empty table. No matter the clothes, you could spot one of these guys at a distance simply by the way he moved—a sort of rolling amble informing the world it could wait for him no matter the inconvenience. After giving each face a quick once over, she turned her head toward the window. Never again, never again, never again played in her mind like the sounds of a scratched 78. So why, against all common sense, did she hope Bill might come waltzing back into her life? Sarah caught her lower lip between her teeth and fought back the catch in her throat.

It was idiotic, really.

Feeling a hand on her arm, Sarah glanced at her dinner companion. The furrows between Agnes's brows were deeper than usual. "Sweet girl, they aren't anything special. Just four more pilots."

Sarah shrugged. "I know it's stupid, but I can't help it. I keep hoping he'll just walk into a room one night."

"And then what? He said he couldn't handle entanglements, and I think he's pretty well proven it."

"Maybe." Sarah hated the edge in her voice, but couldn't stop it. "Or maybe he's flying so many missions he doesn't have time to write. He could have been shot down and be a POW. We don't really know for sure, do we?"

"My darling girl, listen to yourself. You're making excuses for a man who two-timed you while he was here and then left Casablanca with nary a word. He isn't worth your spit. Getting miffed with me isn't going to change that."

Sarah's bubble of irritation deflated as though pricked by a pin. "Please forgive me. I'm really angry with myself, not you. Like I said, it's stupid." Fatigue settled over Sarah like a smothery mantle. She massaged the bridge of her nose between her eyes. "I guess I'm more tired than usual."

"Uh huh." Agnes raised an eyebrow. "So, how many double shifts at the hospital do you think you can pull before you drop? Even Florence Nightingale and Sarah Barton occasionally took a load off and put their feet up."

Sarah shrugged. "When I'm with the patients, I don't have time to think about myself."

"And the times I see you in the ward when you're supposed to be off duty?"

"Some of my guys are just kids straight out of high school. They're scared and terribly homesick. It helps when someone reads to them or writes their letters. Besides, we're short-handed."

"I'll admit we could use another nurse or three, but it'll only make things worse if you work yourself to death. If you won't slow down for yourself," Agnes cocked her head to one side and tapped her chest, then continued, "at least have a heart and think of me, your long-suffering supervisor. I need you upright and healthy. Got it?"

Sarah placed three fingers against her temple in a Girl Scout salute. "Gotcha, Boss."

Agnes's head snapped down and back up in one swift nod. "Good. I'm going to the Ladies'. Don't let that officious waiter grab my drink away while I'm gone."

Agnes's brand of humor was a fresh breeze in an airless room. Sarah smiled as she watched her friend, colleague, and mentor maneuver across the crowded restaurant. Always polite, but ever in charge, Agnes made it to the other side in record time with only one or two angry looks directed her way.

Sarah poked at the remnants of her couscous with an index finger and silently cursed the soft pounding beneath her temples. Why had she allowed Agnes to talk her into coming out tonight? Memories echoed from every cracked tile in the floor mosaic and each tarnished brass lamp hanging from the domed ceiling. Sarah took a bite of the tan glob, then pushed her plate aside. It still tasted like sawdust. No doubt the management had refused to pay the black market price for decent spices. Or maybe the flavor had simply gotten lost somewhere in the blue haze of cigarette smoke hovering over the whole place.

The clattering of metal on the stone floor near Sarah's feet broke into her thoughts and made her jump. She bent to retrieve the object and nearly bumped heads with the diner at the next table. A small man in gray flannel muttered something Sarah didn't quite catch as he grabbed his spoon from the floor. His eyes met hers and grew rounder like he was startled or nervous about drawing attention to himself. He jerked upright, his back rigid against his chair, his eyes darting left then back at Sarah. She smiled sympathetically, but the little man frowned and broke eye contact.

Odd little fellow. As gray as his suit.

A red silk square in his breast pocket provided the only relief in his otherwise monochromatic appearance. Amused, Sarah couldn't stop watching. With a trembling hand, the man in gray reached for the teacup before him. He drained it in one swallow, then lifted the teapot. It clattered against the rim as he refilled the cup. After sloshing tea onto the white table linen, the little man folded his hands in his lap where he began rolling and unrolling the cloth's hem, each time pulling the teapot a little closer to the edge of the table. If he kept it up, he would soon be wearing his tea.

He must have felt Sarah's eyes on him, for he suddenly shot her a disgruntled look. Heat rose in her face as she turned away. The little guy seemed wound up as tightly as a two-dollar wrist watch. This place was a strange choice for someone so clearly uncomfortable in the setting.

Agnes, having made the return trip across the restaurant with her usual efficiency, strolled to her seat and pointed toward the back of the room. "Hey, there's the band." Dragging her chair out, she plopped down. "They're pretty good. Don't you think?"

Sarah wrinkled her nose. "Mmm. That's a bit of a stretch."

"Okay." A crooked smile spread across Agnes's face. "Good enough."

Sarah couldn't suppress a smile. "If you don't mind your jazz played at a dirge tempo."

Agnes hunched her shoulders. "I give. I admit it. They're pretty terrible, but at least they play a lot of American music." Agnes's wink made Sarah chuckle. Irrepressible Agnes. Sarah didn't know what she would do without her.

A five-piece combo trooped onto a little dais and began arranging chairs and music stands, white dinner jackets contrasting sharply with brown faces. Amazing. This city in a Muslim country had nightlife, but then Casablanca always did seem to bend with the prevailing winds. The band probably played a lot of German music two months ago and years of French tunes before that. The restaurant and nightclub owners hardly missed a beat before reopening after the Allies' November invasion took control of the city from the Nazis' Vichy lapdogs.

The opening strains of a sedate "Don't Sit Under the Apple Tree" floated across the cavernous room enticing several couples out onto the dance floor. Lost in the melody, Sarah watched the figures turning round and round. What a joke. It had been Bill's and her song. Maybe it was his song with all of his girls.

A throat cleared behind Sarah's chair, causing her to flinch and turn to see who loomed so near. Ready to glare at the intruder, she looked up into blue eyes so clear she had to stifle a gasp. They were deep set in an oddly attractive face, not exactly handsome, but rugged and appealing in an earthy sort of way. Full lips and fair hair completed the picture. He stepped forward and smiled down at her in a manner that might have been shy except for the automatic air of authority conveyed by his captain's uniform.

"Miss, would you do me the honor of this dance?" His voice flowed in the cadence of the South, but not Sarah's beloved Virginia.

"No. Thank you, but no. I can't."

He smiled beguilingly. "Surely a pretty girl like

you knows how to dance."

"I really can't." Sarah inwardly winced at the sharpness of her tone.

"Ah, can but won't. Too bad."

Sarah could feel heat rising in her face. "I'm not in the habit of dancing with impertinent strangers."

A chill replaced the smile in his eyes. "Forgive me. I meant no offense." He turned to Agnes, smiling once more. "Ma'am, would you care to take a turn? I've been told I'm rather light on my feet."

"Don't mind if I do as long as you mind your manners, young man."

"Of course. Otherwise, my mama would come all the way from Texas and turn me over her knee."

Sarah's foot tapped impatiently beneath the table. Surely no one had ever drawled that slowly—not even irksome cowboys from God-forsaken Texas. Affectation coupled with flyboy arrogance. What a surprise.

Agnes fixed the stranger with a look that only a head nurse can deliver. "Perhaps your mother should book her passage now. Or did she neglect teaching the importance of introductions?"

His face flushed as he chuckled. Bowing slightly from the waist, he added, "It's Heinz. Captain Kurt Heinz at your service."

"Agnes Johnson. And the non-dancer here is Sarah Barrett. Shall we?"

Sarah watched Agnes and the captain move onto the dance floor. True to his word, he maneuvered around the parquet square with grace and fluidity, but every few turns, he grinned at Sarah and whispered in Agnes's ear. Agnes then laughed and whispered back.

After the third of these little episodes, Sarah refused to look at them any longer. They could enjoy their foolishness without having her for an audience.

Sarah's gaze drifted back to the strange little man at the next table. She couldn't keep herself from observing him. He sat all alone in a crowded restaurant, not inviting company with either gesture or smile, while his gaze darted over the room. Intrigued, Sarah watched his wandering eye settle onto the dancers, head swiveling to follow them. When Captain Heinz met his gaze and nodded, the little man's head snapped around and he focused on the tea. Below the table, the white linen cloth's hem jiggled violently. Her neighbor's left foot bounced on its toes. Up and down. Up and down in rapid succession. The words "ticking time bomb" wandered through Sarah's mind sending a shiver crawling down her spine.

Good grief! All the talk and rumors about Casablanca were getting under her skin, giving her the willies. Add to that, weird people in a place she hated. It was putting her imagination into overdrive. That did it. This was positively the last time she would come here.

She and Agnes had been denied entry to their usual haunt, the bar at the Anfa Hotel, and the other decent watering holes had been standing room only. Even this, their choice of last resort, was more crowded than usual. The atmosphere in the city was positively electric. Casablanca twitched in anticipation, of what, no one was exactly sure. The incoming traffic out at the American Army Air Corps base had rumors flying. Men, chests beribboned with fruit salad and shoulder boards filled with stars, had been arriving all week accompanied by staff—lots of staff.

Agnes whirled into her seat, laughing and fanning herself. "Captain Heinz, you dance divinely as promised."

"The right partner makes all the difference. Thank you for saying yes."

"Anytime, soldier." Agnes grinned at Sarah, cocked her head, and waggled her eyebrows.

The captain, slouching hipshot with hands in pockets, lingered by their table. "May I buy you ladies a drink?"

Agnes's lips parted, but instead of speaking, her eyes widened and her mouth formed a small "o".

"It's been lovely meeting you, Captain," Sarah interjected, "but our next shift starts soon. We've got to go."

"Oh. That's too bad. Well…." The captain's face fell, then he looked at his watch and his expression brightened. "It's really early still. Won't you stay a little longer? I hate drinking alone."

"I believe you're here with friends, so you'll be just fine. Happy New Year and good night, Captain." Sarah cut her eyes at Agnes. "You coming?"

Sarah didn't wait for an answer.

At the dining room entrance, Agnes hissed, "Wait up. For crying out loud, what were you trying to do under the table? Break my ankle?"

Sarah stopped and glanced back to find Agnes massaging her foot, her shoe on the floor.

"I'm sorry. I didn't mean to kick you so hard. I just couldn't stand being with that pilot another minute."

"Hmm. So I saw. But you're slipping, my girl."

Sarah raised an eyebrow. "Really?"

"Yeah, really. He's not a pilot. No gold wings. How did you miss that?"

"Because I wasn't looking. I'm not interested." Sarah struggled into her overcoat. "So what does he do?"

"Not sure exactly. He was rather vague about being on some brass's staff, but he seemed like a nice guy. Don't know why you had to be so mean to him."

"I was not mean," Sarah snapped.

Agnes's brows arched. Tilting her head a little to the right, a small smile played across her lips before she responded, "Yes you were, Sweet Pea. All he wanted was a dance with a pretty girl and you practically threw your drink in his face."

Sarah studied Agnes's features for signs of teasing. There were none. "Was I really that bad?"

"Uh huh."

"Terribly rude?"

"You were."

Sarah sighed. "I guess I took my bad mood out on the poor guy. I shouldn't have come tonight."

"You had to get it over with sometime. You can't avoid every place you went with Bill."

"Yeah, but the memories here made me a grump. I'm sorry if I embarrassed you."

"You didn't, and it's not me I'm worried about. If you keep shoving guys away because of one bastard, you'll end up an old maid."

"Must you always sing the same old song?" Sarah snapped, but guilt quickly replaced irritation. Voice contrite, she continued, "Gosh, I'm sorry. That was a nasty thing to say. This place brings out the worst in me. First, I was rude to the captain, and now I've bitten your head off."

Agnes's brow rose as she shrugged. "Me? I can handle it, but you should have been nicer to Captain Heinz."

"Yeah, you're right as usual, but it really doesn't matter. We'll never see him again."

Agnes grinned. "That'll be too bad because he's a great dancer, and I liked him. Leaving at 7:30 for an 11:00 shift is a waste of good free time, and God knows we get little enough of that."

"Stay if you want. I don't want to keep you from having fun."

"And let you wander alone in the wilds of Casablanca? Not on your life. Besides, he's too young for me. Of course, he's just about right for you." Mischief lit Agnes's eyes as she took Sarah's arm to steady herself while she eased her foot back into its shoe.

Agnes was senior in both rank and age, but Sarah had found in her the sister she had always longed for. They never argued, and Sarah usually took the maternal goading with good grace, but not tonight. Her fingernails curled into the palms of her hands and pressed down, a physical reminder to keep her irritation to herself.

Distracted, Sarah brushed too near an attractive couple just entering the dining room. She sidestepped quickly to avoid crashing headlong into the man, who looked down his nose at her in unconcealed disdain. The elegantly dressed woman at his side cast a cool glance over Sarah, who began, "*Pardon moi. Je—*"

Before she could finish, the woman pushed Sarah aside, and the couple strolled away as though Sarah and

Agnes were beneath their notice. Sarah's upper lip curled, then she thought better of it. Nearly running them down gave the couple a right to be abrupt.

Feeling a prickling along the nape of her neck, Sarah glanced back into the dining room where a pair of blue eyes met hers with unblinking interest. Heat crawled up her throat, filling Sarah's face. When Captain Heinz winked, she frowned, turned on her heel, and marched into the night.

Chapter 2

Kurt watched in dismay as the man in gray picked up his fedora and rose from the table next to the one recently vacated by the two women. This had to be his contact. The man had watched Kurt on the sly since he arrived at the restaurant. Moreover, the guy matched the description right down to the red pocket square in his suit breast pocket and the thin, pale scar running along his left jawline. Making a quick decision, Kurt pushed his chair back and tossed some cash on the table.

"It's been interesting guys, but I'm calling it a night. Use this to cover my tab."

"What's the rush, Heinz? We haven't even ordered dinner."

"I guess my sins are catching up with me. It's return to quarters and bed for me."

"You headed back with us on the return flight tomorrow?"

"Nope, I'm here with the Old Man for the duration. You boys have a good trip."

The street was nearly deserted when Kurt stepped out onto its glistening concrete surface. Misty rain created halos around the sparse street lamps and obscured most objects more than a few feet distant. Only the two women, Sarah and Agnes, stood under an umbrella waiting for a taxi. Kurt watched them from the restaurant's portico. Focused on their conversation, they seemed oblivious to anyone behind them.

Glancing to his right, Kurt saw his man in gray scurrying toward the cross street. He stepped onto the sidewalk and crept along a good twenty paces behind. When his quarry slowed at the corner and looked back over his shoulder, Kurt stepped into the shadow of a doorway behind the taxi stand and waited. If this guy didn't want to make contact, he wouldn't appreciate being followed.

Kurt couldn't make out what the women talked about, but by their gestures, it had to be man trouble. Agnes patted the girl's arm while Sarah, the non-dancer, dabbed at her eyes with a handkerchief. She was pretty enough to attract any man—long auburn hair, kelly green eyes, cute little butt—so what could she be upset about? Women. Drama seemed to be their stock and trade, and that was something he had no time for now or in the near future. Certainly not until this war was over.

The echo of retreating footsteps commanded his attention. Glancing a last time at the women, Kurt slipped out onto the sidewalk again and down to the corner. The man in gray had disappeared. There was only one way in which the guy could have gone. Kurt peered down the side street. Nothing. His contact was supposed to meet him at the restaurant tonight, but the man Kurt was tailing hadn't made a move to connect. Still, he matched the description perfectly. If the girl hadn't bolted, her friend would have asked Kurt to sit with them, and he would've been elbow to elbow with the fella. Something must have spooked the man in gray because he practically fled the restaurant in the women's wake. Perhaps the pair of Vichy rats who entered the dining room just as the nurses were leaving sent his man scampering into the night. Whatever it was, something had certainly panicked him.

Drizzle sent clammy fingers down Kurt's neck. As he turned into the side street, he flipped up the collar of his uniform jacket and strained for a glimpse of his man. No street lamps relieved the gloom, but Kurt heard scurrying footsteps. The sound suddenly became muffled, as though the man had gone behind a building. There must be another cross street or maybe an alley farther along. Kurt picked up speed. The sound of the man's movements became louder as Kurt came abreast a narrow alley running behind the restaurant. He turned in and increased his speed again.

No light penetrated the alley from the restaurant or the modest apartment buildings on the opposite side. As Kurt picked his way along the dirty cobblestones, visibility dropped. Footsteps, increasing in speed, echoed farther along. The man might be running from him, or maybe he was just some stranger with no purpose other than getting home before curfew. Perhaps Kurt had been mistaken. Maybe his true contact simply failed to show and he was pursuing some innocent soul, scaring the hell out of him in the process. At one point, the figure fleeing down the narrow passage seemed to slow and look back over his shoulder, but the mist prevented a clear view. The scurrying footsteps picked up speed again, and Kurt did the same. Objects suddenly appeared in the path, forcing him to jump them or risk stumbling and falling flat on his face.

He leapt over a pile of baskets strewn across the path. Landing with a thud that put him slightly off balance, Kurt scrambled for footing and pushed forward with greater effort. He was getting close despite the now almost impenetrable gloom. He could actually hear the man gasping. A moment more and Kurt would be on top of him. What happened after that would depend solely on the other man. Kurt slid a hand onto his sidearm holster and undid the flap.

Without warning, the quality of the man's movement changed and then the alley fell silent. A solid wall loomed out of the dark. Kurt found himself at the end of the passage with no sign of his quarry. Kurt gazed up at the eaves of rooflines three stories above his head. No stairs, no ladders, nothing that would help a man go up top. No doors or windows through which he might pass. A complete dead end. It was as though the man had sprouted wings and flown away.

A shower of gravel hit the alley's cobbles in the corner on Kurt's left. Letting his gaze follow the sound upward, he could just make out a slight hump on the roofline. The clatter of wood striking masonry propelled Kurt into the corner where he leapt at a rope ladder rising just out of reach. The shadowy hump on the roofline rose and pulled out of sight. Stealthy footsteps pattered on roof tiles, muffled by rain that had begun in earnest. Kurt strained to see through the gloom long after any sounds disappeared.

Hellfire and damnation. If the man in gray was his contact, weeks of delicate work might be down the tubes. He would catch hell if they had to start over in building an intelligence network here in Casablanca. But standing in the rain staring at an empty roofline wasn't going to make his situation any better. Kurt retraced his path back to the street and hailed a taxi.

"Anfa Hotel. Drop me by the military checkpoint."

The driver nodded and moved out onto the deserted street. From the backseat, Kurt watched the cityscape change from the Moorish architecture of the Medina, the old city, to the modern outskirts. The contrast between the old section and the new was so marked as to make a man feel like he was time traveling by merely taking a drive. Napoleon had taught the French how to build wide boulevards and grand public buildings. The lessons extended far into their colonial ventures and certainly had not been lost on Casablanca.

When they reached the razor wire protected compound that the Anfa had recently become, Kurt paid the driver, gained admission to the grounds, and hiked toward the front entrance. Light poured into the night from all four of the hotel's floors, including the glass enclosed top floor restaurant and observation deck. The white Art Deco edifice looked down on lush grounds of tropical plantings. Regal palms and flowering shrubs dotted a wide expanse of lawn. The building's rounded ends, narrow width, top floor observation decks, and solid balcony railings gave it the appearance of a ship floating on an ocean of vegetation. Kurt showed his identification to the guards manning the front entrance and strode into the lobby bar. Surveying the interior crowded with American and British uniforms, he spotted the face he sought in a far corner, back to the wall.

"Sit, old boy, by all means do. No need to stand on ceremony." Lieutenant Commander Jeremy Maitland, British Naval Intelligence, eyed Kurt while waving vaguely in the direction of a vacant chair. Kurt slid the chair around beside the Brit so he, too, could watch the traffic coming and going from the bar.

"My goodness, do you not own an umbrella?" the commander asked as he brushed water droplets from the sleeve of his impeccably tailored uniform.

"I didn't realize I needed permission to avoid the rain—only to follow phantoms through the back alleys of Casablanca."

"I take it our man didn't show?"

"Take it however you want. I chased a guy matching the description. If he's working for us, he sure has a funny way of showing it."

"Oh, dear." Maitland drummed the table with the fingers of one hand, a thoughtful expression furrowing his brow. "Something frighten him?"

"Looked like it."

Maitland tilted his head to cut his eyes at Kurt. "Any ideas as to what?"

"Maybe there were too many Vichy rats in the place. The Ahmeds strolled in just before our man bolted."

"Jalal and Laila Ahmed. Unfortunate, that. Did they notice our man?"

Kurt shrugged. "Hard to say. Whatever it was, the guy didn't stick around. Next time you want to send somebody on a wild goose chase, how about sending one of your own."

"Ah, but we haven't anyone with your particular qualifications, now have we?"

Kurt's gaze shifted to the center of the room and he scanned from left to right and back, a habit developed during his training at Bethesda. Wild Bill Donovan himself had selected Kurt because he spoke perfectly unaccented German and looked like a poster boy for Himmler's SS. Now he was chasing shadows across

Morocco for reasons known only to Intelligence High Command in London.

"Remind me to thank my grandparents for making the whole family speak German at home when I was a kid."

"Yes, well we do owe Granny and Gramps rather a debt of gratitude, don't we? Or did you call them Oma and Opa?"

Kurt's mouth narrowed to a thin line. "What do you think?"

"Of course." Maitland picked up his rocks glass and swirled the scotch in its bottom. Watching the amber liquid create little rivers down the sides, he pursed his lips, and then asked, "From where in Germany did they come?"

"Westphalia, outside a little place called Telgte."

"Ah yes, the northwest. And what was it they did?"

"They were farmers." Kurt's eyes narrowed. Maitland was asking for Heinz family history that he probably knew better than Kurt himself. The Brits were a suspicious lot. They really didn't get the idea of America's melting pot or maybe Maitland was just the egotistical snob Kurt had taken him for at first sight. Either way, the man gave every impression of questioning Kurt's loyalty. If it wouldn't land him in the stockade, Kurt would love to wipe the supercilious sneer off his pointy, noble face.

"Texas must have been quite a change for them— an adjustment of epic proportions."

"They managed."

"Do your parents speak English?"

"Yeah, sure…look, as fascinating as my heritage is, I'm beat. I'm going up to bed. It's been a long day."

"Certainly. By the by, you'll find I've placed a uniform in your closet. Please try it on for fit. A tailor is on call if needed. MacFadyen wants you in his office at 0600 for a briefing. Things are developing rapidly."

Kurt nodded and went to the lobby. A line of new arrivals waited at the elevators with luggage piled high. He was in no mood for saluting and kowtowing to a bunch of strange brass, so Kurt walked the three flights up to his room overlooking the front gardens and the Atlantic beyond.

The key turned easily in the lock as would be expected in a building so new. He flipped on the lights, tugged off his jacket, and loosened his tie. Finally a minute to unwind.

He opened the door to the balcony and stepped out for a breath of fresh air. Stars winked here and there between scudding clouds. The rain had finally let up. Just beyond the railing, the fronds of palm trees swayed and rattled in the breeze blowing in from the ocean. Lights from ships at anchor dotted the coastline. It all looked so peaceful now, but back in November, things would have been decidedly different during the Allied invasion of unoccupied French Morocco. Although most of the American troops had been untried in battle, Casablanca had fallen in an hour. Operation Torch had given the Allies an important foothold in North Africa. Intelligence officers like him had arrived shortly thereafter.

Kurt leaned out and filled his lungs with salt laden air. Moments like this had been few and far between since he signed on with the OSS. Peace settled over him and he wished he could stay there admiring the view, but he needed to catch up on his sleep before he faced

MacFadyen in the morning.

After hanging his uniform in the closest, he removed the garment bag that had made its way into his room, undid the zipper, and let out a low whistle. Although Maitland hadn't given Kurt the details of his upcoming mission, it would surely take him somewhere other than the gin joints of Casablanca.

Chapter 3

First week of January 1943

The rat-a-tat-tat of anti-aircraft guns tore through the predawn stillness, sending Sarah's heart lurching into her throat. She braced herself against the doorjamb and took deep, slow breaths. She would never get used to the sudden violence of war.

The sound of scrambling feet drew Sarah's attention from her own discomfort. Her jaw set as her eyes narrowed. Wheeling around in the hospital ward's arched entrance, she marched straight back toward her charges. The walking wounded jockeyed for a better look at the Nazi bombers releasing their payloads over Casablanca while the immobile shouted encouragement from their beds.

"Close the curtains and get away from those windows."

A second lieutenant grinned over his shoulder before he turned back to the fireworks display. "Aw, come on, Sarah. We just want a little excitement. It's boring lying around all day doing nothing."

"You'd like being killed by shrapnel or flying glass better? We're not going to have a repeat of last time. Get back. Now!"

Like so many scolded schoolboys, the men dropped the blackout curtains and shuffled toward the center of the room where they plopped down on their cots. She would have preferred that her patients take cover under mattresses, but she would settle for having them away from the windows. At least the scalawags weren't trying to run up onto the roof like so many of them had during the first raid. This particular ward of wounded infantry officers and Army Air Corps pilots were a difficult lot at the best of times. When they weren't flirting outrageously with the nurses, they were finding evermore inventive ways to break the rules.

The unmistakable whistle of falling bombs made the hair on the back of Sarah's neck stand on end. Several of her patients rolled under their beds. She could hear the men counting the seconds between whistle stop and explosion trying to gage the distance from hospital to bombsites. If you could detect that pattern, you were usually way too close for comfort. Worse, though, were the Stuka dive-bomber sirens. One of her patients had told her that the Krauts, his word, designed the sirens specifically to scare victims witless. The plan was a resounding success. Her heart pounded as a Stuka's scream became ever louder and then stopped as if someone had flipped a switch. Engine vibrations rattled the hospital's windows until a pane shattered. The pilot must have pulled up at the last minute. Why anyone would buzz a hospital was beyond understanding. A lot of things in this war didn't make much sense.

Without warning, a blast shook the building to its very foundations. Sarah sprawled across the body of a patient who was unable to move from his bed. He groaned and then smiled at her with blistered lips, the only part of his fire ravaged face visible through his bandages. Her weight must be torture for him, but she had no other way to keep him safe from flying debris. The floor shifted beneath them and settled back into place. Chunks of plaster crashed down from the ornate ceiling, creating clouds of choking dust. That's what they got for trying to turn the former Italian Consulate into a home for the 8th Evacuation Hospital. The lights flickered and dimmed. Sarah prayed the explosions hadn't brought down the newly strung electric wires put up after the last raid. It was always so much harder to care for incoming wounded by lantern and flashlight.

The Stukas' screams faded as quickly as they had come and gradually the anti-aircraft fire ceased. Coughing and brushing dust from her uniform, Sarah stood and adjusted the bedclothes covering her burn patient as the lights came back—one miracle granted.

"I'm so sorry about that. I hope I didn't hurt you too much."

"S'okay. Like girls in bed. Anytime."

Sarah raised an eyebrow. "I see you're getting better, but don't go thinking you can be too frisky. Not yet, anyway."

Sarah turned her head so that the patient couldn't see the lie in her eyes. It would be a miracle if he lived until the end of the week. His burns were too extensive and the environment was too toxic. This was the part of nursing she hated. Losing even one went against everything she believed, everything she had dedicated her life to.

She shook her head slightly. If she dwelt on morbid thoughts, she wouldn't be any good to anyone. Better to stay busy. The next round of checking vital signs and administering meds was near enough, so she went to the supply cabinet and got her tools: thermometer, blood pressure cuff, syringes, antiseptic solution. Her patients weren't asleep anyway, so better to do it now rather than wake them up later.

Slowly and then more rapidly, raised voices, the scuffle of boots against stone floors, and the squeal of gurney wheels—the sounds of triage—floated into the ward. Sarah straightened up from tucking in a patient's bedcovers and listened. Instead of the constant roar that came with large numbers of admissions, the noise rose and fell in a stop-start manner.

Perhaps there weren't many casualties. Now there was a happy thought!

She smiled and gave the men one last evaluative glance before returning to her table by the door. Under the bulb of a single desk lamp, she worked on her never-ending stack of reports. The noise from admissions gradually subsided until it became a single gurney's wheels crunching over sand and debris littering the hall floor. The gurney stopped outside her ward and the door opened.

"Where you want him?" A PFC bumped through the opening with an unconscious patient.

Sarah went to the gurney and picked up the medical chart lying on its end. She nodded toward the side wall. "Help me move that empty cot over here."

While she and the private placed the cot next to her burn patient, Sarah glanced at the inert form on the gurney. He had multiple chest and abdominal wounds and had lost a great deal of blood.

"His chart doesn't give rank, name, or unit. What happened to his dog tags?"

"Search me. This is the first I laid eyes on him."

"Weren't you there when they brought him in?"

The private shrugged. "Musta been, but I didn't see nothing. They had me running around like a chicken with its head cut off getting supplies and stuff. Some jerk on last shift didn't restock the cabinets."

"Did you help unload the ambulances?"

"Yeah. There was only two and he wasn't in either one. Guess he walked in under his own steam."

"Perhaps."

"Doc said he probably ain't gonna make it."

Sarah gave the young man a stern look and shook her head. Even though the injured man seemed completely out of it, you never knew what he might hear or remember. During her nurse's training at the University of Virginia, she knew of a coma patient who woke up and immediately started yelling at his wife and son because they planned his funeral while sitting next to his bed during the long months waiting to see if he would ever recover. Thereafter, Sarah never made assumptions regarding the unconscious.

"Let's get him onto the cot. Be easy with him."

The injured man groaned softly as they shifted him from the gurney. A strange feeling swept over Sarah as she observed her new patient. His face seemed oddly familiar, but she couldn't place him. In fact, she was quite sure they had never met and yet....Sarah sighed and rolled her head from side to side. Maybe Agnes was right about her needing more rest. Her imagination seemed to be running rampant. Of one thing she was sure, however, silently she agreed with the doctor's prognosis—the man's injuries were extensive.

The private picked up a bundle and shoved it at Sarah. "This here's his stuff, if...I mean when he needs it."

"Thank you, Private. That will be all."

"Sure. See ya."

Sarah didn't know why admissions kept tying up bloody uniforms and sending them with the patients. It wasn't as if most of the clothes were wearable anymore. Furthermore, storage space was nonexistent. She tossed the bundle on her table and sat down to resume the paperwork, but the clothes drew her attention. Instead of khaki serge, lamplight revealed gray flannel under the twine bindings. She picked up a pair of shears and snipped until the string fell away. She held the garments up. This was no military uniform. From the red pocket square tucked in the suit's breast pocket to its cut, there was no way anyone could confuse these clothes for those worn by a soldier. The odors of cigarettes, liquor, and cheap cologne wafted from the blood-spattered coat. Casablanca lounge lizard? Interesting thought, but what would a civilian of that ilk be doing in a military hospital? Next she shook out the shirt. It had once been white, but now the front was stained red from collar to hem. Upon closer inspection, half a dozen thin holes of about a half-inch in width were scattered over the shirt in a pattern indicating a frenzied attack. Whatever had happened to her newest patient, it had nothing to do with Nazi bombs.

A soft sound came from the cot area. Her new patient's eyes were open and his lips moved slowly. She went to his side and leaned down.

"You're safe now. You're in a hospital."

"*Aidez-moi.*"

Puzzled, Sarah said, "Try not to talk. I can't give you anything more for the pain yet, but I will as soon as it's possible."

She rose to leave, but his hand grabbed her wrist in a surprisingly strong grip, considering the trauma he had suffered.

"*Aidez-moi.*" He spoke louder this time, turning his head so that he gazed directly up into Sarah's eyes. A thin, pale scar ran along his jawline.

"I'm sorry, but my high school French is pretty rusty."

"Help."

"Of course. Do you need water?"

The dark head rolled in the negative. "Coat."

"Your coat? It's here. Don't worry. We wouldn't do away with your things without asking you first."

"Get it."

Sarah doubted the man would want the thing when he saw its condition, but he gestured in such agitation that she retrieved it from the desk. When she held out the coat, the man grasped it like a drowning victim grabs a life ring. He turned the garment over in his hands, feeling along the edges of the lining. His fingers came to rest on the lower front left hem where he began picking at the material.

Sarah didn't like the wild look in his eyes. "Why don't you let me help with that?"

The coat fell onto his chest and he nodded. Trembling fingers poked at the garment until they exposed a slightly raised rectangle within the lining. He tapped it and said, "Cut."

When Sarah hesitated, he repeated, "Cut!"

With an uneasy feeling, Sarah got scissors and clipped hand-sewn stitches holding the lining and the suit jacket's flannel exterior together. Once the fabrics separated, a small white card, folded over and creased many times by dirty fingers, fell into her lap. She picked it up and extended it on her outstretched palm. The man pushed the card back toward Sarah.

"Hei…"

His voice faded to an indiscernible whisper. Sarah bent down so that her ear was close to his lips.

"What do you want?"

"Heinz."

Sarah sat up and considered what she thought she had heard. "You want to get this to a person named Heinz?"

The injured man raised himself on one elbow and grabbed at Sarah's arm with his free hand. His eyes were wild with effort and pain. "Heinz. Captain. Anfa."

Having delivered himself of his burden, the man fell back against his pillow. Sarah watched him, hoping that he would say more. Did he want her to find this Heinz or was he warning her against him? She couldn't be sure. If he was directing her to Casablanca's Anfa district, this Captain Heinz probably wasn't a Nazi despite his German name, but that presented a problem of a different sort. She couldn't just march up to the Anfa Hotel or the military encampment nearby, bristling as they were with guards, and demand admittance.

The man's gaze bored holes in her heart. Although he was beyond speech, his eyes held a desperation that was impossible to ignore. There was no real obligation, but Sarah felt bound to help the sick and injured, especially if it was in her power to grant the wishes of the dying.

Turning the card over in her hand, she considered it

for a moment and then said, "I'll try to find your Captain Heinz. Is that what you want?"

There was no response. Her patient's eyes closed and the tension drained from his body. His breathing became ragged. Sarah hurried to the nurses' station in the main hall to ask for the doctor on call. A baby faced young man, surely not a month out of med school, returned to the ward with her. She led the doctor to her mysterious patient.

The injured man's chest failed to rise and fall, not even in the ragged pattern of a few moments past. An unwelcome, but by now familiar, feeling of defeat swept over Sarah. The doctor sat by the cot and picked up the man's wrist. Next, he pressed the carotid artery, leaving his fingers just below the jaw longer than necessary. He waited a moment before running though the procedure a second time. Looking up at Sarah, the doctor shook his head and drew the blanket over the man's face.

The edges of the stranger's card suddenly felt very sharp against Sarah's curled palm.

Chapter 4

The eastern sky was still dark when Kurt's alarm jarred him awake. He groaned and gave the clock a vicious swat. Between the activities of the previous evening and the early morning bombing raid, sleep had become just an afterthought. But adequate rest would have to wait because Colonel MacFadyen, British Army and Allied Intelligence Officer for North Africa, wouldn't. Kurt sat up and reached for the cigarette pack on the bedside table. Nasty habit, one he couldn't seem to break for more than a week or two at a time.

Dressed, showered, and shaved, he arrived at MacFadyen's office with a couple of minutes to spare.

"He in?"

The girl seated behind the reception desk rolled her eyes and grimaced. "Sure. *We've* been in since 0530. I'll let him know you're here."

As she got up, the door to MacFadyen's office swung back. A man in civilian clothes rushed through the opening, bumping into and pushing past the secretary without apology or salutation.

Kurt frowned and turned to follow, but the girl placed a hand on his arm and shook her head.

"Save it, Sir Galahad, for something more important."

Kurt watched the civilian until he reached the elevator. "That jerk needs to be taught a lesson in manners."

"Yes, but not by someone at His Nibs' beck and call."

"So, is that guy somebody I ought to get to know?"

"Not necessarily."

"He sure was in a hurry. What gives?"

Cocking her head to one side, she began, "Ours not to reason why—"

"—Ours but to do and die." Kurt finished with a grin. Tennyson's Light Brigade rhyme was a private joke between them.

Kurt had learned long ago that secretaries, janitors, and other lowly staff were often privy to information simply through proximity to the great and powerful. It was his upbringing to be kind to everyone regardless of their station in life, a trait that he now found important in his work. Initially, Kurt was baffled when he learned the spit and polish MacFadyen had a member of the all female Auxiliary Territorial Service for a secretary. His first encounter with the lovely and intelligent Corporal Hortensia Linthwaite, ATS, however, had cleared up the mystery post haste, despite any misgivings he might have regarding the moniker her parents had hung on the girl. In the short time he had known her, he and Hortensia had formed the kind of bond that people with a common enemy often develop.

"That you, Heinz?" rumbled through the doorway. "Don't stand there all day. Cpl. Linthwaite has work to do even if you don't."

Hortensia winked and muttered under her breath, "The Colonel at his early morning best. Step carefully."

Kurt lifted three fingers in a Boy Scout salute and entered The Presence, as Hortensia called MacFadyen when she was especially irritated with him. The Colonel frowned and gestured toward a chair.

"Our man has completely disappeared, taking the information he carried with him. No sign anywhere. This is a disaster."

"Will the mission be canceled?"

"Oh no, not at all. It simply increases the danger a hundredfold."

"May I ask, sir, what the mission is?" Kurt understood the need for secrecy, but being kept out of the loop was wearing thin. When he left England, he was told only that he would be on loan to the Brits for a special assignment in North Africa. He knew it must be something big, and he needed to prepare himself mentally for whatever the boys in London were planning.

MacFadyen made a bridge of his fingers and let his gaze sweep over Kurt before answering, "Perhaps it is time that you knew." Opening a drawer, he withdrew a piece of paper and threw it on the desktop. "Take a look."

Kurt picked up the blank sheet and turned it over revealing a black and white photograph of a guy wearing a Nazi captain's uniform. Moderately attractive face in an earthy sort of way. Fair hair. Eyes that were probably blue. Kurt's heart jumped into his throat. With a gasp, he let the photo fall from his fingers. It was like looking into a mirror.

The corners of MacFadyen's mouth turned up, but the smile failed to reach his eyes. "Recognize him, do you?"

The blood pounded in Kurt's ears. "Where did you get this?"

"Our usual source. Name's Helmut Heinz. A relation of yours, perhaps?"

"If you have this, you know he is," Kurt growled before he thought better of the tone he used with a superior officer.

MacFadyen appeared unruffled by the insubordination. "Cousin, I believe?"

Kurt wondered if Colonel MacFadyen had enjoyed pulling the wings off butterflies when he was a small boy. "Our fathers are first cousins, but they've never met. Our paternal grandfathers were brothers. Helmut's grandfather died in the Great War."

"Starved along with your great aunt as I understand it. Result of the blockade. Pity, don't you think?"

Kurt's hands clenched. His nails dug into his palms as rage and something akin to fear boiled up inside him. "Sir, what does this have to do with my assignment?"

MacFadyen's face took on the same expression Kurt's ninth grade teacher wore when a student asked a particularly stupid question. "Obvious, really. Surprised you had to ask. We want you to impersonate your cousin. Find out what Adolph has planned now that Monty has the Desert Fox on the run. Rumors stirring, but no sound information. Should be simple enough, given your close family ties."

"We may look alike, but I've never met Helmut." Kurt's mouth tightened to a thin line. "I know nothing about him. We've lost all contact with that part of the family. Never had much to begin with, other than a few letters written before the last war."

"Seems we know more about your cousin than you do. We've a man who knew him at university. He'll fill you in on mannerisms, tastes, and the like."

"University? That must have been ten years ago. Don't you think Helmut might have changed a little?"

"Not in the basics. People usually don't, you know."

Kurt didn't know anything of the kind, but this old college buddy of Helmut's was probably the best he was going to get. "Where is this impersonation going to take place?"

"Here in North Africa. Your cousin's star was on the rise in Berlin until he got himself into some difficulties. Fell afoul of the law over a woman. Now he's banished to the desert. He has great skill with intelligence gathering and code breaking. Rather like you, I might point out. And his father is a high-ranking Nazi Party official. Apparently your German relations have left the farm and come up in the world."

"That's too bad. My parents and grandparents will be appalled."

"By the fact that you have Nazis in the family or by your cousin's fall from grace?"

Refusing to dignify the question with an answer, Kurt simply glared in reply.

"Well, it really makes no difference. I'm sure your loyalty is above reproach or Bill Donovan wouldn't have insisted on this mission being created around your rather particular set of assets."

"I see."

Kurt must have looked puzzled for MacFadyen continued, "You wouldn't be sitting here otherwise, my boy. Donovan says that despite your occasional disregard for the finer points of rank, he would trust you with his life."

"He's a fine teacher and commander. It's a

compliment I'll work hard to deserve."

MacFadyen eyed Kurt for a moment as though inspecting troop formations. "Yes, I'm sure that you will." The colonel leaned forward and pointed at Kurt with his index finger. "You OSS chaps may be in charge of the over-all intelligence work here in North Africa, but this operation is under British command due to our expertise with this situation. It would be best for you not to forget that fact."

"No, sir. I recognize that you are in charge. May I ask when we start?" Kurt might dislike his temporary boss, but he had no intention of letting that interfere with his duty.

"Your tutor will begin instruction this morning. Did I mention that you will be taking up residence with him in a block of flats near the hotel? Here's the address. Get your things over there now. There may be very little time for you to prepare."

Chapter 5

The sun was well over the rooftops when Sarah finally left the hospital. Her left hand toyed with the card in her coat pocket while she stood on the sidewalk trying to decide what to do. Home, a bath, and bed beckoned, but her conscience wouldn't be still. Her promise to the dead civilian replayed in her mind. The man had been so desperate for his message to be delivered that his final words had been a gasped plea for help. She withdrew the card from her pocket and looked at the scribbled inscription. It had to be some kind of code because it made no sense—just a jumble of letters that didn't even look like a language, at least not one she had ever seen. Sighing, she hailed a passing taxi and climbed in.

"*Ou voulez-vous aller, Mademoiselle?*"

Sarah searched the little she remembered of her high school French for a phrase that would tell the driver where to take her. He drummed his fingers on the wheel and asked again with growing impatience.

Sarah latched onto the only sensible phrase she could think of. "*Le camp militaire.*"

"*Ce qui?*" Irritation radiated from the driver's every pore.

Sarah repeated her request.

The driver's upper lip curled. "*L'ha, votre accent, c' est terrible.*" He held out his hand. "*Cinq francs*

37

maintenant."

Fed up, Sarah hissed, "Let's not worry about my accent, shall we? Now, take me to the American camp and maybe I won't report you to the military police for trying to gouge the public with inflated fares."

She was gratified to see the driver's eyes widen. Only then did she drop a one-franc note onto the seat beside him to ensure that he did her bidding. In a huff, he jerked the wheel and moved forward at a pace she was sure exceeded the speed limit. Shortly thereafter, the cab pulled up to a curb and stopped. The outline of the Anfa Hotel's upper floors was visible beyond its barriers and gardens father down the street. A wire enclosed tent encampment squatted brown and dusty some yards away across a large open sand lot.

The guard at the gate post grinned appreciatively as Sarah approached. "Good morning, Miss. How can the army help one of our Nightingales?"

Sarah raised an eyebrow and smiled. "By telling me where I can find a Captain Heinz."

"Know his company?"

"Uh-uh. I'm afraid not."

The soldier stepped into the guardhouse and returned with a clipboard. After flipping through several pages of typed lists, he looked up and said, "Sorry. No Captain Heinz here. We got a Cpl. Heinz, First Platoon, Charlie Company."

"No, it's Captain. I'm sure."

"Well, Miss, I guess we're out of luck."

Disappointed and feeling a little lightheaded, Sarah trudged back to the paved road and hailed another taxi for the ride home. It looked as though discharging her obligation would be more difficult than she had thought, but she had done all she could for the time being. Promise or no, she needed to go home. Agnes was right. Burning the candle at both ends was catching up with her.

****

Sarah dragged herself up three flights of dark, narrow stairs to the top floor of the little residential hotel where she shared an efficiency with Agnes. The damned manager had removed the landing's single light bulb again, rendering the cramped space dark as pitch. She dug her key from beneath the dead stranger's card in her coat pocket and reached for the ancient lock. Without warning, hinges creaked as the door swung back at her touch. Instinctively, Sarah drew back her hand and peered into the apartment's interior. Sunlight poured through uncovered windows. Ebony blackout curtains, ripped from their rods, pooled on the floor. Bureau drawers lay splintered, contents scattered across the wooden floor.

Heart racing, Sarah took a tentative step across the threshold. Their little dining table and chairs had been tossed upside down. Cushions, stuffing popping from large gashes, were across the room from their overturned chairs. Both upper cabinets in the little Pullman kitchen lay in a heap in front of the sink unit, whose doors hung at odd angles from single hinges. A tremor swept through Sarah at the thought of what she might find in the curtained off bedroom area. She looked down at her hands. They were actually shaking.

Dreading every step but determined to assess the damage, Sarah moved to the sleeping area and drew back the curtain partition. She froze in her tracks. The space had received the same treatment as the living area, but the twin beds had been singled out for special attention. The mattresses were no longer recognizable as such. If she had seen them on the street, Sarah might have thought someone was getting cotton ready for the gin. The bedsteads were broken rubble. Involuntarily, Sarah's hand flew to her mouth to stifle the screams welling up inside her.

"Good god, what the hell happened here?" Agnes's voice echoed from the front door. Sarah turned toward the sound, but it seemed to be coming through a long tunnel. She slumped to one side against the wall. Hurried footsteps brought Agnes to her side. "Are you all right? Were you here when this happened? Did those bastards hurt you?"

Embarrassed, Sarah straightened up and shook her head. "I'm fine. I wasn't here."

Agnes eyed the destruction. "There's not a single stick of furniture left. What on earth were they looking for? It's not like we're Vanderbilts or Rockefellers."

"What makes you think there was more than one?"

Agnes made a sweeping gesture. "Just look at this mess. It would have taken one guy forever to do all this. I wasn't gone for more than forty minutes." Agnes pointed toward net bags spilling fruit and vegetables across the landing. "I got up early and went shopping for tonight's dinner. I thought we needed a good meal at home for a change."

The blood drained from Sarah's head. "I don't think the kitchen is in any shape for that." Her voice sounded distant and vague to her own ears.

Agnes wrapped her fingers around Sarah's wrist. "Your pulse is racing and you look like a ghost. You need a warm drink and a hot bath. Get yourself into the tub while I make you a hot toddy."

Bathed and in pajamas, Sarah sipped her whiskey-laced drink. Its sweet fire swept through her. Muscles suddenly released their tension and melted into a rubbery calm. The remnants of the mattress on which she sat didn't feel quite so lumpy anymore. Agnes had done her best to make a bed by turning the uncut side face up on the floor and covering it with undamaged sheets.

Coming into the bedroom with blankets freshly shaken to rid them of debris, Agnes eyed Sarah huddled in the corner. "You look better, my girl."

"I feel a lot better, but a little embarrassed. I'm not a fainter. I don't know what got into me."

"You need rest. Go to sleep."

"But what on earth are we going to do with this place?"

"We'll tackle that job when both of us are up to snuff."

Agnes crossed her arms over her small bosom and gave Sarah "The Look". Grinning in response, Sarah sank down under the bedclothes and drifted into welcome slumber.

****

Several hours later, Sarah jerked awake, her heart pounding. She staggered to her feet and stumbled to the living area where her coat lay over the arm of a righted chair. Grabbing the mac, she searched the pockets. Relief flooded her. It was still there.

Agnes looked up from the most recent copy of Stars and Stripes. "What's with the sudden need for your coat?"

"I was afraid I'd lost this." Sarah held up the

battered card with its coded message.

"Doesn't look like it'd be any great loss."

"I made a promise to a dying man," Sarah began, then went on to explain the odd circumstances under which the card came into her possession, and finished with, "So I have to find this Captain Heinz, but he isn't at the American camp."

Agnes cocked her head to one side and scrunched up her lips, a habit she had when she was trying the remember something. She snapped her fingers. "I think I've got it. I bet it's that cute blond captain from the restaurant on New Year's Eve. The one you were so mean to. His name was something or other Heinz."

"The dancer?"

"Yeah. Now whose staff did he say he was on?" Agnes drummed her fingers on the chair arm. She shrugged. "Sorry, kid. I can't remember his boss's name, but it's bound to be one of that bunch of brass at the Anfa."

"Good luck getting in there. Have you seen that place? Something's up but nobody seems to know what."

"Then forget about it. You did your best."

"That's not true, and you know it. I'm getting dressed and going to the Anfa before it gets any later." Sarah turned and looked around at the mess. "Don't do anything until I get back. I'll help you clean up later."

****

In the end, it had been so simple. Sarah beamed as she replaced the receiver on the checkpoint guardhouse phone. Whoever this Hortensia was, she had given Sarah a full name and residential address. Just for the asking. Well, not that easy really. Sarah had flirted with the Marine standing guard duty at the Anfa front gate. He had checked several lists and made more than a few calls. Finally, she had told a Colonel MacFadyen's aide, the unfortunately named Hortensia, about the card and the dead man. Hortensia put the phone down and Sarah could hear the sound of sensible shoes treading away. After a moment, the girl returned and asked that Sarah come up and leave the card with the Colonel as Captain Heinz was not in the office at the moment. Sarah had adamantly refused, saying she would only deliver it to the captain. It was then Hortensia had given her the address. Just like that.

Sarah turned and headed off toward an apartment building two blocks away. In a few minutes, she would be rid of the blasted card, and her conscience would be divested of its burden.

Chapter 6

"No, no, no, Captain Heinz! You've still got it wrong. Now begin again. And do try to remember the flourish of the wrist."

Kurt ran a finger around his collar and loosened his tie. The last few hours had been intense. Despite chilly winter breezes rattling the windows, the atmosphere in the cramped apartment was stifling. Smoke hung in the air like a veil. Kurt would like nothing better than to tell Phelps, his new flat mate, to go to hell and take off for a long walk by himself but time was running out. Observing his own hands as they clipped a cigar for the third time, Kurt was satisfied that he had the affectation down pat. He glanced up to get Phelps's reaction.

"Yes, that's it." Helmut's college buddy nodded enthusiastically. "You've finally got it. Now walk."

With the stub of one of Cuba's finest dangling between his fingers, Kurt sauntered across the room. He hoped that he didn't look as big a fool as he felt.

"No, damn it! You're still walking like an American. You've got to move like a European, like a bloody German, for Christ's sake. Your cousin Helmut may have been born to pig farmers, but by the time he finished university, he was quite sophisticated, very polished. Watch me."

Leaning against the wall, Kurt eyed Phelps and quashed a laugh. The Brit glided across the floor as if he could have stepped on eggs without breaking them. When he came to a halt, Phelps sort of cocked a hip and turned one foot to the side, more like a woman might stand.

Kurt wiped the smirk from his face as Phelps looked back over his shoulder. "I realize you knew my cousin for several years at Leipzig, but do you really think he'd walk like that in jackboots?"

Phelps turned and placed a hand on his hip. "Perhaps not, but let's get the basics down first, shall we? Then we can move on to adaptations. Go on. Try again."

Kurt lifted himself off the wall and executed a fair imitation of the sashaying he had just witnessed. No man back home in Texas would move like that without having hell to pay. Patriotism came with a price these days.

"That's better, not perfect mind you, but an improvement. By the time he finished his studies, your cousin had become a man of great pretension." Phelps arched a brow. "He even tried to claim noble relatives, but I knew better, having visited his home."

"You knew his parents?" Kurt couldn't keep the surprise from his voice.

"Yes, and his grandparents, too."

Phelps's knowing tone irritated Kurt, but the man's words fascinated him. The German relatives were no more than a few scrawled pages that arrived sporadically over the years of his childhood. These strangers who shared his surname had been given little thought, but now his curiosity to know them became overpowering.

"Were you close to the family?"

"In a small way. Frau Heinz was kind to a poor student far from home. Going back to England for Christmas and other holidays was beyond the limits of my purse. I liked the old people, too." A half smile curled Phelps's lips.

"But not Helmut's father, I take it?"

Phelps hesitated before answering, "Let us say he was of the old school and leave it at that."

"So why did you keep going?"

"Helmut invited me, and his mother was a good cook. She liked to see *ihre Jungen* eat. We were a long time out of short pants by then, but she still called us her boys. She was a sweetly maternal woman. Why are you smirking?"

"Sorry, but this conversation is sort of surreal. They're my close kin, but I've never set eyes on them. Really know very little about them. You, on the other hand, seem to know everything. Did y'all stay in touch after college?"

"Y'all?—Oh, yes. An expression of the American South indicating second person plural, I believe?"

"Yeah. Something like that. My cousins?"

"Yes, well, our friendship—Helmut's and mine— broke shortly before I returned to England. You see, by then his head was filled with Nazi rubbish. Helmut was attracted to the National Socialists early on. I thought he would outgrow it, but in the end, he and his father were both loyal party members. No amount of reasoning could change Helmut's mind. The old man was understandable. But Helmut was so bright, had once been so kind. I couldn't stomach the change in him."

"Why Leipzig University, not Cambridge or

Oxford?"

"Didn't MacFadyen tell you?"

Kurt shook his head.

"I wanted to study the German language and psychology. Leipzig was the natural choice. In Civvy Street, I'm a psychologist specializing in analysis of the criminal mentality. Useful these days when one's country is trying to kick the bloody daylights out of *der Fuhrer*."

"Yes, I can see how it might be."

"Now let's—" Pounding on the front door interrupted Phelps mid-sentence. He turned an eye on Kurt. "Oh, really now. Should we be expecting company so soon?"

Kurt shrugged and ambled toward the noise echoing from the small reception vestibule on the other side of the living room wall. He looked through the front door's peephole. Standing on the other side was a pretty redhead in a nurse's uniform. She looked familiar, but he couldn't place her.

He was about to slip away without answering when the girl called out, "Captain Heinz? Is anyone home? I really need to speak with you." The pounding started again.

She raised such a racket that Kurt stepped back to the door and yanked it open. "I'm Heinz. What do you want?"

"Oh. It's you."

"Yeah?"

"From the restaurant on New Year's Eve."

Kurt was silent for a moment, then it came back to him. "I remember. You're the girl who refused to dance with me."

47

A red flush crawled from her throat onto the apples of her cheeks. "Yes. I'm sorry if I was rude."

"I've been cut dead before. I got over it."

The girl's eyes glittered. "I'm sure you did. Are you going to keep me standing here on the doorstep for everyone to see?"

"Why? I'm not expecting company. Would it be a problem?"

"It certainly might if the people who tore my apartment apart followed me here."

Kurt looked into her eyes with complete attention for the first time since opening the door. Whatever had happened to this girl, she looked terrified and angry. Not a particularly good combination for the covert activities he and Phelps were up to.

Kurt made a quick decision. He stepped back and pulled the door wide while raising his voice. "You better come inside and tell me why you think what happened to your apartment has anything to do with me."

When they stepped into the living area, Phelps had disappeared. Kurt gestured toward the sofa and the girl sat down.

Propping himself on the sofa's arm, he looked down into her frightened eyes.

"Now tell me how I can help you, Miss, uh…"

"Barrett, Sarah. US Army. RN."

"Well, Nurse Barrett, what can I do for you?"

The girl stuck her hand in her coat pocket and whipped out a scrap of paper that she waved in his face. "By telling me what's on this paper and why it's so important that somebody took a knife to my furniture."

Kurt took the paper and unfolded it. His heart

lurched. "Where did you get this?"

"Answer my questions first, and I might answer yours."

Kurt could no longer contain his frustration. He reached down and grabbed the girl's wrist. "You have no idea what you've stumbled into. Now tell me where this came from, or I will have no choice but to have you arrested."

Tears spilled down Sarah's creamy cheeks, but her eyes were fiery. "Let go or I'll scream the house down. Then you can explain to the MP's why you felt it necessary to manhandle someone half your size."

Kurt dropped her arm instantly. Sheepishly, he said, "I'm sorry. Really I am. But for your own sake, please tell me how you came by this."

The girl studied his face for several beats. Finally, she answered, "From a dying man. Your rank and name were the last words he spoke."

"And where was this?"

Listening to Sarah's story of the civilian in gray who had died at the military hospital, Kurt decided that the coded message was probably authentic. He weighed his options before continuing, "Wait here while I check this out. Okay?"

When the girl nodded, Kurt turned and went into the bedroom, closing the door behind him. Phelps lay on one of the twin beds where he was thumbing through a months old magazine. He looked up and raised his eyebrows.

Kurt placed a finger to his lips and jerked his head toward the living room. Phelps nodded as Kurt sat on the opposite bed. From beneath a loose floor tile, he withdrew a small black notebook. Within minutes, he knew what his contact had died trying to tell him. When Phelps had read the decoded message, Kurt rose. Phelps moved as though he might follow, but Kurt shook his head, and Phelps resumed his perusal of the magazine.

Sitting on the sofa next to the frightened girl, Kurt said, "I'm sorry. There is really nothing I can tell you."

"Why?" The question echoed off the bare plaster walls. "Everything Agnes and I own has been destroyed, and you can't tell me anything? I don't believe you."

"I really can't. It's for your own safety."

"Well, I haven't been particularly safe since your mystery man dropped into my ward. So tell me. Exactly how am I to stay safe if I don't even know who to look out for?"

Kurt smiled. He couldn't help it. Not only was she pretty, Sarah seemed to be something rather rare. There she sat telling him a tale that would make most girls run screaming, yet this girl wouldn't back down, not for a minute.

He fought a sudden urge to tuck a stray lock of auburn hair behind her ear. "I suppose you're right about one thing."

With an incensed expression, Sarah spoke through clinched teeth. "And what, pray, would that be?"

"You aren't safe. The best thing I can do for you right now is go back to your place and help you move."

"Now? Agnes and I have to be back at the hospital for our shift by 1500 hours. We don't have time to find a new place, much less move."

"I'll make a couple of calls. You'll be given the time off to make your arrangements. That, at least, I can promise you."

After making several calls from the bedroom phone, Kurt led Sarah out to the street where his Jeep squatted beneath a tall palm in front of the building. What he did not mention was that one of the calls had been to Maitland giving him the contents of the coded message word for word. It gave coordinates. That was all. He didn't know why they were important, but Kurt was pretty sure the location was somewhere on the Tunisian coast. He would deliver the actual scrap of paper it was written on after he and the girl got her things. He had not yet decided what to do with her, but it was certain that she could not stay where she was. With Casablanca filled to bursting, it looked like she and this Agnes would have to bunk down wherever the other nurses from their unit stayed. Why they were so special as to have a place to themselves was beyond him, but Agnes apparently had pull with the brass. At the mention of her name and situation, the request for time off for the women had been granted without question. Of course, being a Senator's sister had its perks.

The ride across town took longer than Kurt ever thought possible. A convoy returning from the desert kept the main roads clogged for over an hour. Sarah's hands chafed one another as vehicle after vehicle passed in a seemingly unending line. The tanks and half-tracks kicked up great clouds of dust. It settled as a blinding, suffocating layer on everything in the vicinity. Slowly, the last of the convoy rumbled past and they were able to resume their journey. When they finally pulled up to Sarah's building, long afternoon shadows darkened the entry to her staircase.

Brushing the dirt from her uniform skirt, Sarah

jumped out of the Jeep and ran up the three flights of narrow dark stairs to her landing at the top of the house, Kurt close behind.

She opened the door and called, "Agnes. I'm back. I have Captain Heinz with me."

Kurt stepped into the room. An attempt had been made to tidy up, but the destruction still lay in piles around the room. Agnes was nowhere in sight. Sarah, a worried frown creasing her brow, headed toward the sleeping area. Kurt followed quickly on her heels. At the curtain partition, both stopped short and stared. A small red pool stained the floor before them. As her fist flew to her mouth, Kurt instinctively put an arm around Sarah's shoulders and pulled her close.

Chapter 7

Sarah jerked away from the arms holding her back and slowly made her way toward the bathroom, kicking debris aside as she went. She would not give in to the hysterics that were trying so hard to overtake her. There had to be an acceptable explanation for the pool of blood. Maybe Agnes had cut herself badly on one of the many sharp edges laying about the room. She could have. It was certainly possible. It wasn't that much blood really. She and Agnes saw more blood while changing surgical dressings.

With her heart pounding hard enough to make her lightheaded, Sarah grasped the doorknob and twisted. She froze, terrified of what she might find behind the door, but common sense took over. If Agnes was in the bathroom, she might be bleeding to death while Sarah dillydallied with her own cowardice. Getting a grip on her fear, she gave the door a little push. Its hinges creaked as the door swung gently inward. Another pool of bright red shone in sharp contrast to the white floor tiles, but there was no sign of Agnes. Sarah turned back toward the captain.

"She's not here. Look at this." With a trembling finger, Sarah pointed to the red stain on the bathroom floor. "There's only one explanation. They've taken her."

"Who are they?"

Sarah stared in disbelief. How could anyone be so dense? She let her arm sweep from one side to the other, taking in the whole of the bedroom. Shaking with fury and fear, she spoke slowly and carefully, as one might to a dimwitted child. "The men who did all of this."

"Look, I know you're upset, but you don't know for sure. She could have stepped out for any number of reasons."

Heat rose in Sarah's face and she glared at him. "She would have left a note telling me. She's very methodical and organized. She wouldn't leave pools of blood on the floor without an explanation. It's completely out of character."

"When people are really upset or have had a bad experience, they sometimes act out of character." The captain's voice was irritatingly soothing and calm.

"Not Agnes. She's the Rock of Gibraltar."

"In that case, gather up some things and let's get out of here."

Sarah felt like screaming. Instead, she forced herself to reply quietly, "No."

"What do you mean, no?"

"I'm not budging until I know what's happened to Agnes." Sarah glared up at the captain through narrowed eyes.

"And just how long do you plan to stay here? Until the men who did this come back for a second look?"

Although common sense shouted that he was right, Sarah couldn't just leave Agnes to the fates. She spoke evenly, enunciating her words with great care though her heart rate rose with each syllable. "Promise me you'll find her."

Kurt put his hands on his hips and cocked his head to one side. "And how do you suggest I go about that when we don't have a clue who has her or if anyone has her?" He snorted and continued, "As if I have time for this. Leave it to the MPs."

Plastering her best faux smile on her lips, Sarah let her tone match his sarcasm note for note. "I'm sure you will find a way. I doubt the MPs will work with the dedication of a guy for whom a coded message was intended."

"Look, if some thugs have taken her, even you should be able to figure out this place isn't safe." Anger and frustration colored his tone. "Come on. Let's go."

Sarah didn't budge. Through clenched teeth she hissed, "Not until you promise to find Agnes."

"Of all the stupid, pigheaded…" Kurt's eyes blazed. His gaze shifted away from Sarah, then snapped back to look directly into her eyes. "What makes you think I can promise that?"

Sarah's chin rose. "Because I'm betting you know a whole lot more about this business than you're telling me."

"So you're a mind reader now too, are you?" Kurt shouted. "Even if it's so, how does staying here help Agnes?"

Feeling foolish and furious, Sarah sat down on the edge of the nearest mattress intent on making her point, but promptly burst into tears.

Kurt knelt down and slipped an arm around her shoulders. "Look, I shouldn't have yelled at you. I'm sorry I made you cry. It'll be better after we leave this place."

Sarah jerked away from him and stared in disbelief.

"You think you made me cry? Of all the presumption! I'm crying because I'm so damned mad. And don't you dare touch me again."

"I wouldn't dream of it. I might get my eyes scratched out for my trouble." Kurt's angry words rang through the apartment and bounced off the walls.

A responding yell bubbled up in Sarah, but when she opened her mouth, raucous laughter tumbled out instead. Sarah couldn't believe the sound was coming from her or how her body shook beyond her control. After what seemed an eon, she went limp with exhaustion. The shaking dissipated. Silence reigned.

Her gaze drifted upward to meet the captain's eyes, which were filled with concern. She smiled ruefully. "I guess I'm more upset by all this than I wanted to admit."

"So it would seem. You aren't going into shock on me, are you?"

Sarah pressed her fingers to the pulse point on her wrist. "I don't think so."

She fell into a thoughtful silence and let her gaze drift about the room. Maybe the captain was right. She had to admit it would be the height of foolishness to hang around waiting for the intruders to return, and she really couldn't bear the sight of all the destruction any longer.

Letting out a long, slow breath, she spoke quietly. "I think I'm ready to leave now."

"Good." Satisfaction and something close to relief filled the captain's voice. "Pack enough clothes for a couple of weeks."

"Where are you taking me?"

"To my place." When she shot him an angry look,

he cut her off before she could speak. "You really don't have a choice."

"And just what makes you think I will blithely follow your orders?"

His eyes narrowed and his mouth became firm. He lifted his arm in a gesture that took in the whole room. "Look at this place. I think even you will agree it's uninhabitable. And because it beats sleeping on the street."

Chapter 8

Kurt glanced sidewise at Sarah's profile beside him in the Jeep's passenger seat. Her temper matched her red hair perfectly. He wasn't sure what he would have done if she had continued to refuse to leave the wrecked apartment. Bodily carried her out, most likely. He didn't want to tell her that in all likelihood her roommate was dead and that she would probably be next unless measures were taken to ensure her safety. Stashing the girl at his place for a while looked like the best way to keep her alive. The MPs would have to solve the mystery of the roommate.

A car horn's blast snatched Kurt's attention back to the road just in time to avoid sideswiping an oncoming vehicle. He shook his head. Pretty enough to break a man's heart and stubborn enough to get him killed. She was trouble. You could take that to the bank.

Sarah must have caught him looking at her. Out of the corner of his eye, he could see a little half-smile on her Cupid's bow lips.

"Penny for your thoughts, Captain."

"They aren't worth that much. And it's Kurt. If we're going to be living together for a while, I think we ought to be on a first name basis, don't you?"

"Living together? You better not be getting ideas, *Captain Heinz*." Her emphasis on his name made her meaning unmistakable.

For crying out loud. This girl was something else. Here he was trying to help her and she wanted to set the terms. Kurt couldn't keep the irritation from his voice. "I didn't mean it that way. I'll sleep in the living room on the sofa. You'll have the bedroom all to yourself. I will have to use the same bathroom, though. We've only got one."

"We? Do you have a roommate?"

Stupid slip of the tongue. "Uh, no. Did I say we?"

"Yes, you did. Get this straight, mister. I'm not living with two men, so you can take me to the hospital. Now. They'll squeeze me in somewhere. And since you don't want to do anything about Agnes, I'll camp out in the Anfa's lobby. I bet that'll get your boss's attention."

Snippy broad. Thinks every guy she meets wants to climb into bed with her. He forced back a grin. Of course, there were lots of sex-starved soldiers around, but he didn't need to trick a girl into his bed.

"Slow down. I live alone except when a friend needs a place to bunk down. And you can forget my boss looking for one missing nurse. You could dance naked in the general's office and all it will get you is a round of applause, if you're lucky. As I said, I'll sleep on my lumpy, too short sofa. You'll be more comfortable and safer with me. Does that meet with your approval?" Sarcasm. That was a nice, mature touch, Heinz.

She turned doe eyes on him and graced him with a tight smile. "That will have to do, I suppose."

Well, sister, it's the best offer you're likely to get. It was on the tip of his tongue. He wanted to say it aloud, but something gave him pause. He glanced at her out of the corner of his eye. She looked so unhappy, so tired. He'd like to leave her to her just desserts, but he wouldn't, in fact couldn't. For all her bossy, demanding ways, he could feel this girl getting under his skin. The role of knight-errant sat uncomfortably on him, but it was one he seemed to be embracing against his better judgment.

He would have to break Phelps to her gently, maybe as a friend who got bombed out of his own billet. But in reality, there was really nothing else he could let her do. Until Kurt knew who was behind his contact's murder, it was best to keep Sarah close. She would be safer where he could keep an eye on her.

Another reason, one that made him cringe inwardly, reared its ugly head. She might prove valuable in trapping his contact's killer. He had a strong hunch—find the people who had taken this Agnes woman and he would find a big piece in the puzzle that had High Command in London and Washington OSS in such a lather they were willing to risk sending him into the lion's den. His conscience shouted that he was a jerk to even think about using the girl as bait, but he hadn't been the one who had gotten her involved in the first place. And besides, conscience was a commodity no one could afford these days. His jaw tightened. He had been taught to take maximum advantage of all situations regardless of how personally repugnant they might be to him. God, he hated war and the espionage he seemed so good at conducting. It made him feel dirty; sometimes he wondered if he would ever feel clean again.

MacFadyen, and probably Maitland, would have to be told about Sarah, but it could wait until Kurt could shake himself free from Phelps. Fortunately, Phelps hadn't actually seen Sarah when she first came to the flat, so he wouldn't know she was the bearer of the coded message. For reasons Kurt couldn't put his finger on, he was relieved that Phelps wouldn't recognize the girl. He wasn't completely sure he trusted his new roommate. Even though Phelps was MacFadyen's boy, there was something about him that put Kurt on edge. Phelps would probably react poorly to having Sarah move in, but he didn't have a say in the matter either. As to the explanation Kurt would give for her being there, he would think of something. For now, all that mattered was to make sure she stayed alive.

A sudden flash of fury swept through Kurt. Damn the Nazis and their web of spies and double agents. He would never have involved mere nurses in this mess, but the stranger in gray had made keeping them out of it impossible.

The Jeep's tires began rumbling as they hit a rough patch of road. He could feel her body relaxing a little when her shoulder bumped against his. He'd never thought of potholes as useful until that moment. Glancing again at her winsome profile, a wave of protectiveness swept through him.

Kurt's hands tightened on the wheel until his knuckles turned white. Being so close to Sarah was messing with his head. With what he had coming up, the fate of two army nurses shouldn't even be a blip on his radar, but Sarah and her problems seemed to be taking over his mind and his will. He hoped Agnes would turn up okay because he didn't have time to think about her, much less try to find her. Then the memory of Sarah's frightened, bewildered face surfaced, demanding that he find her roommate, and he suspected that against all common sense he would look for this Agnes no matter the cost. Of course, Agnes was probably dead, her body dumped in some Casablanca back alley, but Kurt didn't have the heart to say it aloud.

Damn. What the hell was coming over him? He couldn't get involved with this girl right now or any time in the near future. The risk would be too great to everyone.

Chapter 9

Kurt pushed the door to his apartment open. Sarah stepped through the vestibule and into the front room. Her nose wrinkled as the sights and odors of male habitation greeted her. Dirty dishes overflowed a sink in the corner of the room that served as kitchen. Clothes, shoes, and socks lay strewn about the furniture and floor. It seemed Captain Kurt Heinz, despite his know-it-all attitude, had his share of faults.

She raised her brow and asked in a sticky sweet voice, "Maid didn't come today?"

Kurt grinned as he snatched dirty clothes from the sofa and piled them on a chair. "Today and every day. Sorry about the mess. Why don't you sit here while I get some of this stuff picked up?"

"Nope. Four hands will make quicker work. I'll work on the kitchen while you see to the clothes."

The captain's face was an evolving picture of what he must be thinking. Surprise, followed by relief, and topped off with sheepish gratitude all made their way across his rugged features. "You sure? KP duty is definitely not expected or required."

"I'm quite sure."

"But you've had a rough day. Why don't you put your feet up with a drink? There's a decent bottle of scotch somewhere around here."

The way he was trying so hard to reject her help

when it was so obvious he really wanted it made Sarah feel like laughing aloud. In the tone she used for soothing frightened patients, she said, "Thanks, but no. If I stay busy, I won't think about what's happened."

"I guess that makes sense." He hesitated for a moment and then another emotion that looked a lot like guilt appeared in his eyes. "Look, this is probably not the time to say this, but maybe it would be better to get it out in the open now. You've asked me to find Agnes, and I'm going to try. But I don't want you to build up false hope, and I'm not promising anything. Am I being clear?"

A physical shock coursed through Sarah at mention of Agnes. She concentrated hard to keep her voice from shaking. "Crystal, but until we find Agnes, I don't think I'll be able to rest."

"Hold on. I said *I* would try. There is not going to be any *we*. No way. Got it?"

Sarah had no intention of acknowledging such an absurd demand. Just when she thought he was one of the good guys, he became all dictatorial and demanding. She turned toward the kitchen corner before he could see the tears of anger and fear in her eyes. She'd be damned if she would cry in front of him again. That would wait until she could bury her face in a pillow. Then she would let it all out.

With emotionally fueled energy, Sarah set to the task of scraping heaven only knew how many days, maybe weeks, of food from the load of encrusted plates, pots, and pans overrunning the sink. The clanging and banging she created drew some quick glances from the captain, but she didn't care. If her muscles ached, then her mind didn't need to think. When she dropped a plate and it shattered, Captain Heinz came to her side.

"Why don't you let me finish up here?" His voice was filled with concern and caution.

"No. I said I'd do this, and I will. I don't need your help. I'm sorry about the plate." Sarah's voice sounded rude and petulant, but it was just too bad. She needed to decompress and that meant time to force her mind to become blank and drift without conscious thought. The very idea of having to make polite conversation left her feeling drained. She didn't have the emotional strength for it. Blowing out a breath of irritation, she began picking up the broken shards. The captain wisely removed himself to the sofa.

By the time she draped the dishrag over the tap, night darkened the panes of the room's single large window. She observed her reflection in the glass. A thin face with wide eyes holding a rather haunted expression stared back at her. Her uniform was baggy and beginning to fray at the cuffs. Stray locks, having escaped their pins, hung here and there around her face and neck. She pushed one strand behind each ear and let out a little sigh of disgust. What had become of the girl who loved pretty clothes and to dress up for a night on the town? War was turning her into a drudge just as her mother had warned, but at least she had the satisfaction of knowing that what she was doing was important. It was the consolation to which she could cling until this nightmare ended.

Damn it! She had to get a grip on herself. Being maudlin wasn't going to help the situation or find Agnes any faster. Sarah splashed her face with cold water and rubbed it hard with a dishtowel.

She turned to the sofa where the captain sat

reading. "I think I'll take that drink now. After that, I'll see what you have to make supper."

"The drink's a go, but no way are you going to cook. I'm taking you to a little restaurant around the corner. They serve a decent lamb dish. I strongly suspect the owner has ties to the black market, but he claims he's got a cousin with a farm south along the coast. Who knows? Maybe it's true. After supper, you will take a bath and go to bed."

Sarah's first instinct was to argue. She disliked his giving her orders, but then she thought better of it. It was clear he was trying to be kind, wanting to take care of her. Maybe she should let him. Something that felt an awful lot like relief spread through her. It had been a long time since she had been on the receiving end of being cared for and pampered. At any rate, she was too exhausted to do battle over anything, certainly nothing as meaningless as what she would eat.

She gave him a tired smile. "Lead on, MacDuff. I've learned to love lamb since coming to Casablanca."

"A misquote of Macbeth just before he was killed by the said MacDuff. Let's hope our evening turns out better than his did."

"Misquote?"

"It's actually, 'Lay on, MacDuff.' Early modern usage."

"Are you a Shakespeare scholar as well as being whatever it is you do for the army, Captain Heinz?" Sarah winced a little at the derisive edge in her voice, but she had a hard time picturing him as anything other than an officious military man.

The captain cocked his head to one side and put an exaggerated expression of professorial displeasure on his face. A prissily wagging finger and theatrical flare to his lips completed the picture. "What's that? To whom are you speaking?"

Sarah laughed in spite of herself. "*You*, Idiot."

"Well, I refuse to answer your question, *Sarah,* until you call me by my Christian name."

"Okay, *Kurt*." Sarah raised an eyebrow. "You do a fair imitation of a British aristocrat. Are you an actor in addition to being a general's aide?"

"First, I'm a colonel's aide. A good bit lower down the totem pole, Ma'am." Kurt's Texas drawl was back in force. "Second, I'm good with impressions. Comes in handy at parties and family gatherings. Third, I minored in English Lit. Now let's go eat. I'm hungry."

A short walk brought them to a heavy wooden door behind which lay a little four table restaurant. Sarah's eyes took a moment to adjust to the interior lit only by candles and oil lamps, creating an exotic, otherworldly atmosphere. It might have been very romantic if she had been with the right man.

Kurt led her to one of the traditional Moroccan tables covered with colorful tile mosaics and held her hand as she knelt onto the brightly patterned floor cushions surrounding it.

"I'm getting the feeling we are going to dine in the traditional Moroccan style."

Kurt smiled gently. "Would that be so bad? To try something different?"

"I guess not. When in Rome…"

Sarah paused and broke eye contact with Kurt. The trite saying was rushing her headlong into banality and that was the last word she wanted the captain to associate with her. Surprised and flustered by the thought, she traced the mosaic pattern on the tabletop with her fingers.

"Moroccan tiles are really pretty, don't you think?" Another trite comment. Why couldn't she think of anything brilliant or interesting to say?

An expression of surprise followed by gentle amusement filled Kurt's eyes. "Yes, they are beautiful. I'm partial to the really colorful ones."

His mirth at her expense made Sarah want to crawl under the table, but she doubted she would fit as it was so low to the floor. Why did she care what he thought anyway? They were nothing to one another, except that she needed him to find Agnes.

To her relief, the waiter arrived, preventing another of Sarah's inane comments and covering her confusion. Over a luscious lamb *tagine*, tangy with apricots and sweetened with a touch of honey, Sarah began to feel better than she had thought possible. She even enjoyed the Moroccan custom of shoveling food into her mouth with her fingers.

While they ate, she discovered Kurt was actually rather good company. He entertained her with tales of his Texas childhood spent on a dairy farm where German was spoken exclusively. She learned he had graduated from Texas A&M with a degree in history and dreams of becoming a lawyer, but couldn't afford law school, so he joined the Army instead. The war came shortly after he graduated from OCS. He was sent overseas after some additional training about which he was rather vague.

Sarah was glad he did most of the talking, but she wondered what he left out. He really was a contradiction. It seemed he liked talking about his early life, but couldn't be drawn out about anything since he joined the army. He would be a difficult man to live with.

Now where had that thought come from?

At the end of the meal, she looked across the table into his smiling face and found that she liked what she saw. He wasn't exactly handsome, but he was attractive in a very masculine, virile way. Better yet, he had a winning smile and kind eyes. He wasn't her type. She had always preferred them tall, dark, and handsome, but he seemed like a nice guy, the kind that the right girl could fall hard for. Then a shadow fell and another face suddenly interposed itself on Kurt's. Her heart dropped to the pit of her stomach. She hadn't seen Bill, the cheating pilot, since he flew away from Casablanca without so much as a goodbye, but Sarah still found herself wanting, no yearning to see him come walking through any door, any time. Her mind told her it was stupid, but her wayward heart refused to listen.

She closed her eyes and massaged her temples. When she looked up at the figure on the other side of the table again, he was the captain once more. It was definitely time for bath and bed.

****

Kurt looked at Sarah in complete confusion. He was quite sure he hadn't said or done anything to produce the expression he saw etched on her face. "Are you okay? You're as white as a sheet."

Red flooded the apples of her cheeks as she shook her head. "I'm just tired. I've been working double shifts for a while, and I guess it's catching up with me."

Kurt had an inkling that she wasn't telling him everything, but he really had no right to press for more information. Although she would be sleeping in his bed, they hadn't known each other long enough for him to demand full and complete disclosure of what was on her mind. He had secrets he must keep at all costs. Why should she be expected to tell all simply to satisfy the curiosity of a near stranger? Unfortunately, he found he rather wanted to know all there was about Sarah Barrett, RN. Instead of pursuing that dangerous train of thought, he unfolded himself from the low table, stood, and held out his hand.

Sarah placed her hand in his and he assisted her to her feet. She must be descended from birds because she was as light as a feather and graceful as a swan. The urge to place his hands around her waist was almost overwhelming. His fingers would probably meet tip-to-tip. When she shot him a quizzical look, he realized he must have been staring—his turn to be embarrassed.

Heat filled his face as he shifted his gaze to a spot over her head on the back wall. He tossed more than enough cash on the table to cover their meal and forced as casual a tone as he could muster. "Let's get you home before you go to sleep on your feet."

He glanced at Sarah out of the corner of his eye. She was looking up at him as though something had amused her no end. Perhaps she could read minds after all. He smiled as much to himself as at her and taking her elbow, steered her toward the door.

The chill night air sent a shiver down Kurt's spine despite the weight of his winter uniform jacket. He instinctively wanted to put a protective arm around Sarah's thin shoulders, but the gesture would most certainly be rebuffed. Not wanting to create any more tension between them than already existed, he willed his greedy hands to stay at his sides and prayed that keeping them there wasn't going to become a problem for him.

Chapter 10

Kurt glanced up at the four-story building where his flat lay sandwiched between the street level shops and the floors above. A chink of light glowed from the single front window between blackout curtains that weren't drawn quite closely enough.

Phelps had returned. A cover story for his presence in the flat couldn't be put off any longer. Kurt's mind churned as he led Sarah through the small entrance alcove and up the dark staircase, their shoes tapping out their ascent on the tile covered risers. For once, Kurt was grateful for the ringing echo that announced the arrival of anyone coming up from the street. He hoped Phelps didn't choose tonight to become a dullard. The man, if nothing else, had thus far shown himself to be quick on the uptake.

A new worry popped up. Would Phelps recognize Sarah? He wasn't sure whether Phelps had heard Sarah's voice and name when she first came pounding on their door. He played the scene over in his mind. The flat's reception vestibule prevented anyone in the living area from seeing who came through the door and Phelps had already slipped into the bedroom when Sarah entered the front room. He was fairly confident Phelps hadn't seen her. A sense of relief swept through him.

Like Kurt, Phelps was deep into intelligence

operations. Unlike Kurt, Phelps was a civilian who had been snatched from his position as psychological warfare advisor to the big boys at Bletchley Park and hustled off to Casablanca for the sole purpose of teaching Kurt to pass himself off as his Nazi cousin, Helmut. Phelps didn't have actual field experience, so it came as no surprise that he didn't want to have direct contact with casual, unexpected visitors. And like Kurt, Phelps was a man of many secrets.

For reasons Kurt couldn't explain or maybe didn't want to admit, he wanted to shield Sarah from Phelps. The coded message, her vandalized apartment, her missing roommate were secrets that were better kept for fewer people knowing them. It would be safer for her. And then there was Phelps himself. In his way, Phelps was a suave, sophisticated man, the kind women often found attractive. Kurt mentally shook himself. Jealousy and protective instincts were a dangerous combination for someone in his line of work.

Kurt took his time rattling and fumbling keys around, trying to insert one into the lock. At length, the door moved inward.

He turned to Sarah and said louder than necessary, "After you, M'lady. Your bath and chamber await." Corny, hokey, and possibly insulting, but it was the best he could think of at the moment.

She tossed him a quizzical glance and proceeded through the vestibule into the front room where she came up short at the sight of Phelps lounging prone on the sofa, a cigarette dangling from his lips dropping ash onto the front of his open collar shirt. Phelps jumped to his feet and crushed out his smoke in an overflowing ashtray.

He flapped at the gray haze hanging over the sofa. "Oh, I say. Dreadfully sorry. Wasn't expecting company."

Sarah looked from Phelps to Kurt with growing suspicion reflected in her eyes. Kurt quickly stepped forward.

"Phelps, you're early. I thought you weren't coming until next week."

Phelps looked startled for only a heartbeat and then recovered his usual aplomb. "Sorry. There has obviously been a most unexpected change of plans."

Damn the man's sly attempt at humor. Kurt glanced at Sarah to see if she had caught the double meaning in Phelps's comment, then said, "Yeah, unexpected would be the word for it."

"At any rate, couldn't get clearance for sending word to you." Phelps chuckled. "The war office will have its pesky little rules, you know."

"Of course." Kurt strode to the sofa, his hand extended. "Glad you're here. Did you have a calm trip?"

Phelps took Kurt's hand and shook it as though they hadn't seen one another for years. "A bit choppy, but nothing too rough." His gaze shifted toward Sarah, an inquiring smile playing over his features.

"This is Nurse Sarah Barrett with the 8th Evacuation Hospital. She needs a place to stay until something opens up. I've given her the bedroom."

Sarah's face flushed as she looked up at Phelps. "I'm so sorry. Captain Heinz, you'll have to find me another place to stay or take me to the hospital. You can't expect your guest to sleep on the sofa."

"Like I told you, there's nothing. Not even a

closet." Irritation made the overheated room feel even hotter. "Believe me. I tried everyone I know. And Phelps won't be sleeping on the sofa. He'll sleep on the mattress that we'll drag out here while you have your bath. It'll be okay. We're both gentlemen." Kurt didn't look at his roommate, but he felt the man's eyes boring into his back. He pointed to the bedroom door. "The bathroom is through that door on the far side of the room. Clean pajamas are in the cupboard." Kurt mentally held his breath. If she insisted on going to the hospital, Kurt wasn't sure what he would say, but he would think of something, even if it meant taking Phelps into his confidence and revealing to Sarah the extent of the danger she was in.

Sarah hesitated, looking from Phelps to Kurt and back. Without a word, she nodded and picked up her suitcase from its place by Kurt's feet. The click of the bathroom door's lock sounded a few seconds later followed by the thunder of water gushing into the tub.

Kurt started toward the bedroom, but was waylaid by Phelps's hand on his arm. "Have you taken complete leave of your senses, man? Whatever do you mean bringing a girl here?"

Kurt thought for a second before answering. "She's good looking and she needs a place for a few days. Her place got ransacked by thieves. It's in a bad part of the city. A nurse shouldn't have been billeted there in the first place."

"And how did you meet said good looking girl?"

"New Year's Eve. At a restaurant. Now, let's get the bed in here before she's finished in the bathroom."

Phelps's eyes narrowed and he looked as though he wanted to pursue the subject, but Kurt went into the bedroom and grabbed a mattress from the nearest twin bed.

"Come help with this unless you want to sleep on the floor."

"Heinz, MacFadyen will hear of this, and he will not be best pleased. I admit we can't turn her out in the dead of night, but she must go tomorrow. That's final."

Kurt's eyes must have bulged because the top of his head felt like it was about to blow off. He didn't trust himself to speak until he had taken a couple of deep breaths. "The last time I checked, you have no authority over military personnel, so I'm not sure where you get off giving orders. There aren't any rooms left in the city. I've already checked it out. Even MacFadyen couldn't shoehorn her in anywhere." Kurt watched Phelps's reaction. His face was a study in pop-eyed consternation, making Kurt grin maliciously. "Yeah, I've already told our boss, so keep out of it."

Phelps's face flamed, but he kept quiet and grabbed the other side of the mattress. Neither man spoke as they wrestled the bed into the living room and shoved it against a wall. Kurt's mind roiled with the lie he had just told. The damage would be easier to control if he could get to MacFadyen before Phelps did.

His boss would probably bluster and shout, but in the end he would have to accept Sarah's being in the flat unless he was able to pull rabbits out of hats. And after things settled down and Casablanca was back to normal, or as normal as a city under armed occupation could be, a room would surely become available. He would see that her name was at the top of the billeting list. MacFadyen would owe him that much. With that accomplished, he would be free of any feeling of obligation to the girl. Once his mission was completed, he could fly back to London without ever seeing her again. It would be for the best. And he would be rid of this inconvenient need to protect and comfort her no matter what. Hell, that came dangerously close to cherishing, something he didn't want to feel until this damned war was over. There was no place for emotional entanglements in intelligence work. Yes, the sooner this is over, the better for everybody. He blew out a long breath in a surge of resolve. He would feel a certain amount of regret, but making these assurances to his boss would get Sarah a safe place to stay.

At least that was how Kurt envisioned it playing out. MacFadyen could be difficult and unpredictable at the best of times. Kurt glanced at his watch. The hands approached midnight and that meant a short night's sleep. There was nothing for it but to make sure he left for the Anfa office before Phelps woke up in the morning.

****

Sarah tested the water's temperature with her big toe, and finding it just right, plunged in up to her chin. She should probably be ashamed to use up so much of the precious commodity considering the city sat at the edge of the desert, but for once she didn't care. The last thirty-six hours had been just possibly the worst of her life. Although she saw terrible injury and death everyday at the hospital, it was never so personal. She couldn't afford for it to be. Medical personnel had it pounded into them during training. In self-preservation, she never allowed herself to become personally involved. She had kept her patients at a professional distance, but Agnes was a different story altogether.

Whatever Captain Kurt Heinz said or thought, she was determined to see that they found Agnes. He could go on about having a job to do. So what? Didn't everyone in this war? Feeling like she was going to shout because she was suddenly so angry, Sarah dove completely under the water and blew rage fueled bubbles until the absurdity of it brought her to the surface, smiling ruefully and choking.

She might as well try to enjoy herself. This was the first real bath she had taken in ages. She reclined against the enamel back of the tub and luxuriated in the steamy warmth. She hadn't seen a tub since they left Virginia. The minuscule shower in the apartment she had shared with Agnes had been a godsend after weeks on board the ship that brought troops and medical staff alike to Casablanca from their point of deployment at Newport News. Sarah had always dreamed of being a world traveler, but so far all she had seen was a naval installation on the English coast and Casablanca. She supposed it wasn't bad for a girl who never thought she would ever get out of the Shenandoah Valley.

Thinking of home brought Agnes's plight back to her full force. Agnes was the older sister Sarah never had but always longed for. If it hadn't been for the captain's man in gray and his blasted coded message, none of this would have happened. When they found Agnes and things were back to normal, she would say farewell to the secretive Captain Kurt Heinz and his odd friends. Until then, she wasn't going to give him any peace.

Chapter 11

The stars were just bidding farewell to the dawn when Kurt slipped out of the flat, down the stairs, and out onto the street for the short walk to the Anfa. He hadn't been able to get into the bathroom to shave because Sarah, suspicious untrusting girl that she was, had locked the bedroom door. At any rate, it was probably for the best. Moving around too much might have awakened his other roommate. Kurt had left the flat with the sound of Phelps's light snoring filling the front room. He ran a hand over his chin. The stubble itched and MacFadyen demanded clean-shaven officers. Maybe the hotel concierge would rustle up a razor and toothbrush for him.

A brief chat with the assistant manager accompanied by a nice gratuity admitted Kurt to the manager's private bathroom, grooming tools in hand. Looking at himself in the mirror over a steaming basin of water, he saw dark smudges under eyes set in a faintly gaunt face. He supposed he had lost weight since arriving in Morocco. There weren't really too many overweight soldiers. Probably would lose a few more pounds before all this was over. Shaking his head at his own morbid thoughts, he glanced at his watch and lathered his chin. He made quick work of his beard and then headed toward the elevator.

The elevator doors opened on an all but vacant

floor. The one exception was the lovely Hortensia at her post outside MacFadyen's office.

Approaching her desk, Kurt smiled and asked, "Keeps you chained here all hours, does he?"

There wasn't even a break in the clacking of the secretary's typewriter keys as she glanced up at Kurt and murmured, "Hmm."

Jerking his head in the direction of MacFadyen's office door, Kurt continued, "How's the weather this morning?"

Hortensia smirked as her fingers continued to fly over the keyboard. "Oh, fair to partly cloudy, I'd say. Only one smallish thunderstorm so far, but the day is young."

"Anything I should know about?"

"Not really. Just the usual." Hortensia glanced at the paper in her typewriter carriage. "Oh, blast! Just look at what I've done. Now I'll have to start over."

Kurt chewed his lip while he watched the girl snatch at the object of her frustration. He really needed to know how to handle his boss today. Shifting from one foot to the other, he cast about for something to say to prolong lingering by her desk. "Uh, other than wasting typewriter paper, you doing okay this morning?"

Hortensia's hands ceased fumbling with the ruined document. She looked up fully for the first time since Kurt arrived, her mouth a straight line and one eyebrow arching toward her hairline. "Captain Heinz, as much as I enjoy our tête-à-têtes, I really do have too much work to continue this little dance. What do you need?"

"Sorry. I've got a problem to talk over with the boss."

"Well, my advice is get on with it. He's already called for a second pot of coffee, never a good sign. Knock on the door and go in."

"I don't think so." Kurt mustered his most ingratiating grin. "Let him know I'm here? Sorta smooth the path? He likes you a whole lot better than me."

She smiled and picked up her telephone receiver. "I suppose you're right."

Kurt stood at attention in front of MacFadyen. The man did not deign to acknowledge his presence. Out of the corner of his eye, Kurt could just see the clock perched on the corner of the desk. The second hand made two complete circles of the clock face. Losing patience with this little cat and mouse game that his boss occasionally liked to inflict on his subordinates, Kurt loudly cleared his throat.

MacFadyen looked up with a frown. "Heinz, couldn't it have waited until a decent hour? I arrive early for the sole purpose of getting work done before the daily onslaught."

"Sorry, sir. Thank you for seeing me." Kurt paused, trying to decide exactly how much he would tell the colonel about Sarah. Initially he had thought he should tell all, but something was holding him back now that the moment had arrived.

"Well, do get on with it. I haven't got all day."

"I thought I should let you know I have a girl staying in my apartment."

MacFadyen's eyes bulged ever so slightly under his bushy, ginger colored brows. "Really, now. That so?" The sarcasm could have been cut with a knife. The colonel's face reddened. "Under ordinary circumstances the romantic dalliances of junior officers would be of little interest to me, but considering the circumstances of your present assignment, I am dumbfounded you would be stupid enough to take up with some woman. Get rid of her."

"Please let me explain, sir." Kurt spent the next few minutes telling how an army nurse with a top secret coded message came to be under his roof. "So you see, I really felt I didn't have a choice. She isn't safe after the break-in at her place. She's about your daughter's age, I think. I've called everyone I know without any luck. If you could recommend a secure billet for her, I'll move her immediately."

Sarah's being the same age as the Honorable Miss MacFadyen, presently serving safe and sound in the London War Office, seemed to have appealed to his boss's sense of honor and his paternal instincts.

MacFadyen's eyes softened ever so slightly and his color faded to its normal freckled strewn pallor. He harrumphed once and said, "Young woman, you say?"

"Yes sir."

"Whatever did we think we were doing sending young girls to war? I don't care if they are trained nurses and secretaries. I'll look into a better place for the girl. In the meantime, I suppose she'll be out of the flat at the hospital much of the time. See that you transport her to and from."

"Yes, sir. Thank you, sir." Kurt saluted. "Will that be all, sir?"

"Actually, no it isn't. It's just as well you showed up this morning. Was going to send for you anyway. Why don't you take a seat, my boy." The sudden shift in MacFadyen's voice to something akin to camaraderie set off warning bells in Kurt's head. The old man rarely showed emotion and now he had done it twice in so many minutes. Something was up. Kurt wanted a smoke in the worst sort of way.

MacFadyen took an envelope marked top secret from a drawer and tossed it on the desk in front of Kurt. "He's been located. Those coordinates that nurse of yours stumbled upon were on the money. Your target arrives there day after tomorrow. Get your bag packed. You leave in three days."

****

Sarah awoke with a start. The vision of Agnes lying in a pool of blood lingered after the dream ended, leaving Sarah muddleheaded and tired, her head on a damp pillow. She swiped at the tears that traced their way down her cheeks, then sat up. Her forehead felt like it was trying to detach itself from the rest of her skull. She massaged her temples trying to ease the headache thumping just behind her eyes. It was no wonder her head pounded. She had tossed and turned half the night.

She snatched her wristwatch from the nightstand. Early still, but she could see daylight shining through the space at the bottom of the closed bedroom door. Throwing a borrowed robe over borrowed pajamas, she tiptoed to the door and opened it a crack. The front room was empty. Apparently Capt. Heinz and his guest had already left the flat. Perhaps she shouldn't have slept so long. The men must have left the flat without being able to clean up. A little pang of guilt pricked her conscience. Not a very nice way to repay the captain's kindness. Padding over to the kitchen nook, she gingerly tapped the side of the coffee pot. Good. Still hot. The men must not have been gone too long. While she poked around in the single cupboard for sugar, she took stock. She needed to stop by the Quartermaster and request new uniforms. Sarah sighed and bit her lip to keep from giving in to all out bawling. The vandals had managed to rip apart her clothes while they destroyed the furniture in the apartment. She and Agnes had thought themselves so lucky because they had been placed in a real furnished apartment unlike many of the girls who were billeted in rooms at the hospital. Sarah hadn't even asked who they might have displaced from their home in the process or what magic Agnes must have conjured with the brass. It had seemed like a godsend not to be sleeping on an army cot at the hospital. So much for luck.

She glanced at her watch again. It was time she reported for duty. No matter what the captain said about her needing a little time off, staying away wasn't an option. Inactivity would make her crazy. As much as she wanted to hunt Kurt Heinz down and demand he begin the search for Agnes, she didn't know where to look for him. Or rather, she didn't know which office in the Anfa he might be in, if she could get into the place, if that was where he really worked, if he was who he said he was at all. All she had to go on was his word and that of a female voice on the end of the telephone that had given her an address. She knew so little about him, and yet she had willingly followed him to his flat where he lived with another man. She really must be losing her grip, but then the whole situation with the man in gray, her apartment, and Agnes's disappearance had thrown her into a tailspin.

She drained the last of the dark, sweet liquid from

the tin cup and washed it. Before she pulled on her only remaining uniform, she brought it close to her face. Her nose wrinkled when she sniffed the underarms, but too bad. It was all she had. Slipping the offending garment over her head, she made up her mind to tackle Kurt when her shift was over. The war and the wounded wouldn't wait because two nurses had run up against trouble.

The odor of antiseptics mixed with pine oil greeted Sarah as she passed through the double doors of the 8th Evacuation Hospital's temporary home in the former Italian Consulate. The smells were so familiar now that they brought a feeling of coming home with them. No matter the medical facility or location, they all had this in common. It never ceased to remind Sarah that she was part of something important, something bigger than just being a girl from Virginia with little experience of the world.

She found the shift charge nurse, clipboard in hand, strolling among the beds in Ward C, Sarah's usual assignment.

"Hey, Lois. I'm back. I'm sorry I've missed my shifts. Where do you want me?"

The charge nurse looked up from her paperwork and peered at Sarah over the rims of her glasses. "Hey, yourself. We are all desperate to know about Agnes. Any word?"

Sarah didn't trust herself to speak and simply shook her head. Between the lack of sleep, stress, and worry, she felt on the verge of tears at the mere mention of her best friend's name.

"We got a call about you. You've got friends in high places."

"Not that I know of."

"A certain Commander Maitland attached to a Colonel MacFadyen's office at the Anfa. British, no less." Lois's eyebrows rose and her voice implied a question rather than a statement. "He told us about Agnes being missing and your apartment. He said his office had found you a new billet and that you wouldn't report for duty for a few days. He cleared it through the hospital CO."

"Oh. He must work with Captain Heinz."

"And who is Captain Heinz?"

"A friend that Agnes and I met a while back. He helped me after I found the apartment all torn up."

Lois looked as though she would like to pursue the subject of Captain Heinz, but Sarah was reluctant to share more than she already had. Something was wrong with all of this. She didn't know what, but even she knew that a captain in the American Army didn't usually report to a British colonel. Sarah put on her brightest smile and cut Lois off with, "I'm really anxious to get back to work. Where do you need me?"

Lois's eyes swept over Sarah from head to foot. "You look terrible. How long has it been since you've slept?"

"I'm having a little trouble sleeping, but I'm ready to go to work."

"Hmmm. I don't think so. You've done more than your share around here already. You've worked double shifts for weeks now. I think you've earned some time off, and I'm giving it to you. I don't want to see you back here for at least three days."

"But—"

"No buts. We don't need another patient, and you

look dead on your feet. Now, get out of here." When Sarah hesitated, Lois's face became a study in military authority. "That's an order."

"Yes, ma'am. See you in three days."

Sarah felt almost giddy with an emotion she couldn't quite put a name to. It certainly wasn't joy considering what had happened. Perhaps relief was closer, but why? Then it dawned on her. Instead of going back to the apartment and to bed, Sarah had a better idea. She knew exactly what she would do. A small detail, apparently hidden by her subconscious for some maddening reason, surged forward in her memory. It was suddenly all so clear. That she hadn't remembered it before made her want to kick herself.

Chapter 12

Sarah hailed a taxi and gave the driver directions. One sure way to begin the search for Agnes was by tracing their connection to the man in gray. The place wouldn't be open for business at this hour, but maybe the staff would be in. If anyone could give information, it would likely be a *maître d'* or the manager. The restaurant wasn't far, but the short ride gave her time to think. Why hadn't she remembered before now? She barely noticed the man on New Year's Eve, but something had made him register with her. Sarah couldn't explain why she hadn't recognized him later on at the hospital. Perhaps the circumstances and his condition had gotten in the way. After all, it had taken a crisis to jar loose her memory of him.

When they pulled to the curb, she tossed a couple of bills on the front seat and scrambled onto the sidewalk without waiting for her change. Memory grew stronger as she pushed through the restaurant's door.

"*Pardon, mademoiselle. Je suis désolé, mais nous ne servons pas jusqu'à cinq heures.*"

Sarah's heart skipped a beat. She was looking up into the eyes of the *maître d'* who greeted patrons on New Year's Eve. His white tuxedo shirt strained to cover heavily muscled arms and chest. Maybe he was the bouncer as well. Unfortunately, her French didn't extend to forming the questions she wanted to ask.

Mustering her most winning smile, she said, "I'm so sorry to bother you. I'm not here to eat. Do you speak English by any chance?"

Solicitude and hospitality slipped from the man's expression. "If you are not here to dine, what is it you want?"

"I'm hoping you can help me with a problem."

The *maître d's* eyebrows rose ever so slightly. "With what could I possibly help you, if not with food?"

Sarah hesitated for a moment, trying to decide the best way forward. She settled on being direct. "I am looking for someone. I think you might know him."

"I know many people through my position here. What is the name?"

This was going to be tougher than Sarah had thought. In her eagerness for action, she hadn't stopped to formulate a real plan. She had just blundered into this place and gotten lucky. This man was neither friend nor acquaintance, yet she expected him to freely give her information on someone who had died under mysterious circumstances. What an impulsive nitwit she had been. Maybe she really did need more rest than she was getting. Heat filled her face.

"I'm afraid I don't know his name."

"Then how can I possibly help you?"

"Maybe if I described him, you might be able to place him?"

The man studied Sarah for several beats and gave a curt nod. She pointed to the cluster of tables where she and Agnes had been sitting on New Year's Eve. Her dead civilian patient had been within arm's reach at the very next table.

As Sarah described the man in gray, the *maître d's* eyes narrowed. She could feel an icy distance growing between them. He literally took a step back from her. His gaze traveled the length and breadth of the room as though he feared someone might overhear their conversation. Her every instinct shouted that this man knew something important.

Sarah opened her mouth to ask another question, but before she could utter a sound, the *maître d'* grabbed her arm and squeezed hard.

Sarah tried to wrench free. "Hey, who do you think—"

Between tightly smiling lips, he muttered, "Not now. Cooperate silently or I'll snap your arm like a matchstick." Sarah winced from the sudden increase in pressure. In full voice, he continued, "Of course you may not qualify, but we are always looking for attractive hostesses for our small coffee shop in the next street. If you will accompany me?"

He dragged Sarah through the restaurant door and out onto the sidewalk. Blinded by the abrupt change from semi-darkness to bright daylight, Sarah blinked back tears and locked her knees. "Look, mister, I don't know who you're used to dealing with but—"

"But nothing. Come quietly."

Sarah gasped as the pressure of his grip increased again. Her hand went numb. Her upper arm felt like it was in the jaws of a massive vise. There was no doubt in Sarah's mind that he could tear her arm from its socket if he chose. Dizziness clouded her mind as her knees buckled, but the man's grasp on her arm prevented her falling.

"Shut up. Not another sound. Is that clear?"

Sarah nodded.

The *maître d'* propelled her to the end of the block and around the corner into an alley that ran behind the restaurant. He turned Sarah to face him and shook her. "Who are you? What is your interest in the man you described?"

Anger surged through Sarah, mixing with her growing terror. She tried once more to yank free, but the vise encircling her arm bore down to the breaking point. She moaned involuntarily. Her eyes widened in surprise as the man's grip loosened ever so slightly. His expression told her that regret, maybe even chivalry, lurked somewhere under the surface of his aggression. Perhaps if he knew why she was seeking the information, he would help her.

Sarah answered in a low, measured cadence, trying desperately to maintain some sort of control over her emotions. "Since sitting beside that man, my apartment has been vandalized, my clothes have been ripped apart, and my roommate has disappeared. I think I have earned the right to know more about him."

"Sitting beside someone in a restaurant doesn't produce such a chain of events. You are withholding information. Tell me everything, or you may not live to return to your comrades, whoever they are."

Sarah's hand trembled as she pointed to her name patch. She couldn't keep her voice from shaking. "Look, I'm exactly who my uniform says I am. That man was brought into my ward after a bombing raid. Before he died, he asked me to do something for him. I did it, and that's when all the trouble started."

"Why would you do the bidding of a complete stranger? Are you really so stupid?"

Rage displaced terror. "I did it because he begged me to. It was the only comfort I could offer a dying patient. And I keep my promises. If you believe that's being stupid, there is something very wrong with your values, *Monsieur*."

The *maître d'* looked down into Sarah's eyes. After what appeared to be a rather intense internal struggle, his grip on her arm loosened enough to allow the blood to circulate again. Sighing, his mouth turned up at the corners, but the smile did not reach his eyes. "You are right, *mon cher*. My values have become somewhat skewed of late."

His voice held such longing that some of Sarah's anger slipped away. She spoke quietly. "It's the war. Everyone's been changed by it."

The man's features softened, his expression almost wistful. "Yes, and living in occupied territory tends to have an effect on one as well. First the French and the Spanish, next the Germans via control of their Vichy puppets, now you Americans and British."

"But you're French. Wouldn't you want your country back in control?"

His mirthless laugh held only bitterness. "I am not French, although I spoke that language before any other. My mother was French, my father Moroccan. I was born in Casablanca. Now tell me who you are."

Sarah bit her lower lip as she thought about what to say. Unfortunately, how to go about extracting information from a source hadn't been part of her training. If she was going to get the *maître d'* to reveal anything, she decided she was going to have to tell more of her own story than she really wanted. Everyone said Casablanca was full of spies and double agents from every corner of the world, that you never knew whom you could trust. The medical staff had been warned about this before being deployed from the base in England. Don't say too much. Don't inadvertently give aid to the enemy. Loose lips sink ships. Beware, beware, beware. In the end, she settled on telling him about joining the army nursing corps and that she hailed from Virginia.

"So, now will you tell me who my patient was or who I can talk to for more information?"

"I do not know his name, and even if I did, I would not tell you. Such information gets people killed."

"Then please let me go. The only thing I want is to find my friend and get back to caring for my patients."

"If you keep up this line of inquiry, it is most probable that neither of those goals will ever be achieved."

Sarah's pulse raced. If she looked down at her chest, she was sure she would see her heart's rhythmic bumping against her breastbone. The muscles of her upper arm jumped and trembled beneath the *maître d's* fingers.

Sympathy crept into his expression. "Do not look so frightened. You really have nothing to fear from me unless you are a German saboteur. Now, tell me the whole truth. Why you are seeking information on the man who died while in your care."

Sarah repeated what she had already told him, and added the one important detail she had previously omitted. She explained what the man in gray had asked her to do.

"So, he had a message to deliver. Yes, that makes sense. Would you like to know what happened after you

93

departed the restaurant in December?"

Sarah nodded.

"Your man followed on your heels in something of a rush. I thought he might have become frightened by someone he saw."

"Wait. I remember. A well-dressed couple passed us at the door. They were coming in as we were leaving. Could it have been them?"

Surprisingly, he didn't ask for a description. He seemed to have very clear memory of the couple. "Perhaps. They are people not to be trusted."

"So exactly who are they?"

The *maître d'* tilted his head slightly to one side and studied Sarah for several beats. "I don't suppose this is anything you could not learn from anyone you cared to ask. The man was once a highly placed Vichy official. Very chummy with the German high command that passed through Casablanca. Catered to their every demand, whether it was for black market items or lists of names. The woman was very popular with the German officers as well, but for reasons, shall we say, of a more intimate nature. Now these two pretend to be loyal Moroccans."

"They must have been the reason he ran. Don't you think?"

"It is hard to say. The restaurant was very crowded that night. Some of your countrymen were very loud that evening. I noticed your man kept glancing their way."

"The pilots? Yes, they were hard to miss."

"Very true. In fact, one of them left shortly after your man rushed away."

Sarah's pulse quickened. "Do you remember which

one?"

"Oh, yes. He made quite an impression. If he hadn't been in an American uniform, I would have taken him for German. Blonde, tall, typical SS type."

Sarah's heart fell to the soles of her feet.

The *maître d'* must have sensed her alarm, for he spoke quickly. "Miss Barrett, you seem to be a well-intentioned but naive young woman. I am going to give you some advice, and I hope you will follow it. Forget the man who died in your care. Forget his message and the person to whom you delivered it. No good can come of your becoming involved."

"That's all well and good, except I'm already involved. They took my best friend, and I intend to get her back."

"That would be a very foolish quest. It pains me to say this, but your friend is most likely dead, and her body will probably never be recovered. Leave this alone before it claims your life as well."

"Look. You know my name and life history. At least tell me whose advice I'm supposed to follow."

He let his hand slide from her upper arm to her wrist, which he lifted to his lips. Bowing slightly, he smiled and said, "Philippe Badouri at your service."

Sarah's mouth lifted at one corner. "Nice to meet you...I think."

The *maître d's* smile faded. "Please, Miss Barrett. I beseech you. Forget these events and anyone connected with them. You have no idea into what you have stumbled."

"Maybe not, but I'm learning fast." Sarah tugged at Philippe's grasp. "Are you going to let me leave? I'll be missed, and the MPs will come looking for me here."

Sarah inwardly winced at how easily the lie came to her.

"I doubt that, but yes. I will let you go." His hand dropped from her arm. "And Miss Barrett, if you are determined to chase spies and saboteurs, please learn to draw less attention to yourself, and do not so readily tell all that you know. One never knows whom one can trust in Casablanca. Better to trust no one."

As she walked to the taxi stop in front of the restaurant, Sarah thought about the *maître d's* parting words. It went against her nature to be so suspicious, but he was right. She must be more careful. While she waited, "trust no one" echoed in her mind. As much as she wanted to ignore it, Philippe Badouri had included Captain Heinz in his warning.

Surely she had misunderstood. Kurt was clearly involved with some unsavory people, but he was a captain in the US Army, for crying out loud. If Sarah was honest, she would admit that he had been nothing but kind to her. She owed him some loyalty, didn't she? The scene from New Year's Eve returned in force. Maybe he wasn't seeking a dance partner after all. That must be it. He just wanted an excuse to get close to the man in gray and that made her want to spit or cry. She wasn't sure which. Who was this man she had so willingly allowed to order her around? If he had tried to use her and Agnes to get close to the man in gray at the restaurant, he might be using her in some way now. But that made no sense. Sarah had no idea what his purpose could be. She knew nothing more than she had already told him.

Without warning, an unwelcome realization formed. She reviewed every word she could remember from the night the man in gray died. She thought he had asked her to find Kurt and give him the message, but now she wasn't so sure. All he had actually done was utter Kurt's name. Had she misunderstood? The dying man could have been trying to warn her against Kurt instead.

On New Year's Eve, Kurt must have been after the message carried by her patient. In light of what she now knew, his actions that evening all pointed in that direction. So how far might Kurt have been willing to go to get the message? Slowly, an answer presented itself and it chilled her to the bone.

Chapter 13

Kurt sat alone in the flat, the envelope marked top secret resting in his lap. For once, his ever-present shadow, Phelps, wasn't around. Kurt had no idea where the man was or what he could be doing. His sole reason for being in Casablanca was to prepare Kurt for the mission, and time was running short. Under other circumstances, Kurt would have been glad for the rare moment of solitude. As it was, Kurt feared the man might be spilling his guts to their boss and messing up things for Sarah. She had disappeared too, and it worried him. Maybe she had gone to the hospital. At least, there she would be out of trouble. He had expected to find her still sleeping or at least relaxing, but only the sun pouring through the large front window greeted him upon his return from MacFadyen's office.

He drew his penknife from his trouser pocket, slit open the envelope, and held it on its side. A flurry of paper slid onto his lap. Sifting through the sheets, he found a map, deciphered Enigma messages detailing the movements of Rommel's executive staff, and German identification papers in the name of Helmut Heinz. A plan of operation was sealed within its own thin envelope, which he laid aside while studying the maps and messages.

A key rattled in the front door lock. Kurt

instinctively stuffed everything back into the large envelope and tucked it under the sofa cushions. The door clicked open, and Phelps's tread sounded in the vestibule.

"Went out rather early, didn't you, old man?" A note of suspicion colored Phelps's question.

Kurt had no intention of being drawn into revelations. "I had business at the office."

"I don't suppose it included clearing the path for your lady friend?"

The man seemed to take pleasure in punching Kurt's buttons at every opportunity. "What's with you, Phelps? You act like you're my keeper. Knock it off. And since you brought up the subject, where the hell have you been?"

"My, but we are touchy this morning. Like you, I had business to attend. Commander Maitland. Apparently my services are soon to be made redundant. I am to return to London shortly. Looking forward to getting home, actually."

"Well, good for you." Kurt winced inwardly at the schoolyard tone in his voice. Letting Phelps get to him wasn't helping anything. Better to get on with their job. "What do you want to work on first? My walk or the way I hold a fork?" Kurt couldn't keep the small note of sarcasm out of his voice.

Phelps drew a long, slow breath and cocked his head to one side. "Actually, I think we might take a break. You've really made tremendous progress. I'm not sure how much more I can teach you. Perhaps we could begin again this evening, just to tie up loose ends. You really are ready, you know."

Kurt stared at Phelps. The man was just full of

surprises. Being judged ready for the mission was news to Kurt, but he decided not to argue. Visions of Sarah's tear-stained face kept coming back to him. "Whatever you say. You're the professor. By the way, did you speak to Miss Barrett this morning?"

"No, I presume she was still sleeping when I left. The bedroom door was locked. Dashed inconvenient, that." Phelps ran a hand over the light brown stubble on his chin.

"Well, she's not here now. Bathroom's free."

When the bathroom door clicked shut, Kurt dug the envelope from under the sofa cushion. Studying the documents it contained would have to wait. Kurt couldn't shake the feeling that something was wrong with Sarah. She should have been lounging about the flat, taking advantage of the days off he had arranged. Knowing her, she was probably wandering around Casablanca looking for her missing roommate instead and getting herself into trouble. Jeez, the girl was a pain in the ass, but one he couldn't seem to get out of his head.

Kurt went to the kitchen area and snatched back the cabinet door under the sink. If he was going to trail around Casablanca looking for the missing Agnes, he couldn't carry sensitive documents with him. Sticking his upper body into the opening, he shoved the envelope into a crack behind the adjoining cabinet where the wooden back didn't quite meet the plaster wall. Kurt had discovered the space a few days back in anticipation of needing it for a situation like this. Half-way out of the cabinet, he winced. Damn the cast iron sink. He had managed to give his head a good whack on its underside.

Rocking back on his haunches, he rubbed the tender place just behind the crown of his head and sucked on his lower lip. He had no business getting so worked up over this dame. He didn't owe her a thing. She wasn't his responsibility. Not really. He wasn't even sure that she appreciated what he had done for her. In fact, she seemed to blame him for what had happened to her and her roommate. He really should let it go. If she came back to the flat, maybe he'd try to help her, if there was time.

Hell, who was he kidding? Her face would haunt him forever if he didn't do what he could to protect her. He had three days to take care of her, find out what happened to the roommate, and prepare for the most important mission he was ever likely to be given. Might as well get on with it.

Kurt scribbled a note for Phelps saying he was gone for the day, needed to clear his head, planned to wander at will, don't expect him back until late. He hoped that would keep Phelps's curiosity at bay and the man himself out of his hair. Kurt taped the scrap of paper to Phelps's scotch bottle, the thing the man reached for at some point every morning. A bracing pick-me-up to get the day started, he said. To Kurt, it seemed more like a necessary crutch, and he wondered if their boss knew how much liquor the man put away in a twenty-four hour period. Not enough to declare the man a full blown alcoholic, but in Kurt's opinion, more than was good for someone who had access to sensitive information. Whatever the case, after the next three days, Phelps would be MacFadyen's problem and out of Kurt's life.

****

Kurt was pretty sure he knew where to start looking for Sarah. He steered his Jeep into the only available spot near the 8th Evacuation Hospital and climbed out onto the sidewalk. He wanted to make sure she stayed out of his way too, so he might as well tackle the issue with her head on. A promise to search for Agnes would be offered with a price. Sarah was to stay out of it.

The smell of ether and disinfectant greeted Kurt as he strode into the reception area and approached the corporal on duty. At Kurt's inquiry, the corporal indicated an area not far along the first floor. Kurt stared down the hallway, considering his options. This could all end right here, and no one would be the wiser. He could walk away now, telling himself that Sarah would act sensibly and remain safe. After all, she had returned to work, hadn't she? Or, he could listen to his instincts and confront her.

Shaking his head at his attempt at self-delusion, Kurt silently acknowledged that he didn't really have a choice. Sarah had already proven she would tackle trouble on her own. She had to be made to see reason.

He slowed as he approached an arched entrance, pausing just short of entering Sarah's ward. The scene playing out there stayed his step. Sarah sat on the edge of a cot holding a patient's hand. The face looking up at her from the bed couldn't be more than twenty at most. The kid looked scared and in considerable pain. The sagging bedclothes where legs should have been told a lot of the story. Sarah bent closer as the boy's lips moved, her head nodding. Her patient stopped speaking, and Sarah must have replied, but Kurt couldn't hear what she said. She ran her free hand over the boy's hair as a mother might when soothing a fretful child. If Kurt had ever seen adoration, it was there in the young patient's eyes as he gazed up at Sarah. A hiss of whispered words drifted from where she sat. The boy's body visibly relaxed, and he closed his eyes. Sarah placed her fingers ever so lightly against the boy's cheek. Kurt's chest tightened. He didn't speak or move. He didn't want to break the spell.

Sarah must have felt his eyes on her because she suddenly turned toward the doorway. After one more glance at her patient, she got up and came to block Kurt's entrance to the ward.

"Captain Heinz. What are you doing here?" Her tone lacked warmth, was even confrontational.

Surprised by her attitude, Kurt kept his voice even with difficulty. "I might ask you the same thing. You're supposed to be relaxing at the flat. Getting some rest."

"I got all the rest I needed last night. Thank you, but I won't be troubling you and your guest any further. They've squeezed in a cot for me here."

"I see." Anger and something akin to distrust darkened Sarah's eyes. Confused, Kurt cast about for an explanation. "Well, I can understand why bunking with two guys might not be ideal."

"That has nothing to do with it. Now, excuse me. I've got to get back to my patients." Her tone was cold, almost hateful.

"Look, I've tried every way I know to help you and keep you safe, then you turn around and spit in my face. Hell, woman, what's the matter with you?" Kurt grabbed her upper arm to prevent her leaving. Sarah winced. He unwrapped his fingers, but didn't release her entirely. He lifted her arm toward a hall sconce glowing above their heads and drew back her sleeve with his free hand. Four dark purple lines ran across her bicep.

"Where did these bruises come from? Who did this?"

"I seem to be running into all sorts of men who want to manhandle me today. Let me go."

"Not until you tell me what happened."

"It's not your concern."

"I think you've made it my business."

"Really? How?"

"By pounding on my door and dumping your problems in my lap."

"I was fulfilling a promise and delivering a message you were glad to get. Remember?"

Her words were like a bucket of cold water poured over his head. Kurt let out a long, slow breath. He released her arm and stepped back a pace. "Yes, you were, and I'm grateful that you found me. Look, arguing isn't getting us anywhere. I just want to help. No more, no less."

"Well, let's see. If I understood Philippe Badouri correctly, you may have killed my patient and maybe Agnes." Sarah paused for breath, her eyes burning bright with emotion. "Exactly how does that help me? Who are you? Whose side are you on?"

Badouri. Where in the hell had she come across him? If it hadn't made Kurt so angry, he would have laughed aloud. The girl actually seemed to think he had killed two people in cold blood.

"When you jump to conclusions, lady, you make it the Grand Canyon. For your information, I happen to know Badouri." Sarah's eyes grew wide and her mouth snapped shut. Gratified by her reaction, Kurt continued, "He's kind of shady, but I doubt he'd say I'm a killer. He would probably warn you to stay out of things that'll get you killed. Sounds a lot like what I've been telling you, doesn't it?"

Sarah's face filled with heat. She felt the urge to slap his face, but his question brought her up short. Kurt was right. Both he and Badouri had said essentially the same thing. Sarah's instincts screamed that Kurt Heinz was dangerous and that she should have no more to do with him. In his favor was the fact that he could have done away with her at several points, and he hadn't. He didn't have to give her a place to stay last night or take her to dinner, but he had. Maybe her sleep deprived brain and emotions were creating a threat that didn't exist. Philippe didn't actually say that Kurt had harmed anyone. He had simply warned her to forget him and to not trust anyone. Fears, warnings, facts, imaginings all tumbled through her mind. What did she really know for certain? Very little. One thing was clear, however. If she had any chance of finding Agnes, Kurt was probably her best, maybe her only hope.

Chapter 14

Kurt looked down into Sarah's eyes. They were filled with anger and confusion. Taking a long, slow breath, he tried to make his tone conciliatory. "Look, I don't want to argue with you. I'm going to search for Agnes. But only if you make me a promise."

"Depends on what it is."

"Stay out of this and let me do the work."

"Wait just a minute, buster." The darkness in Sarah's eyes deepened. "How do I know you'll do what you say?"

Kurt's lips compressed into a thin line. Breaking eye contact, his gaze landed on a spot just over her head on the entrance archway. He struggled for civility, enunciating each word with utmost care. "Because you have my word."

"Sorry, but that's not good enough. All I've heard for weeks on end is not to trust anyone in Casablanca, so I'm starting with you."

"Of all the pigheaded, mulish, stubborn, idiotic…" Walking away now would serve her right. Kurt wished he could do it.

With a fist on each hip, Sarah glared up at him. "Where you go, I go. And I happen to have an idea where to start looking."

"Yeah? Where?"

If Sarah noticed the schoolyard tone in his reply,

she didn't give any indication. She charged on, earnestly describing the couple who passed her and Agnes as they left the restaurant on New Year's Eve. "I bet Badouri can give us an address for them."

"I don't need Badouri for that." Kurt would have laughed if he hadn't been so frustrated. "Trust me. I know where to find them. I noticed them that evening at the restaurant as well. They are real lowlifes with dangerous friends." Anger swept through Kurt. This stupid, meddling girl was going to get herself killed. "Why didn't you let me know you were going to talk to Badouri?" His voice was sharp, almost vicious, but he didn't care.

Sarah's head snapped back, her face inflamed with fury. "Why would I tell you anything? You've told me nothing but half-truths and lies from the very beginning." Her volume crescendoed with each syllable. "You weren't even honest about why you asked me to dance that night. Why should I trust you?"

So she'd figured it out. Maybe it was time he told her a little something. Not enough to give away his true military identity, but enough to keep her quiet and out of the way.

Kurt lifted his hands in surrender. "Got me there. I came over to y'all at first because of the man sitting at the next table. I admit it. But after I saw you, I really did want that dance." Kurt mustered what he hoped was a charming smile.

"I see." She didn't sound convinced.

He reached out and tucked a stray lock of hair behind Sarah's ear. Encouraged that she didn't automatically flinch and duck from his gesture, he said, "I'm sorry to be so mysterious. There's a lot I can't tell

107

you—can't tell anyone. But please believe I would've prevented what happened to Agnes if I could have."

It must have worked because Sarah's expression became less guarded.

Kurt made his voice gentle and conciliatory. "Are we going to keep arguing?"

Sarah held Kurt's gaze for several beats before answering, "I guess not, as long as you don't try to keep me in the dark."

"Good. I'll go see our Vichy friends." His jaw relaxed with his smile.

"Oh, no. Not without me, you're not."

Kurt tried, but failed to control the edge in his voice. "I thought we agreed you were going to let me handle this."

Sarah's eyes flashed. "I agreed to no such thing."

None of this made sense. The girl was an infuriating, walking contradiction. Beyond caring that he might hurt her feelings, Kurt allowed condescension and sarcasm to color his words. "I thought you didn't trust me. If I've already killed two people as you seem to think, why follow me around?"

That brought Sarah up short. Her face became a study in sorrow as she fought back tears. She hiccupped and tilted her head back a little. "I'm sorry. I don't think you're a killer, not really. You've been kind, and I appreciate it. But if all I do is hang around the hospital, I'll go crazy."

"Don't you have patients to take care of?"

Sarah shook her head. "No. I'm not really on duty. Please understand. I've got to be involved."

Kurt's better judgment yelled for him to walk away now, to let the MPs do the work, but when he looked down into those eyes bright with tears, common sense flew out the window. He sighed and took her hand. "If I ever go missing, I hope I have a friend like you to come looking for me. I guess it can't hurt anything for you to meet two of Germany's favorite Vichy lapdogs."

Sarah threw her arms around Kurt's neck and kissed him on the cheek. "Oh, thank you. I promise you won't regret it."

He took her arms from his neck and eased her away from him before he completely lost his composure. "I hope not. Go get a coat."

Sarah gave him a watery smile. "I'll just be a second. Don't go anywhere. Stay right here."

Kurt smiled. She was so very earnest. He pointed at his feet and asked, "Right here?"

"Yes. Don't move an inch." Sarah turned to walk away, then stopped in her tracks and frowned over her shoulder. "Are you laughing at me?"

"Maybe just a little."

"Well, don't. This isn't funny."

"You're right. I apologize."

Sarah nodded and scurried off toward the end of the hall. How did she do it? One minute she was so infuriating, so absolutely maddening, and the next she was so…what? Cute? Winsome? Endearing? Yeah, that was the word. So endearing.

****

"My goodness, Sarah. You come and go like we have a revolving door in this place. Are you sure you're okay?" Beatrice, the administrative head nurse, could be a real harridan at times, but you could count on her when it was important.

"I'll be fine once Agnes is found."

Beatrice took off her glasses and rubbed the bridge of her nose. Placing the glasses on the desk, she looked up at Sarah. "Honey, give it a rest. Leave finding Agnes to the MPs."

"I'm sure they are doing what they can."

"But you don't think it's enough."

Sarah shook her head and hesitated. She wasn't sure how much to admit. "I have a friend, an army captain, who has promised to help."

Beatrice raised an eyebrow. "He must be a close friend."

Sarah knew what Beatrice was getting at, but she feigned ignorance. "He's very kind, and he knows Agnes."

"You know how the brass feels about nurses and officers fraternizing."

Sarah could feel the heat rising in her cheeks. "Yes, but it isn't really against the rules. And besides, we aren't fraternizing. We're just friends."

Beatrice cocked her head to one side. "Your friend seems to have an unusual amount of free time for an army captain."

"He's an aide to some colonel at the Anfa." Sarah's fingers played an imaginary tune on her forearm. She hated it when she fidgeted, but her hands seemed to have a mind of their own.

"That so? Well, I would think those boys ought to be working around the clock with all the incoming traffic lately."

"He's made arrangements," Sarah snapped.

Beatrice shook her head in apparent resignation. "I can't talk you out of this, can I?"

"I don't know what you mean."

"Oh, yes you do."

"Look, Agnes is in trouble. I know you care as much about her as I do. I've got someone who may have an inside track on what happened, and I'm going to follow up on it."

Beatrice studied Sarah and sighed. "If you are that determined, at least tell me who you're running off with. You still have three days of official leave, but I want to know what's going on with you. We can't afford to lose any more good nurses."

Sarah gave Kurt's name and address. "He works for a Colonel MacFadyen."

"Ah yes, now everything is making more sense, my dear. Apparently your Captain Heinz has considerable pull. Someone from the colonel's office talked to the hospital brass about your time off." Beatrice's mouth became a thin line. "You really should take a break, instead of chasing around town doing the MP's job."

Sarah clasped her hands together to keep them from pounding on Beatrice's desk in frustration. "I can't."

"Well, see that you stay out of trouble." Beatrice's words followed Sarah down the hall. Kurt was exactly where she left him, grinning at her as she approached.

"I've followed orders to the letter."

"So I see. Ready?"

****

Where was the wisdom in having Sarah actively involved in this mess? There was none, but there seemed no choice other than to go along with her wishes. Kurt stood aside and gestured toward the front entrance.

The sun beamed high overhead as Kurt led Sarah to

his Jeep's passenger side. She grasped his hand tightly as she jumped up into the seat, sending a tingle up his arm that he unsuccessfully tried to ignore. After settling into the driver's side, Kurt slipped the shift out of gear, turned the key, and pressed the starter button. Nothing. He jiggled the ignition. The engine spluttered and died. Muttering an oath under his breath, he graced her with a lopsided grin. She nodded and smiled encouragingly. The girl really was a puzzle, at least in his experience. She got so angry with him when his concern for her safety put him at odds with her determination to be involved, yet a quarrelsome ignition seemingly caused her no concern. Kurt thought of how former girlfriends might have reacted in the same situation. They would have at least commented, several would have complained loudly, but Sarah just bit her lip and gave every indication she believed he would soon have them underway. She was different, perhaps something rather special.

As they barreled along the broad avenue leading them from the modern city outskirts into the heart of the medina, the city's oldest quarter, Kurt found his attention wandering from the road. From the corner of his eye, he could see the breeze lifting wisps of reddish gold from around her face, creating a halo effect. She sat beside him with her hands clasped in her lap, a quiet, determined angel. What he wouldn't give to see that troubled frown disappear forever from her face, but that would require a commitment he wasn't at liberty to make until this war was over. Damn the Nazis. Damn them for wanting to rule the world. Damn them for hating and killing innocent people. Fighting their evil was the most important thing he could be doing, might be the most critical thing he would ever do, but it was playing hell with his personal life. If he needed additional reasons to hate fascists, he now had them.

After they passed through an arched gateway in the old city wall, the streets narrowed, forcing Kurt to keep his mind on his driving. Several left and right turns later, Kurt pulled to a stop in a narrow cobbled lane between rows of squatty three story buildings.

He leaned against the steering wheel and turned toward Sarah. "Are you sure you want to go through with this? Once you start down this road, it may be difficult to turn back."

She met his gaze and held it without a blink. "Are we going to sit here all day, or are you going to get on with keeping your promise?"

"I guess that will have to do for an answer." He got out of the Jeep and came around to her side. Before he rounded the front fender, Sarah hopped down and began smoothing the wrinkles in her crumpled uniform.

The buildings on either side of the street seemed to lean in toward each other, creating dimness even at high noon. Kurt stepped into a shadowy alcove set in an otherwise featureless wall and pounded on a heavy wooden door. Some minutes passed before the door's small communication portal opened and a male voice spoke in Arabic.

Sarah hovered behind Kurt's shoulder, telegraphing her anxiety through the trembling hand on his elbow. He reached back and took her arm, giving it a gentle squeeze as he pulled her to his side. Addressing the man at the door, he asked, "Is your master in?"

The presumed servant plastered a quizzical expression on his face and hunched his shoulders as though he didn't understand.

"I know you speak English. Go tell Jalal that Captain Heinz is here to see him."

From out of the darkness deeper within the house, a female voice spoke. The man frowned and turned away. What followed sounded like a heated exchange. The female spoke in a loud, angry voice and then silence descended. The man slipped from sight but left the communication portal open. The click-clack of approaching high-heeled shoes echoed before the entry door cracked open an inch. Dark kohl-rimmed eyes peered out at them. The woman ran her gaze over Sarah, taking in the rumpled uniform and military issue shoes. A corner of her upper lip curled slightly as a frown creased her brow. With a sniff, she turned her attention to Kurt.

"Captain. I did not think to see you again after our last encounter." The woman made no move to open the door wide enough for them to enter.

"You can never count me out, Laila. We're here to see Jalal."

At mention of the man's name, the woman's eyes grew wide. "That is not possible. He is away from the city."

"Where did he go?"

"I do not know."

Kurt's eyes narrowed while he studied the woman. "You're lying, Laila. Tell me where he."

"I have told you. I do not know." With that, the woman Laila moved to shut the door, but Kurt placed his boot in the opening, grabbed her by the arm, and twisted. The manservant rushed forward from the shadows, but Laila waved him off.

Increasing the pressure on Laila's forearm, Kurt continued, "Tell me where he is, or you can explain to the police how you came by certain items in your possession. I'm sure they'll be very interested in the contents of your store rooms." Kurt gave her arm a hard yank. "Help me out here with Moroccan law. Does dealing on the black market carry a stiff prison sentence, or do they just cut off your hands? I can never remember."

Laila's eyes grew large with panic. "Hush. Do not be so loud. Someone might hear you."

"Then call off your watchdog, and let us inside."

With a swift glance up and down the street, she nodded. Kurt relaxed his grip, allowing Laila to wrench her arm free. She stepped back and Kurt pushed the door wide enough for Sarah to precede him inside, then Laila snapped it shut behind them.

After passing through a dark passage, they were momentarily blinded by sunlight pouring through an opening in the roof. Beneath the opening, water splashed over a tiled fountain into a small pool at its base. Pots of foliage and small palms were scattered around the courtyard. Kurt heard Sarah's intake of breath. Glancing down, he watched her eyes fill with awe as they wandered over three stories of open air hallways lined by intricately carved railings and supported by colorfully tiled columns.

Kurt chuckled and asked, "Surprising, isn't it, after seeing the outside?"

"You can say that again. I would never have guessed. It's really lovely. Are all the houses here like this one?" Sarah directed the question to the other woman, who ignored it by looking away and rolling her eyes.

Kurt's lips curved into a smirk. "I doubt there are any others quite like this house. I believe Laila and Jalal did rather extensive renovations over the last two or three years. It's amazing how much Nazis will pay for information about your neighbors isn't it, Laila?"

The woman's eyes flashed. "I don't know what you mean. Jalal was born in this house. His father started improvements long before the Germans or you Americans arrived. What do you want?" Laila's voice held no warmth or hospitality.

"Like I told you. We need to see Jalal."

"And as I told you, he is not here."

"So where is he?"

"Away."

"You said that. Where?" The question thundered and rolled around the courtyard's enclosed space.

Laila lifted her chin in defiance, but a quiver in her voice betrayed her. "He did not say."

Kurt made no attempt to hide his exasperation. "Look, we can play this cat and mouse game down at the MP's post, or you can make it easy on yourself and tell me now. The choice is yours."

Laila met Kurt's gaze without uttering a word or breaking eye contact. No doubt she was gaging the sincerity of his threat, weighing it against the cost of telling him the truth. After several moments of staring, she made her decision.

"You will find him in El Jadida. More than that I truly do not know. He has gone into hiding."

"And left you here to fend for yourself? How gallant of him."

"I will be safe here as long as persons such as

yourself are not indiscreet. It was not I who failed in performing an important task."

"Yes, my contact's death was truly unfortunate. Too bad Jalal felt the need to kill him for nothing." Kurt wondered if she would take the bait. He had suspected Laila and Jalal Ahmed all along of being involved in the murder of the man in gray.

"Jalal is sometimes a fool, but he did not kill your man."

"Then why hide?"

"He made promises to the wrong people. Jalal needed your man alive. But he was killed and Jalal failed in finding an important document the man carried."

Kurt felt, rather than saw, Sarah jerk beside him. He reached out and grabbed her shoulder, pulling her under his arm. He hugged her hard against his side. She shook all over, but whether it was from grief or rage, Kurt couldn't say. Probably a mixture of both.

Kurt returned his attention to Laila. "An American Army nurse named Agnes Johnson disappeared from the apartment Jalal tore apart. Is she with him?"

"I don't know. Perhaps. He only left a scribbled note. I did not speak with him. He was desperate to get away."

"What about the servants?"

"There is only the one who answered the door, and he did not."

Kurt released Sarah and grabbed Laila's wrist. "It'll go hard for you if you've lied or withheld information."

She struggled against his grasp, speaking through clenched teeth. "I have told you all I know. Please do me the courtesy of leaving my home."

Laila's servant, if that was what he was, stepped from the shadows and hovered menacingly on the edge of the little group. Sunlight glinted off the tip of a dagger's scabbard visible below the hem of his loose fitting jacket. The man was large, well over six feet and probably in the neighborhood of 250 pounds.

Kurt eyed the Moroccan. He might be able to take the servant, but he would probably have to kill the man in the process. That was a complication he didn't need just now. Kurt nodded and turned toward the entrance passage, pushing Sarah ahead of him. He glanced back over his shoulder as they neared the exterior door, but Laila and her servant had disappeared. Maybe he should go ahead and call the Casablanca cops on general principle. Maitland said she was working for the Allies, but Kurt still didn't trust her. He knew who she had allowed into her bed when the Nazis controlled North Africa.

****

When they were sitting in the Jeep again, Sarah finally stopped shaking.

She turned to Kurt. "Where is El Jadida?"

"It's a small port city about sixty miles south of Casablanca."

She grabbed his arm. "Do you really think Agnes might be there with that man?"

"Maybe. If not, he probably knows where she is."

Her intake of breath was audible. "When can we leave?"

She looked so hopeful, so pleading, so in need of his protection and care. Kurt's heart skipped a beat. He had less than three days until his mission took him away from Casablanca. Although there were things he needed to do in preparation for the journey, he knew he would devote all of the remaining time to helping this girl.

Against his better judgment, words flew from his mouth as though they had a will of their own. "Is now soon enough?"

Chapter 15

Sarah grabbed the handle on the jeep's dashboard as Kurt swerved to miss a large pothole.

She cocked her head to one side. "If you're trying to get rid of me, you'll have to do better than that. I grew up riding in an open truck bed."

Kurt grinned and yelled back, "Sorry about the…"

The rest of his words blew away with the wind coming off the Atlantic. Road noise increased as the jeep accelerated once more, making conversation difficult. Sarah turned to watch the scenery whipping by. Rock strewn sand dotted with patches of scrubby, green salt cedar lumbered down to meet azure water. Bits of windblown foam danced along the tops of waves. A low wintery sun hovered at the edge of the world, tinting water and land in shades of orange, pink, and gold. It was a scene straight out of *Tales of the Arabian Nights*, but Sarah took little joy in the stark beauty. She ought to close her eyes and try to rest while they drove, but she dreaded sleep. Since stumbling on the bloodstains in their apartment, Sarah's nights had been disturbed by strange dreams in which Agnes and the mysterious patient blended together in scenes filled with blood, violence, and chaos. She was tired—beyond tired—and more than a little frightened by what the next few days might bring. The best they could hope for was that Agnes was being held captive, but Sarah sensed that Kurt didn't hold out much hope. Perhaps her boss, Beatrice, had been right. Maybe she should be leaving this to the MPs. Her training in no way prepared her to deal with killers.

Oh, God. She had actually said it. Even if only to herself, admitting that Agnes might be dead sent her heart rate soaring. Sarah sucked in her lower lip to keep it from trembling. She had already shed too many tears in front of Kurt.

The miles between Casablanca and El Jadida passed in what seemed a never-ending crawl until Sarah couldn't see anything but patches of dusty road illuminated by the jeep's blackout headlight. Shaded, shuttered, and mounted on the fender, it gave barely enough light for safety on good roads. Every jolt and swerve set Sarah's nerves singing, but every mile brought them closer to a possible answer to Agnes's fate.

Long after nightfall darkened the countryside, an outline of human habitation appeared on the horizon painted silvery blue by a nearly full moon. Kurt slowed the jeep and pulled onto the shoulder.

When they were at a full stop, he switched off the engine and turned to Sarah. "We need to talk." His voice was filled with quiet authority.

Sarah studied him for a couple of beats, a prickle of anxiety fluttering just under her breastbone. "I get the feeling this is going to be a one sided conversation."

"You're right. It is. Before we go any farther, I need to know that you are going to do what I ask without argument."

Heat rose in Sarah's face. "You mean follow orders." Her fear and exhaustion were making her stubborn and jumpy.

"If you want to take it that way, yeah. I agreed to help find Agnes, but it will be on my terms. That means without your misguided interference."

"So, you wait until we are in the middle of nowhere to set terms. My interference found Badouri, didn't it?" She could hear the belligerence in her voice, but she couldn't seem to stop. It was either that or she would break down completely. She lifted her chin, glaring at a point in the middle of his forehead.

"Yeah. And you're lucky you survived that little escapade." His voice held an edge of rising anger. "This is a deadly serious business. Amateurs playing spy usually get themselves hurt or worse."

Had Kurt just revealed his true military identity? The thought was intriguing, but it in no way dampened Sarah's irritation. She wanted him to see her as an equal partner. Being actively involved would keep her from climbing the walls. She knew the words were foolish, but she couldn't stop them flying from her mouth. "I think I know the dangers as well as you do."

"No, you don't." His voice was hard and angry. "You have no idea what these people are truly capable of. Don't make me wish I'd left you in Casablanca."

"Then don't make me regret coming to you for help." Sarah winced inwardly at her ungrateful response, but his attitude had set her exhaustion-fueled temper alight. That he thought so little of her abilities and common sense made her want to scream and slap his face.

Kurt's nostrils flared, his eyes dark with emotion. She held his gaze, mentally preparing herself for the dressing down she deserved. Although he was right about her being foolishly stubborn, she was damned if she would be the first to break eye contact. Her pride had already taken too much of a bruising.

With the suddenness of a summer storm, Kurt reached out and wrapped Sarah in a tight embrace, pulling her close. A frown made his expression hard, almost cold. Sarah could see his fury, but somehow she didn't have the will to break free. His arms were strong, safe, even in anger. When his mouth covered hers, she closed her eyes and melted into him, meeting his tongue thrust for thrust, matching his heart rate beat for beat. One hand broke its grip on her shoulder and inched forward, stroking and circling until it covered her breast. Soft kneading and a quick pinch of her nipple sent warmth surging throughout her body. She gasped aloud.

"Sarah?" She opened her eyes. Kurt's face was in profile. His voice, devoid of emotion, came to her as though it passed through fog. "I'm sorry. I don't know what got into me. It won't happen again." He released her, pushing her back into her seat.

Sarah couldn't speak. This was the decamped pilot all over again. Bring her to the point of letting down her defenses, and then leave her alone and confused. Damn both of them. As though it had a will of its own, her hand flew up and smacked his cheek. Kurt must have seen it coming out of the corner of his eye, but he did nothing to stop her. Still seething, Sarah crossed her arms over her chest, each hand gripping the opposing arm. She couldn't remember when she had last so wanted to claw a man's eyes out. But worst of all, she wasn't sure whether it was because Kurt had brought her to the edge of reason or because he had stopped.

She leaned back against the seat and closed her eyes. She didn't trust herself to look at him.

The clutch popped. The engine roared. Gears clashed and ground. With a hard jerk, the jeep was back on the road again. She hadn't noticed Kurt driving so roughly before. Was he taking out his frustration on the Jeep's internal workings? Perhaps Captain Heinz wasn't as in control as he pretended. Good. She shouldn't be the only one in a tailspin.

****

Kurt gripped the wheel until his hands ached. What was he thinking? Had his self-control totally deserted him? A large rock loomed in the headlight's soft glow. Kurt gave the wheel a vicious jerk. Was he completely losing perspective? God, he hoped not. If he was, then he and Sarah were in big trouble. He needed a clear head for both missions—the personal and the military.

The outskirts of El Jadida did little to reassure travelers—dusty rutted streets, low mud brick structures little more than hovels, a few tired palms. Once inside the city walls, however, things improved. El Jadida was an old Portuguese port whose history brought together a blend of European and North African Moorish architecture and culture.

While stopped at an intersection blocked by an overloaded cart with a recalcitrant donkey tied to it, Kurt cut his eyes at Sarah. She stared straight ahead, her mouth turned down at the corners, deep furrows between her brows. She had every right to be angry, but they couldn't continue with so much tension between them. Too much depended on their working as a team, not as quarreling lovers. Lovers? Hell, he might as well admit it. It was too late. He was already off the deep end over Sarah.

He reached out and put his hand over hers. She tried to jerk away, but he held tight. "Look, I'm really sorry for what happened on the road back there. I'm not a jerk who jumps on every pretty girl I see."

"So what was it? Your way of commanding your female troops?"

"I guess I deserve that." Kurt thought about how to answer her question. He could lie, or he could tell her how he felt. Neither seemed a winning proposition. Feeling like a schoolboy with his first crush, he continued, "The truth is I think I'm falling for you. Not great timing, but that's how it is."

Sarah's head snapped around, her eyes wide with surprise. "Oh."

"Oh? That's all you have to say?"

"What do you expect me to say? One minute you treat me like an incompetent child, the next you expect declarations of love and devotion?"

"I've been trying to maintain a professional distance for both our sakes. Can't you understand that?"

An angry shout in Arabic came from behind them. Sarah jumped and looked toward the intersection.

"The cart's out of the road. You can go."

"Not until you say I'm forgiven."

Another shout, in shrill heavily accented French, made Sarah flinch. With a blast of a car horn, Sarah muttered, "Okay. You're forgiven. Now go before that guy behind us has a coronary."

****

Sarah remained silent until Kurt steered the Jeep down a dark lane, more alley than street, which lay between blocks of adobe buildings. He pulled to a stop in the deepest shadows. Shutters covered the few windows and doors set in the walls. Farther down the alley, a single sign hanging from chains screeched in a light salt laden breeze. Kurt got out and came around to the passenger side.

Sarah took the hand he offered gratefully. Her flagging energy and courage welcomed his warmth and strength. Without warning, the desire to throw herself against him like a frightened child, to be held in the safety of his arms, was almost overwhelming. He had to be a good guy. Otherwise, he wouldn't be helping her, would he?

Sarah took in the surrounding buildings as she rolled her head from side to side to ease the tension in her neck. Here and there, large chunks of stucco had fallen away exposing the mud bricks beneath. The odor of decaying garbage drifted toward them from farther along the alley.

"Where are we exactly?"

"Near the harbor in the old Portuguese section."

She squinted at the luminescent hands on her wristwatch. "It's getting late. Shouldn't we look for a hotel?"

"No. Our presence here needs to be kept quiet."

Sarah cocked her head to one side and raised an eyebrow. "Don't you think an American military jeep parked out in the open is just a little conspicuous?"

"Once we're settled inside, the jeep will disappear."

"I guess that means restaurants are out of the question?"

"It does." Kurt grinned. "Don't tell me you aren't willing to suffer a little for the mission."

"You're laughing at me again, aren't you."

"Guilty. Come on. There's someone I want you to meet."

He led her along the alley, stopping under the swaying sign. Sarah could just make out the words *Maimaran Marchand de Tissus et Tailleur*.

"A tailor shop?"

"Patience. All will be revealed." Kurt pulled a rope hanging beside the shuttered door. Somewhere deep within the building a bell tinkled. After what seemed an age, hinges creaked, and a voice spoke from behind the shutters.

"*Nous sommes firmes. Revenu demain.*"

"It's Kurt Heinz, Jakob. Open up."

Bolts slid from their holds and the shutters parted. Kurt drew Sarah behind him into a darkened courtyard built in the traditional Moroccan style, but this one bore little resemblance to the opulence of the woman Laila's house in Casablanca. No water splashed in a fountain and the only plants were a few herbs scattered about in pots. The courtyard tiles were plain clay devoid of decoration.

Before them stood a portly gentleman holding an oil lamp. He wasn't quite as tall as Sarah. A white beard, wire rimmed spectacles, and smile lines around his eyes gave him the appearance of a pleasant gnome. The little gnome motioned for Kurt and Sarah to follow him through a door that opened into what was clearly the shop workroom. Bolts of cloth lay scattered about on the floor and worktables. Partially clothed tailor's dummies stood in two corners.

The little man blew out the oil lamp and pulled on a cord. Electric light bathed the room, bringing everything into sharper focus. The sudden brightness made Sarah blink. Once her eyes adjusted, she examined her surroundings more closely. An object high on a shelf caught and held her attention. Their host noticed Sarah staring.

His eyes twinkled. "Ah, you see the menorah. Yes, my dear. We are Jews. You are perhaps surprised to find any of us left in this part of the world?" He spoke stilted English with a French accent.

"No, I…" To cover her embarrassment, Sarah held out her hand. "I'm Sarah Barrett, Mr. Mairan?"

The little gnome took her hand and bowed slightly while maintaining eye contact. "Maimaran, but call me Jakob, please. My family has been here since the 1500s. We take our surname from the city itself." Sarah must have looked even more confused, for Jakob added, "Maimaran means 'from Mazagan' as El Jadida was known under the Portuguese."

Kurt shifted beside her and let out a long breath. "Jakob, I'm sure Miss Barrett is as fascinated by your family history as you are by pretty girls, but we don't have much time."

Jakob's lips twitched with humor. "Then tell me what brings you to my door at such an hour."

Kurt described his man, but Sarah noticed he did not reveal why he sought Jalal. Jakob stroked his beard, his lips pursed as though he drew on a pipe. "And you are certain that this man Jalal Ahmed is here in El Jadida?"

"According to my source, he is."

"If it is so, our friends will locate him. Do you wish him dead?"

Sarah gasped. "No! We need him alive."

"I see. Then perhaps a kidnapping is to be arranged?"

Kurt's mouth curved upward in a half smile. "A meeting will be sufficient, but it's got to be no later than tomorrow night."

"That makes your quest more difficult. I cannot guarantee success with so little time."

Sarah leaned toward Jakob and grabbed the sleeve of his tunic. "We've got to find him. It's a matter of life and death. We have important questions only he can answer." Her voice bounced off the room's thick mud walls.

Kurt's hand clamped down on Sarah's arm. She refused to look at him, but she sensed the irritation radiating from his every pore. "What Miss Barrett means is that I will meet with Jalal while she stays *here* with you and your wife."

Sarah opened her mouth. "But…" Pressure from Kurt's fingers dug into the tender flesh on the underside of her arm just above the elbow. Her first instinct was to jerk free, but the urge gave way as she suddenly relaxed under his grip. She was too tired to fight. Perhaps she should give in and let him be in charge. He would take care of her, if she let him. Her heart told her that much. Besides, he was right. She really didn't know what she was doing. Chasing killers and spies was apparently his area of expertise.

Kurt glanced at Sarah, his eyes reflecting surprise. His features softened as his hand released her arm and dropped to his side. To Jakob, he said, "Make sure Jalal understands his survival depends on his cooperation."

Jakob nodded. "Of course." The little gnome looked at Sarah and turned back to Kurt. "I see that you have not changed since our last meeting."

Kurt's brows rose. "Probably not, but what's that got to do with anything?"

"God has seen fit to equip you with a ruthless nature, my friend. Bodies tend to fall in your wake. And I fear this charming young lady is going to be the next casualty of your dogged determination."

Kurt snorted. "Jakob, you couldn't be more off base if you tried. She's the one driving me."

"Tut-tut, Captain." Jakob wagged his index finger. "How ungallant. I will make arrangements for food and rest."

Jakob stepped to the shop door and opened it. He leaned out into the courtyard and clapped loudly. Within minutes, a tiny woman appeared. She paused in the doorway, her eyes moving from Kurt's face to Sarah's and back, then she nodded.

"This is my wife Rebekah. If you will follow her, Miss Barrett, she will see to refreshment and sleeping quarters."

A spasm of fear fluttered in Sarah's midsection. It hadn't occurred to her that she would be separated from Kurt. She found that was the last thing she wanted. The realization that he alone gave her a sense of security hit her full force. "But what about Captain Heinz?"

Jakob lowered his gaze, but his smile broadened. "His needs will be met, but elsewhere. We are a very traditional household, I'm afraid."

Sarah's cheeks burned. Jakob must have assumed that she wanted to sleep with Kurt. "Oh, I didn't mean it like that."

The little woman beside her laughed and took Sarah's hand. "Come. My husband likes to tease beautiful young women." She shot Jakob a stern look over her shoulder. "An annoying habit that I am unable to break in him."

Rebekah led Sarah deep within the house to a room containing a single bed and little else.

"You can feel safe here. The arm of the Boche has never reached within these walls. I will return with food. Eat, then rest."

"Thank you." Sarah hesitated, unsure if she was about to say the right thing. "I hope I didn't give your husband the wrong impression. Captain Heinz and I are just friends, nothing more."

"Pay my husband's teasing no heed. He is an old man who enjoys creating reactions in others. As to our friend the captain…" Rebekah paused, eyeing Sarah before continuing, "my instincts tell me that he thinks of you as much more than a friend. It is there in the way he looks at you. Do you return his affection? I indeed hope it is so. He is doing important work that could be damaged if he became distracted by unrequited love."

Sarah hoped she didn't look as stupid as she felt. "I hardly know how to answer. We've known each other such a short time."

Rebekah fixed Sarah with a maternal glare. "In times of war, an hour can be enough to know one's heart. I will return with food." Rebekah departed before Sarah could think of a sensible reply.

She plopped down on the edge of the bed and pondered her hostess's words. Perhaps war did accelerate the process of falling in love. It certainly had been like that with Bill, the two-timing pilot. She had fallen hard for him in a matter of days. After his defection, she had closed herself off from any chance at love or romance. Her heart had become a locked safe to which she had lost the combination. A vision of Kurt's rugged face evolved in her mind's eye, bringing confusion and another emotion she didn't want to name.

Rebekah returned with a tray that she placed on Sarah's lap and departed without another word. After a simple meal of flat bread and cold lamb, Sarah crawled into bed and instantly sank into dreams filled with faces of the injured and dying. Agnes, Kurt, and the mysterious civilian patient seemed to blend into one tragic individual who desperately needed her help, but who was just beyond her reach.

From some distant place, a voice called to her. "Sarah. Sarah, wake up."

A hand jostled her shoulder. When she opened her eyes, bright sunlight filled her little room through its single narrow window. She had no idea how long she had slept, but by the angle of the sun, she guessed the time must be approaching noon. She couldn't believe she had slept so long. Her head felt like it was filled with cotton balls. Looking toward the source of the voice, she saw an Arab in a red hooded cloak standing over her, a bright blue turban covering his head. Sarah's heart jumped and she grabbed the sheet, dragging it over her chest. She blinked and the face came into focus. Kurt's blue eyes smiled at her from beneath the turban.

"I didn't want to leave without saying goodbye."

Without thinking Sarah sat bolt upright and grabbed Kurt's arm, her heart pounding. "Leave? Where are you going?"

"To meet our friend Jalal."

"But—" Without warning, he gathered her in his arms and kissed her hard and fast. Sarah's body seemed to have a will of its own. Her arms coiled around his neck, pulling him closer. She returned his kiss as if it would be their last.

Breaking the kiss, his lips brushed against her ear. "Don't worry. You'll be safe here with Jakob and Rebekah."

He removed her arms from around his neck and quickly turned to go. He did not stop to answer when she called after him, "But what about you?"

Chapter 16

Kurt strolled the cobbled streets of El Jadida's old quarter with a lightness of heart that made no sense, except for the possibility that Sarah might be falling for him as hard as he had fallen for her. If her response to his kiss was any indication, he was destined to be a happy guy. The girl should be the farthest thing from his mind considering what he had coming up, but she hovered in his thoughts like an obsession. He hadn't answered her question because of the fear he saw in her eyes and her reluctance to let him go when he took her arms from around his neck. If he had stopped to respond, he might not have left. His appointment with Jalal was for noon, an appointment he intended to keep.

Ten minutes later, he passed the Church of the Assumption in the heart of the old Portuguese town. Beyond the church, an adobe wall, once white but now faded to a dirty sand color, rose on his left. A few paces more and he stood beside a portal in the wall. Its thick iron doors were opened wide to admit any tourists brave enough to be traveling in North Africa during such times. The porter seated at the entrance glanced up from his newspaper. Seeing what he must have assumed was one of his countrymen inexplicably wishing to sightsee, his gaze dropped immediately back to his paper without comment.

Kurt walked along a dimly lit corridor, its rib-domed ceiling reminding him of what he had always imagined the inside of ancient crypts must look like. In places, stucco had fallen away exposing the mud bricks beneath. At another pair of open iron doors, Kurt turned and passed under the lintel onto the small landing of a staircase. His heart rate quickened as he descended the stairs. A damp, musty odor drifted from below. At the bottom of the staircase, he stopped to let his eyes adjust to the netherworld spread before him. Twenty or so fat columns supported another rib-vaulted ceiling. In the middle of the space, a shaft of sunlight poured in via a hole in the ceiling open to the sky. Beneath the skylight, stood a low circular wall like the ones found around Middle Eastern water wells. The most startling feature, however, was the thin layer of water covering much of the floor. Walls, ceiling, and columns floated across the water's calm mirror surface. Jakob told him that the space had once been used as a fresh water cistern in times when the city was besieged by enemies.

Kurt's jaw tightened. Besieged was exactly what he hoped Jalal felt. Maybe it would loosen the man's tongue. Of course, the promise of safe passage for one to neutral Portugal had been the bait that brought him out of hiding. How like such a man to think of his own survival while not giving a second thought to his lover's fate: Laila would have a difficult time after Jalal's defection.

Jakob's source said Germany's former lapdog would be waiting on the cistern's far side in an alcove beyond the last columns. After getting his bearings, Kurt walked around the cistern's outer wall rather than across its water covered middle. If Jalal were here, he would be aware of Kurt's approach. Kurt slipped his hand under his djellaba, the red cloak, until he found the slit Rebekah had cut in his white tunic. He fingered the sidearm secured in the waist of his loose fitting trousers, releasing the safety.

A scraping sound echoed softly across the cistern making the hair on the back of Kurt's neck stand on end. Something wasn't right. Kurt didn't believe in second sight or any other form of hocus pocus, but his wartime experiences had honed his instincts for survival to a keen edge. He darted behind a column and then slowly peered around it toward the staircase. He wanted to laugh out loud. A rat the size of a small dog jumped from the top step followed by a scrawny black cat. The rat raced past Kurt with the cat in hot pursuit. Well, good luck to the cat. The world contained too many vermin at the moment, especially the kind that wanted to goose step across the face of the world and grind its peoples under the heels of their jackboots. Kurt couldn't decide which was worse, the Nazis or the collaborators who betrayed their own people. Kurt gave himself a shake. Letting his anger get the better of him would not help his present situation, and it certainly wouldn't find Agnes. He drew a long, calming breath and resumed traversing the cistern.

When he was about three yards from the alcove, a figure stepped out of the shadows. Reflected sunlight highlighted the Luger in Jalal's hand. He motioned for Kurt to approach.

Kurt raised his hands level with his shoulders and moved forward. "There's no need for guns."

The Moroccan smirked. "I wish to live long enough to reach Lisbon. What is it you want of me?"

"Information. That's all. Then you can scamper

away with the rest of the rats."

"What information would that be?"

Before Kurt could respond, an object cut through the air followed by the sickening sound of human flesh and bone splitting. Jalal's eyes grew wide. His mouth sagged. A trickle of spittle dribbled toward his chin. Dropping the Luger, his hand rose toward his left shoulder as though he was trying to grasp at something on his back. He gasped once and collapsed face forward, sending up a thin spray of water when he hit the floor. A stiletto protruded from his back just to the left of his spine near his shoulder blade. Grasping the Moroccan's collar, Kurt dragged Jalal behind the closest column and rolled him over.

"Where is the American nurse you abducted?" Kurt hissed, but the spark of life had already left Jalal's eyes.

Kurt released the body and stood up. Drawing his pistol, he peered in the direction from which the knife had come. He neither saw nor heard any sign of another living person, but the assailant had to still be in the cistern. There was only one way out and no one had gone near the stairs. Kurt would have heard them.

Shoes scraped on the brick floor, but whoever moved was still hidden in shadow. Kurt froze as blood pounded against his eardrums. Footsteps echoed across the cistern. Kurt bent around the column in time to see a cloaked figure reach the bottom of the staircase. The figure turned and looked directly at Kurt, but he couldn't make out the man's features. A hood made his face all but invisible. Kurt raised his pistol, then thought better of it. The booming report of gunfire would bring the police and far too many questions for comfort. Kurt couldn't afford to be detained in El

Jadida. His only choice was to follow the man running up the stairs. Exhaustion must be playing tricks with his mind. Something about the way the man moved seemed vaguely familiar, but that was impossible. Kurt knew no one in El Jadida other than Jakob, and he was fiercely anti-Nazi for obvious reasons. Jakob would have no reason to interfere with Kurt's quest for information. Besides, the retreating figure was much too tall and too thin to be Jakob.

Kurt ran to the stairs just as the hem of the assailant's brown djellaba disappeared into the entrance hall. Mounting the steps two at a time, Kurt skidded onto the tiles of the upper hallway in time to see his quarry turn right out of the main entrance where the porter sat, still reading his paper. The porter barely looked up as the brown-cloaked figure sped past him. Kurt bolted through the doorway and ran straight into a caravan of camels loaded down with goods probably destined for the markets behind the cathedral. Kurt scanned the street. Brown cloaks were everywhere, but if his man was among them, Kurt couldn't find him. Breathing hard, he gave the cistern's wall a couple of hard slaps.

Hellfire and damnation. Where could they turn for information now? Kurt's eyes swept the street again. Still no sign of his quarry.

He ran a hand over his face, then scanned the street one more time searching for that tell-tale something. What was it about the man that seemed familiar? Try as he might, the answer remained elusive. Worse yet, he must now return to Sarah no wiser than when they left Casablanca. Sarah's tear-stained face surfaced in his memory. She would be devastated when he told her they had wasted two days without obtaining even a hint to Agnes's whereabouts. Hurting her was something he couldn't bear to do. His fists clenched until his fingernails cut into his palms. He wanted to beat the living crap out of somebody, but the logical target for his frustration lay dead on the floor beneath the street where he stood.

From the bowels of the cistern, a cry of alarm poured through the open entrance. Kurt glanced back and saw that the porter was no longer at his post. He must have gone below for some reason and discovered Jalal's body. Kurt had no desire to be caught up in a murder investigation. Moving casually so as not to draw attention to himself, he slipped in among the camels and their handlers. They proceeded up the street to the market entrance beside the church. There, Kurt left the caravan and drifted into the shadows of an alley across the way. Once he felt sure he could not be seen by anyone on the main streets, he shrugged out of his red *djellaba* and stuffed it inside his tunic. In this town where brown seemed to be the color of the day, the red cloak stood out, not something he wanted to do.

The alley emptied onto a street Kurt didn't recognize, but using his innate sense of direction, he eventually wound his way back to Jakob's shop. Rebekah showed him to the kitchen where he found Sarah at the worktable kneading dough.

He stood in the doorway without saying a word. He just wanted to watch her for a moment before he had to deliver his disappointing news. Sunlight played across her hair giving it the appearance of a rosy spun-gold halo. A smudge of flour trailed across one cheek where she must have pushed back the errant curl now threatening to dangle in her eyes. Instead of the uniform she had worn on the trip down from Casablanca, she was dressed in a plain white cotton kaftan. The sun outlined her body tantalizingly through the thin fabric. The garment couldn't belong to the much shorter Rebekah because it reached the floor in the traditional manner. Sarah had rolled the sleeves up to her elbows, but they still bore the marks of her work. She looked rested and at peace for the first time since she stumbled into his life. An overwhelming need flooded his heart and mind. He wanted to take care of Sarah and protect her forever.

She stopped pounding the dough and looked his way. A smile lit her face. "Thank goodness you're back. We've been worried. You were gone longer than Jakob expected. How did it go?"

Torn between the desire to scoop her into his arms and the need to be honest, Kurt fumbled for words. Finally, he settled on the simple truth. "I'm afraid we don't know any more than when I left."

Her eyes grew wide. "Nothing? He told you nothing?"

After Kurt described Jalal's grisly end, Sarah was quiet for a few beats. Frowning, she asked, "So what do we do now?"

Kurt answered honestly. "I don't know. I've got to get back to Casablanca. Duty calls."

Sarah's face fell. She looked like she was fighting tears, but whether they were for him or for Agnes, he couldn't be sure. Wiping her hands on a cloth, she walked across the kitchen, coming to rest at the doorway. Her arms went around his neck. "I know you did the best you could. Promise me one thing."

"If I can."

"Promise me you won't disappear on me. I've been down that road before. I don't think I could take it again. I know you have work that you can't talk about, but at least say goodbye when you leave and give me some inkling of when you'll be back."

The uncertainty in her eyes sent a knife to his heart, but what she asked wasn't possible given the task that lay ahead of him. "I'll do my best. Nothing in this war is certain except how I feel about you. You believe me, don't you?"

"Maybe if you told me exactly how you feel, I might."

The challenge in her voice caught him off guard. Kurt leaned back so that he could look Sarah fully in the face. She felt stiff, tense in his arms. It hit him like a punch to the gut. She really didn't understand how much he cared for her. But then, why should she? He hadn't said anything she could count on. He had been as guarded with his words and emotions as he was with his work. It was insane to get involved right now, but the deed was done and he wouldn't turn back.

Kurt pulled Sarah close against his chest. Resting his lips against her hair, he whispered, "I love you. Falling in love isn't what either of us should be doing, but I guess the heart has its own timing about these things."

Sarah relaxed against him. She melted into his kiss and returned it in full until the growl of a throat clearing brought them back to reality.

"The bread must go into the oven."

Kurt looked over his shoulder to see Rebekah, hands on hips, smiling up at him. Heat rose in his face,

141

settling in the tops of his ears. Sarah's face glowed pink as well. They stepped aside, and Rebekah walked between them, patting Sarah's arm as she passed. Rebekah stopped on the other side of the kitchen door and looked up at Kurt. A maternal softness filled her eyes.

"In times like these, my son, we must cherish love and be glad of it. Too many go to their graves without knowing what I see between you two."

Kurt grinned. "You must have second sight, Rebekah."

"No, simply eyes in my head." Rebekah took the hand of each and clasped them between her gnarled ones. "Take care of this girl. You won't find another like her."

Kurt looked at Sarah. "I will, if she'll let me."

Chapter 17

Sarah pulled her coat closer and crossed her arms over her chest, but the Atlantic wind whipping through the open jeep still crept under her collar. Its icy fingers gave physical meaning to the despair that chilled her throughout. The slap-slap of jeep's tires over the miles back to Casablanca was like relentless taunting. Two days lost and no word or sign of Agnes's fate. Sarah wanted to scream and tear something to shreds. She bit her lower lip to keep it from quivering.

She glanced at Kurt beside her in the driver's seat. His face bore signs of too little rest and too much stress. Dark circles smudged the flesh beneath his eyes. His brow had worn a perpetual furrow since he returned from the cistern without being any wiser. Jakob had promised to send any information his group might uncover, but he held out little hope of anything substantial. Acceptance, the thing that Sarah feared most where Agnes was concerned, hovered beneath the surface calm she was trying so hard to maintain.

Selfishness wasn't a trait she admired, but it now ballooned in her. Sarah wanted time with Kurt all to herself. She didn't want to share him with the war or his army bosses, not anyone, not even Agnes. And she wanted all of him. She wanted to give all of herself to him in return. He was a good man, the kind her parents would think her lucky to have. If it weren't for this

143

infernal war, they could have it all, all the things that couples who were in love eventually had—a home, children, a life together. Then it hit her. Without the war, their paths might never have crossed. She would still be in the Shenandoah Valley, probably married to the boy down the road. Who knew where Kurt would be or what he would be doing. Being glad of the war tinted her happiness with a small feeling of shame, but not enough to make her wish it had never happened. Kurt had proven himself a knight in shining armor by keeping his promise, and they had fallen in love in the process. Now the reality of the greater world crashed about them. They were at a dead end in the search for Agnes, but it no longer had the urgency of a few days ago. Selfish fit her to a "T". Guilt mixed with shame. Sarah would return to work at the hospital as though nothing had happened to Agnes, and Kurt would return to whatever it was he did. The thing that she could accept without guilt was that he loved her and she loved him. Of that she was sure.

Without conscious thought, her hand rose to his cheek where her fingers traced a line. Delighted surprise lit his eyes when he turned to look at her. He caught her hand and brought it to his lips. His kiss was warm despite the cold night wind blowing around them. Instead of letting her reclaim her hand, he tucked it into his jacket pocket, pulling her closer until he could get her under his arm. In the warmth of his embrace, Sarah drifted between waking and sleep. In her dreams, she saw two blond, tousle-headed, little boys with Kurt's blue eyes playing in the yard of a whitewashed cottage. Her dreams were somehow simpler, and at the same time, much more complicated than those of just a few days ago.

****

The jeep's slowing brought Sarah fully awake. They were on the street where Kurt's building stood a few blocks ahead. The hands on her watch showed 2:00 a.m.

Kurt kissed the top of her head. "Welcome back. Feel better?"

"I'm so sorry. I didn't mean to nod off. You should have woken me."

"And have you go back to your own seat? Not a chance."

Kurt pulled to the curb beside his building, his face taking on a somber expression. He glanced up at the flat's windows and then down into Sarah's eyes. "This is going to sound like a line from a cheap movie, but I promise you it isn't. Sarah, I love you. If this damned war is ever over, I want to spend the rest of my life with you. But the war isn't over, and who knows what kind of future we can expect. Stay with me at least for tonight. Nothing will happen that you don't want to happen. If all we do is hold each other, it will be enough. This may be all the time we will ever have together."

"Don't say that! We've got to believe that both of us will survive. We've just got to."

"I'll do everything in my power to come back to you, but I'm going away soon. I can't tell you where or why."

"When and for how long?"

"I can't tell you that either. It's the war and my part in it. That's all I can tell you. Will you trust me on that and about tonight?"

"What about Phelps?"

Kurt nodded toward the building's upper stories. "I think he'll understand and be discreet. Under all the condescension and bluster, a normal man surely lurks in there somewhere. I suspect he brought home his share of girls back in London or wherever it was he lived before the war. Anyway, after our last exchange about you, I doubt he'll open his mouth."

Alarmed by Kurt's tone, Sarah asked, "You didn't hurt him, did you?"

Kurt chuckled, but the sound held little mirth. "Heck no. I outplayed him with our boss. That got his goat much more than a beating would have."

Sarah sat back in her seat and studied Kurt's face. He looked exhausted and troubled. He deserved her comfort after all he had done for her and she would gladly give it. She gazed into his eyes and smiled. "Lay on, MacDuff."

The flat was dark with no sign of habitation.

Kurt touched the light switch and called, "Phelps? You here?"

No answer came.

"Looks like we have the place to ourselves. Want a bath or bed?"

"Bed. Definitely."

"Pajamas are where you left them."

"Do you really want me in pajamas?"

"Have something else in mind?"

"Hmmm. How about nothing?"

"I'd be the luckiest guy in the world." He took her hand and led her toward the bedroom. At the door, he stopped and put his hand under her chin so that her gaze met his. "Are you sure this is what you want? I can wait for you forever if I have to."

She kissed his cheek and murmured, "Yeah, but I can't."

****

Sarah awoke feeling like a well-fed cat lying on a sunny windowsill, contented and lazy. Their early morning lovemaking had been cut short by their mutual exhaustion, but it had been passionate and fulfilling all the same. Kurt had proven himself a skillful, considerate lover who held himself in check until she relaxed satisfied and complete in his arms. Only then did he give in to full release. How she had ever thought the two-timing pilot was the best there could be was now a mystery. Of course, he had been her first, so she had no basis of comparison until now. If last night was what she could expect from now on, she looked forward to many years of blissful fulfillment.

Kurt's side of the twin beds he had shoved together last night was empty. The sound of water splashing in the sink told her he was getting ready for the day. She sat up and was dismayed to see clothes and a pack set out for packing. From the closet door hung a garment bag with the zipper pulled halfway down. Well, if he had to leave, she wanted him packed so that his clothes made the trip with as few wrinkles as possible. She knew from watching her brothers how men usually tossed and stuffed their things into bags without regard to condition. She quickly dressed and set about gathering up his clothes obviously set out for his trip. After folding his under things and rolling his socks into pairs, she undid the pack's buckle straps and opened it wide. She glanced inside to gage the amount of available space. Her fist flew to her mouth as her heart jumped and banged in her chest.

In the bottom of the bag, a uniform lay neatly folded, but it wasn't American. It didn't even belong to another Allied nation. The eagle and swastika of Nazi Germany winked up at her from a patch above the chest pocket of the khaki tunic. Sarah lifted a corner of the garment. The odor of freshly laundered clothes drifted up. Beneath the tunic lay the rest of a full German army uniform, all pressed and starched. Under the uniform was a pair of lace up boots that bore signs of a recent attempt at covering scuffs with polish. Someone had gone to a great deal of trouble to make a battered uniform look presentable. Sarah knew very little about German uniforms, but even so, she thought this one must be for an officer because of the two golden yellow stars on the tunic's epaulets. She felt, rather than saw, Kurt watching her from the bathroom door.

"I shouldn't have left that out, but of course I didn't expect you to go snooping." His voice held a razor's edge.

"I wasn't snooping. I was helping you pack." Sarah's cheeks flamed.

"I don't need help packing." He strode across to the bed and held out his hand. Sarah stared at him, not sure what he wanted. Following his gaze to her hands, she realized that she still held a stack of his under garments. She let them fall onto the bed in a heap.

"Why do you have that thing? Where are you going?"

"I can't tell you."

"Can't or won't?" Anger boiled up, making her jaw rigid and her eyes narrow.

"Sarah, I would tell you if I could, but I can't." He

studied her for a moment and seemed to reach a decision. "I think it's time for you to go back to the hospital. I'll drive you. We can stop for breakfast and talk before I drop you off."

"No. I'll take a taxi. I don't want to inconvenience you any longer." Sarah's heart shattered into pieces. She had been such a fool.

"Don't be stupid. I have things in my life that I can't talk about to anyone, not even to the woman I love. Now, let's go. I need to know you're safe."

"Are you going to call me a cab, or do I need to start walking?" Anger, fueled by pain, made her voice strident and overloud.

"Calm down. You'll have the neighbors calling the cops." Kurt yanked up the telephone receiver and barked a few words into it. "Taxi is on its way. Now, sit down and let me tell what little I can."

Reluctantly, Sarah sat on the edge of the bed where Kurt joined her. He let out a long, low breath and took both of her hands in his. She tried to pull away, but he held firm.

"I'm leaving Casablanca under orders. I can't tell you any more than that. What I can tell you is that I love you. If I make it through this war, I hope you'll become my wife. We'll go home to Texas—raise dairy cows and lots of kids. It's unfair to ask you to wait for me, but I'm selfish that way. If you don't want to, I'll understand. Too much is uncertain. I can't even promise when you'll hear from me or where we'll next meet." He smiled weakly, a quizzical expression in his eyes.

Shock waves coursed through Sarah leaving her slightly giddy and completely off balance. A moment ago, she had been prepared to walk away from Kurt and never see him again. The thought that he might be a traitor chilled her to the bone, but her heart wouldn't let her believe it. She would have known somehow. She would have sensed it. She couldn't be in love with a Nazi spy. He was too good a man.

The blast of a car horn from the street below broke through the battle raging between her mind and heart. Tears welled up as she realized that she might never see Kurt after today.

His hand traced the line of her cheek. "So, what do you say? Marry me when the world is sane again?"

Sarah's voice failed her. She blinked back tears. It was foolish to love a man she knew so little about. Common sense screamed to let him go and be glad of a lucky escape. Her heart shouted back that she might never find love like this again. She couldn't send him into danger without the answer they both longed for and the one he deserved. Slowly, she nodded.

****

Kurt watched the taxi bearing Sarah away until it disappeared around a corner some distance down the street. He didn't need the distraction of worrying about her, but he would never regret her stumbling into his life. She was perfect, everything he could possibly want—beauty, brains, courage, loyalty, integrity, kindness. He hated himself for extracting her promise to marry him, but a guilty conscience was a small price to pay for such a prize. When the rear of the taxi was gone from sight, he turned and ascended the stairs to the flat. He had put off the task he dreaded as long as he could. The time had arrived for him to open the detailed information his orders contained.

He checked the bedroom, the bathroom, and front room. Nothing remained of his former roommate except his three quarters empty bottle of scotch. Strange that Phelps didn't say goodbye or at least leave a note, but then the man was odd in more ways than that one. Well, good luck to him on his trip back to England. They may not have become friends, but Phelps had done his best to prepare Kurt for his upcoming mission and he was grateful for it.

Kurt poured himself a stiff one and removed the envelope containing his orders from its hiding place under the sink. Sitting on the sofa, he opened the slim envelope detailing what he was to do once he was away from Casablanca. He scanned the first three pages of directives he would memorize before burning the sheets of paper they were written on. Nothing particularly surprising given where he was going. He placed them on the sofa beside him and continued reading. The fourth page's paragraphs made his heart rate gallop. The last sentence at the end of the page stopped it cold.

Chapter 18

Kurt steered his jeep to a stop beside the last hangar at Casablanca's Allied air base and peered through the darkness toward a lone Beechcraft C-45 poised on the tarmac, twin props spinning slowly in anticipation of the journey that lay ahead. Kurt sat for a moment and observed the scene. It felt as though he were an actor in the wings awaiting act one, scene one of a play for which he wasn't completely prepared. It was the role of a lifetime, but one that might carry a terrible price. His stomach tightened. A metallic taste flooded his mouth. Funny how fear had its own distinctive flavor. Kurt drew a deep breath. It was now or never. Grabbing his pack, he went to greet the airman who ran from the hangar.

"Pilot's ready for you, sir. Let's get you aboard." The airman took Kurt's pack, then helped him into a parachute. Eyeing Kurt's army uniform, the young man asked, "You done much jumping, sir?"

"Enough, but you really have no reason to ask, do you, Airman?"

"No, sir. Sorry, sir. Will that be all, sir?"

Kurt nodded. The airman led the way to the plane's side entrance where a member of the flight crew held the portal open. Swinging up into the interior, Kurt glanced down the two rows of single seats and found himself alone with a two-man crew.

The co-pilot secured the portal door and turned to Kurt. "Sit anywhere you like. Flight time should be about four hours, barring complications from Gerry."

Kurt dropped down into the closest seat. "Are we anticipating trouble?"

The pilot, wearing captain's insignia and looking all of twenty-five, glanced over his shoulder and nodded at Kurt. "Not if our luck holds. Nobody knows this flight is taking off, not even the brass. Your boss was clear that it was need to know only. We got the flight plan just before you arrived." The pilot returned to the final inspection of his gages.

Kurt furrowed his brow and smiled ruefully. "So, I guess it's 'once more into the breach, dear friends.'"

A puzzled expression crossed the co-pilot's face. He couldn't have been more than twenty, certainly wasn't old enough to have attended much college, and thus encountered the Bard's *Henry V*. Probably didn't even need to shave regularly.

"Uh, yeah. I guess so, sir. Well, we need to get going."

The boy turned and settled himself in the co-pilot's seat. The engines revved. Through a small porthole, Kurt watched the tarmac become a narrowing ribbon of black. Soon they were aloft in the moonless sky. Stars became brighter as Casablanca's dim haze faded away. Although he couldn't see it from the plane, an ocean of sand now spread beneath them, sand for which the nations of the world fought and died.

Kurt had already committed his orders to memory and burned the paper documents, but the extent of what was expected of him made his stomach churn. By all accounts, this was probably a suicide mission. He prayed that he would get his job done before the end and that Sarah would be able to forgive him for eliciting her promise to marry him. He was a selfish bastard. She deserved better. Kurt took a pen and small notebook from his pocket. This should have been done before they parted, but he couldn't bring himself to say the words—now his conscience wouldn't let him rest. Opening the notebook, he began to scribble.

When it was done, Kurt stared at the letter for several beats. Except for telling Sarah he loved her, Kurt hated the words he had written, but he cared for her too deeply to leave her hanging. He tore the page from the notebook, folded it twice, and wrote Sarah's hospital address on the back. Sighing, he leaned back, and pulled his cap down over his eyes. Might as well try to get some rest since sleep wouldn't be on the agenda after he reached his contact. Sarah's beautiful face floated in his dreams, marred by anxiety and tears. He awoke with a start from a hand shaking his shoulder.

"We'll be over the drop zone in twenty minutes, sir."

"Thank you, Lieutenant." The co-pilot returned to his seat.

Would he see the single light from his contact? It was anyone's guess. These nighttime jumps had an unfortunate record, but there had been no other way to get him close enough to Helmut's position in time. He had asked why he couldn't come in by sea, but the distances between the Allied occupied territories and his destination were too great. Kurt checked his buckles and the position of the ripcord handle one more time and positioned his personal pack for the jump. The young co-pilot left his seat again.

"It's time, sir. You ready?"

"As ready as I'll ever be."

Kurt went to the portal. A whoosh of cold air washed over him. Wishes, hopes, regrets all vied for supremacy as he peered out into the vastness of the night sky. He could do nothing to change the past, but he could do the right thing for Sarah's future. He turned to the co-pilot.

"I really need a favor."

"If I can, I'll do my best."

"See this address? When you get back to Casablanca, could you deliver this note to my girl personally?"

The boy's eyes softened. "Sure thing. Should be easy enough." After slipping the folded sheet in his flight vest, he extended his hand. "Good luck, sir. Godspeed with your mission."

Kurt grasped the offered hand. "Thanks. Same to you guys for your return flight."

"There, sir." The boy pointed down toward a pinprick of light in the near distance. "Another few seconds."

Grasping the portal's edges with each hand, he paused. Cold air poured into his lungs. Drawing a long, calming breath, he positioned himself for the jump.

A hand gripped his shoulder. "Now, sir."

In the next second, there was nothing but air beneath his feet. His legs blew to the side as he counted seconds to ensure he and his chute cleared the departing plane. When the stars were his only visible companions, he gripped the metal handle on the chute's pack. He yanked the ripcord, setting white silk billowing, which in turn created a considerable drag on his body. Again his body jerked and lunged to the side. Straps dug into his chest with the upward draft, then he settled into the descent. His head swiveled, eyes searching the void for the speck of light that would lead him to the next phase of his mission.

The ground rushed up to meet him. Kurt's boots hit the earth with a thud and he fell on his side. The wind filled the chute, dragging him over the rough terrain. Scrambling for purchase in shifting sand, he grappled with the chute's latches. Finally upright, straps dropped from Kurt's shoulders and he began gathering the lines and silk into a bundle while his gaze roamed over the countryside. Still no sign of his contact. Perhaps they had overshot the drop zone. If so, the mission was probably doomed, and he would most likely find himself in a POW camp or worse.

Stuffing the chute under his arm, Kurt dug in his pack for a flashlight. Three shorts, three longs, three shorts. Nothing. Again, Kurt flashed the SOS signal. This time he was rewarded by an answering flash guiding him over low, rock-strewn sand hills until he reached a small ravine. Rolling and sliding down the last hill, he came to rest at the feet of a figure dressed in Saharan nomad garb, a ship of the desert kneeling in the sand behind him. Extending from the folds of the Bedouin garment, Kurt could just make out the shadow of a pistol muzzle.

"Identify yourself." The voice floating above the pistol sounded British.

Kurt lifted his hands to shoulder height. "Kurt Heinz, captain, US Army, number 18 904 025."

"And the password?"

"Hortensia."

"By Jove, I was beginning to fear we'd lost you."

Kurt stood and extended his hand. "You have no idea how happy I am to find you."

"Your flight was uneventful, I hope."

"Clear sailing all the way."

"From Casablanca, I believe?"

Kurt nodded, but his eyes narrowed. This was not the direction he expected the conversation to take.

"You're attached to MacFadyen's group?"

"Uh huh." Kurt's heart rate picked up speed. Something was off about this guy. He had no business asking so many questions. Kurt cocked his head to one side as his mouth hardened.

The Brit broke eye contact and seemed to be struggling with some internal demon. Finally, he looked back at Kurt, his words tumbling out in a rush. "I say. Did you by any chance meet a girl by that name in Casablanca? A real beauty?"

"Hortensia, you mean?"

"Right."

"Yeah. Great girl. Beauty and brains all in one neat package."

The Brit fairly bristled. His free hand made a fist. "Is she seeing anyone at the moment?"

Kurt studied his contact for a second. "No. She's pining away waiting for some guy called Reggie." The tension visibly drained from the contact's body. Kurt grinned. "That wouldn't be you by any chance, would it?"

The contact sucked on his teeth for a second. "I'm sorry. I shouldn't have asked those questions. It's just that we're not allowed to send personal communication in any form. It's been so long. I was afraid she might have…moved on."

"She's still wearing your ring and gives the cold shoulder to any guy who tries to get too close. Feel better?"

"Much. Thank you." A pained expression crossed Reggie's face as he reached out and put his hand on Kurt's arm. "I would be most grateful if you didn't mention this to MacFadyen should you happen…" Reggie's voice trailed away into embarrassed silence.

"You were going to say if I manage to return. Sure. Any message you want delivered to Hortensia?"

Reggie's eyes grew unnaturally bright. "Tell her she is the dearest person on earth and that I love her more than words can express. Is that too much?"

"Nope. Sounds about right to me."

Reggie shifted from one foot to the other and looked off into the distance, before clearing his throat. "Yes, well, I think we should get down to business. Time is at a premium. Your man will only be in his present location for a week at most."

While Kurt transformed himself from Kurt Heinz, US Army into Helmut Heinz, the Desert Fox's *Abwehr* officer, his contact strode to a nearby dune and grabbed what looked like a handful of desert brush. With a flick of his wrists, a tarp snapped in the air revealing a German *Kübelwagen* beneath. The German equivalent of the US Jeep, the vehicle wore the expected desert tan paint with the white palm tree painted on the sides. Although two wheel drive, it purportedly skidded over sand and snow alike with a minimum of trouble.

Reggie patted the front fender. "This was found undamaged along the coast road west of El Alamein. It seems some Gerry ran out of petrol and left it. Fortunate for us, that. It is hoped in the confusion of Rommel's retreat, no one will have made note of this particular vehicle's identification number."

"Yeah, getting thrown in a German stockade for being in possession of the wrong car would pretty much ruin my day. So, any last minute details that will make my job easier? I was told you might have later intelligence than what we had when I left Casablanca."

"Quite right. You do need to be on your way, but I have something for you before you go." Reggie went to his camel and fumbled through a saddlebag. "Ah. Here it is."

He laid a map out on the sand and held his light over it. "This is a map of the city with your man's place of lodging marked here." Reggie pointed to an X on a street close to the sea. "Lovely little hotel by the port. His is a corner room facing the street with a side wall balcony overhanging an enclosed garden. Fortunate for you, he spends his evenings alone in his room which is at a distance from the others."

Kurt studied the map and tapped the X. "Just like the Nazis to commandeer the best accommodations even when they are on the run."

One corner of Reggie's mouth turned up in a crooked smile. "Quite."

"Do we know why Rommel sent staff officers to Sfax?"

"Planning to converge with von Arnim is our guess. Something which, I shouldn't need to point out, must not happen. Perhaps he is planning an escape route as well. Whatever Rommel's purpose, your man seems to be part of something rather different. A mission directly from the *Führer* by all accounts."

Kurt pursed his lips and gave a soft whistle. Apparently Cousin Helmut had returned to grace or his father had more friends in high places than MacFadyen was led to believe. "Must be something big to take Rommel's intelligence officer away from tactical operations with Montgomery hot on their heels."

"We believe that the outcome of the war could depend upon it."

"Do you know what they have planned?"

"No, but Berlin is apparently agog regarding a certain upcoming Allied event."

Kurt's head snapped up, and he looked directly into Reggie's eyes. "Do they know what and where the event is?"

"We're not completely sure, but it wouldn't be surprising for them to have the information, considering the number of spies the Krauts have in North Africa."

Kurt sucked on his lower lip. His orders were to impersonate Helmut and discover what he was working on. Nothing had been said about Nazi awareness of the upcoming Allied event in Casablanca. Important details had apparently been kept from him. Nothing like working in the dark with incomplete information to make a guy feel secure.

Kurt cocked his head to one side. "Anything else?"

Reggie drew another map from beneath his robes and pressed it into Kurt's hand. "You have a little less than forty-eight hours to reach your destination and locate your target. The distance is about 130 miles east and then north for a short jog. Your route takes you near both German and Allied forces. Be careful. The lines of demarcation are shifting with the sands. Once we part, you will be completely on your own. You can ill afford unplanned contact with either side. Stay well out of sight of all traffic. Wouldn't want you shot for a spy by your own people."

Chapter 19

Rain lashing the hospital windows sent a shiver down Sarah's spine. The weather had prevented opening the windows to admit fresh air for almost two weeks now. The smell of unwashed bodies, disinfectant, and musty plaster must be permanently burned into the linings of her nose. She looked up from her paperwork and let her gaze wander over her patients. Sure enough, her double amputee had thrown his covers off again. Shaking her head, she went to his side and tucked the blanket loosely over the frame covering the lower half of his body. Trying to keep him warm and in as little pain as possible had become a full-time job. His groaning even in near coma drew Sarah's eyes to her watch. Fifteen more minutes and she could give him another dose of morphine. Blessing and curse all rolled together in a syrette.

She straightened up and massaged the small of her back. It had been a long shift, but work was a welcome distraction. With Kurt disappearing to God only knew where and no word of Agnes, Sarah needed something, anything, to keep her mind occupied. Footsteps echoing in the hallway slowed and stopped at the entrance to Sarah's ward. Her gaze shifted toward the source, finding her boss, Beatrice, standing in the entry. She wore an expression akin to regret or at least of hesitation. She no doubt needed to ask Sarah to work yet another extra shift. Well, so be it. She had nothing better to do.

"Sarah, I need to tell you something. When we're finished talking, I want you to take a long hot bath, have a double hot toddy, and rest for a bit."

A feeling of unease set off butterflies in the pit of Sarah's stomach. "Should I sit down?"

"It might be best."

Sarah led Beatrice to the desk where they sat in chairs facing each other. Beatrice reached out and cupped Sarah's hands in both of hers. "This is difficult for everyone, but for you most of all. You were her best friend."

"They've found Agnes, haven't they?"

Beatrice nodded. "I'm afraid it's very bad news."

Sarah sighed and fought to keep her lunch from coming back up. "Tell me everything."

"They said she didn't suffer. That she was already dead when she went into the water. Her body washed ashore south of the city late yesterday."

"If she's been in the ocean all this time, how can they be sure it's Agnes?"

"Dental records and dog tags. Somehow her tags managed to stay around her neck."

"Can I see her?"

"It would be better if you didn't. Remember her as she was."

"Who's writing to her family?"

"The colonel, of course. As her immediate superior, I will as well."

"Thank you. She would want her folks to know what happened, but please spare them the worst."

"The official story is that she died in a boating

accident during an R and R outing. As if anyone would be taking pleasure cruises here, but it seems there is something rather top secret associated with what happened at your apartment. Perhaps your Captain Heinz can shed some light for you."

"He tried his best, but we were too late. It was always too late. She never had a chance." Sarah buried her face in her hands, unable to keep the tears at bay any longer. Agnes had been with her from the beginning, first as training supervisor, then sometime older sister, but most importantly, as the closest friend Sarah had ever known. Life without her now seemed unimaginable.

Beatrice's arm slipped around Sarah's shoulders. "How about that toddy?"

When her storm passed, Sarah stood. "You're probably right about getting some rest, but I'll never be able to right now. I'm going out for a little while. Maybe a walk will help clear my head."

A watery sun peeked from behind scudding clouds when Sarah stepped through the hospital's front doors. A stiff breeze off the Atlantic made her pull her sweater closer, but she welcomed the change after long hours caring for the wounded in the stuffy hospital ward. Without a plan, she wandered for several blocks before stopping at a cafe for coffee and *fekkas*, light delicately flavored cookies filled with toasted sesame seeds, almonds, and raisins. Munching on the twice-baked sweet, Sarah watched the passing traffic without really seeing it. Her mind was miles away, somewhere in the desert or maybe in an unspecified city. She didn't know where to picture Kurt or how to think about the dangers he faced. Being left in such darkness was already dragging her down. She was usually so sensible about things, but her guard had been completely shattered by a rangy Texan with a whole lot of secrets. That she loved him deeply, perhaps desperately, became clearer to her with each passing hour since they parted. It would eventually become unbearable. If only she could check in from time to time with someone who at least knew if he were alive.

Sarah brushed crumbs from her fingers. Placing her elbows on the table, she rested her chin in her upturned palm and sighed. There had to be someone she could talk to about Kurt. Then it came to her.

Stuffing the last of the fekkas in her mouth, she washed it down with coffee and stepped onto the sidewalk beside the café. Looking left and right, she charged off toward the nearest taxi hovering at the corner.

"The Anfa Hotel, please. I'm in something of a hurry."

The Moroccan driver looked at her in the rearview mirror, frowned, and moved with all the urgency of a slug having no particular destination in mind. Sarah fidgeted with impatience. If she said anything further to him about the necessity of speed, the man would probably only go slower, so she sat back and clasped her hands in a tight ball to prevent her fingers drumming on the metal window ledge. As the buildings of the city's older section crawled away and were replaced by the outskirts' newer Art Deco buildings, Sarah planned what she would say to get herself admitted to the hotel which was now rumored to be on complete lockdown. Nothing brilliant came to mind.

The cab rolled up to the front gate and disgorged

Sarah unceremoniously onto the sidewalk, then sped away as though it was a fire truck answering an alarm. Men could be such jerks. She gazed at the hotel secured behind its bristling barbed wire enclosure. Everywhere she looked there seemed to be a rifle-toting soldier. The place really was an armed camp. Feeling someone watching her, she turned toward the front gate. The soldier at the guardhouse watched her with interest. He appeared less than pleased.

"Can I help you, miss?"

Drawing a deep breath and plastering her best smile on her face, she answered, "Why yes, thank you. I need to speak with one of the secretaries in the hotel."

The guard looked unimpressed. "I can't let anyone but authorized personnel inside, ma'am."

"Oh. Well, I don't really need to see her, just to speak to her. Could you maybe call her on your phone?"

"No, ma'am."

"May I leave a note to be delivered to her?"

The guard pursed his lips and cocked his head to one side.

"Is there any way I can reach her?"

"Do you have her direct number and clearance to use it, ma'am?"

"No, I'm afraid not."

"Then I'm afraid you're out of luck." An approaching vehicle's tires crunching to a halt behind Sarah drew the guard's attention. "I have to ask you to move along, ma'am."

Sarah stepped back while the guard bent toward the window of a car bearing British insignia. An involuntary gasp escaped her lips. She had only met him once, but the face gazing at her from the backseat was well remembered all the same. Phelps, Kurt's former roommate, apparently hadn't returned to England after all and he looked as surprised to see Sarah as she was to see him. The guard returned paperwork to the driver and opened the gate. Phelps peered through the back window until the car disappeared behind foliage near the hotel's front entrance.

Sarah watched until the car was out of sight. If anyone could give her information, it might be Phelps. He and Kurt had pretended to be friends, but Sarah had sensed that they were more colleagues than buddies. They were too different. Most tellingly, there had been none of the easy camaraderie one sees between people who enjoy one another's company. If they did work in the same department, unit, or whatever it was, Phelps should be her man, but how to go about contacting him was another matter. She didn't know his position, title, not even his first name. Further complicating things, she had no idea where he was staying and gaining access to anyone having an office in the Anfa was clearly beyond her reach.

Feeling dejected and at a loss for what to do next, Sarah walked for blocks. Random thoughts and images drifted through her mind. She thought of everything and nothing. One moment there was crystal clarity, the next it was all just a jumble. Finally she gave in and flagged down a cab.

"Your destination, Madame?"

Sarah hesitated. Maybe Beatrice was right. Rest and work were the answer. They always had been. Back at the hospital, she went straight to her cot and stretched out. She was somewhere between waking and sleep when one of the girls called from the entrance to the nurses' dorm.

"Sarah, you have a caller at the front desk. Do you want me to tell him you aren't available?"

Sarah opened one eye and mumbled, "Who is it?"

"Some Brit named Phillips, at least I think that's what he said."

Sarah thought for a moment. She didn't know anyone named Phillips. "Could he have said Phelps?"

"Yeah. Maybe."

Sunbeams slanted through the hospital windows at a late afternoon angle. Sarah must have slept for an hour or so. Running her hand over her eyes, she sat up and rested arms on knees. She couldn't be so fortunate that he was here to tell her what she so desperately wanted to find out. Her luck hadn't been running in that direction for a long time.

"Know what he wants?"

"He didn't say. Nice looking guy, though. Since you're taken, how about passing this fella on to me?"

"You can have him, but I'm not sure you'd want him." Now what had made her say that about a man she hardly knew? Phelps was nice looking in a bookish sort of way. He had the terrific manners that only the British upper crust managed to pound into their kids. Girls who went for intellectuals would probably find him devastatingly attractive.

Sarah stood up, straightened her skirt, and ran her hand over her hair. Exhilaration filled her as she considered the prospect of asking him questions, but still she could think of no reason why he wanted to talk to her. Checking her reflection in the hall window just outside her ward's door, she decided her rumpled skirt and blouse would have to do. As to Phelps's sudden unexpected appearance, why look a gift horse in the mouth?

She found him leaning on the security guard's desk talking with the nurse who had come to get her. When he caught sight of Sarah, he politely disengaged from the other girl, who frowned at Sarah and stuck out her tongue behind his back. Sarah chuckled before she could stop herself. A puzzled expression crossed Phelps's face, which he quickly adjusted to a gracious smile.

"Miss Barrett. Thank you for seeing me. I apologize for dropping by unannounced, but I didn't know how else to contact you."

"Actually, I'm glad you did, Mr. Phelps."

"Ah. Rather providential, then." Suddenly confused and shy, Sarah broke eye contact and focused on a space over her visitor's shoulder. After a moment, he drew an audible breath and said, "Yes. Quite. Might there be a place where we may speak undisturbed?"

"Not here in the hospital, I'm afraid. There's a cafe not far down the road."

"Brilliant. May I treat you to a coffee?"

A short walk brought them to a bistro style establishment with tables inside, as well as outside on the sidewalk under an awning. They chose one outside. It was really too chilly for al fresco dining, but the surrounding tables were deserted, providing the privacy Phelps seemed to want. He went to the counter inside and returned with two steaming mugs and a plate of pastries.

Settling himself in the chair across from Sarah, he

offered sugar and cream before taking two lumps and a splash for himself. After stirring for what seemed an inordinately long time, he placed his spoon on the table and took a sip while peering at Sarah over the rim of his mug.

Sarah couldn't bear the tension any longer. "Mr. Phelps, why did you want to see me?"

His eyes grew a little wider as he placed his mug on the table. "I wished…Well, you see…Oh, dash it all. When I saw you standing outside the hotel gate earlier today, I thought you looked rather downcast and might be in need of cheering up. Presumptuous, I know, but there it is."

"Oh, no. It's not presumptuous at all, especially since it's true. I do need cheering up. Have you heard about my friend Agnes Johnson?"

Phelps's eyes widened slightly, then softened. "Yes. So sad. Please let me offer my sincerest condolences."

Sarah's gaze dropped to her cup. Taking the pitcher, she added more cream to the already tan liquid. She picked up her spoon and set the whitish liquid swirling. Without taking her eyes off the coffee, she replied barely above a whisper. "Thank you. Agnes will be missed by everyone." Sarah paused to fight the lump rising in her throat. When she could speak without her voice trembling, she continued, "She was a terrific nurse and a wonderful friend."

Another awkward silence ensued. Sarah nibbled on a pastry and looked up, smiling encouragingly at her host.

"Miss Barrett, you said you wished to speak to me, as well. Is there something with which I may assist you?"

"Look, Mr. Phelps, I know that you and Kurt are involved in work you can't talk about, but I'm so worried about him. After what happened to Agnes…I may have no right to ask you this, but have you heard from him? Could you tell me if you had?"

A studied sympathy filled his eyes. "I see. As to having heard from Captain Heinz, the answer is, alas, no. And even if I had, I would not be at liberty to speak of it." He took a couple sips of coffee while gazing pensively at Sarah. He returned his cup to its saucer and tilted his head slightly to one side. "I say, may I ask why you have connected the fate of your friend Miss Johnson with that of Captain Heinz?"

Sarah gulped her coffee and spluttered as the liquid found the wrong pipe. When she could speak again, she answered, "I'm sorry about that. I don't know what got into me."

"Not at all. No need for apology." His eyes narrowed. "About the connection between the captain and Miss Johnson?"

Sarah was at a loss for what or how much she should say. "I guess I'm seeing assassins behind every bush and door. I'm sure I'll hear from him when the time is right. Please forget I asked."

"Of course, if that is your wish."

With the skill of the well brought up, Phelps changed the subject to the weather and entertained Sarah with tales of his childhood spent in the Yorkshire Dales as the son and heir of a minor nobleman with an estate near Ripon. Finding they had a rural upbringing in common, Sarah shared some of the stories her grandmother had told about how their ancestors got from England's midlands to Virginia's Shenandoah Valley. They passed a pleasant forty-five minutes.

With nothing else she could think of to say, Sarah glanced at her watch. "My goodness, look at the time. My shift starts soon." She rose and extended her hand. "Thank you for the coffee and the cheering up. I feel much better, Mr. Phelps."

He grasped her hand. "I'm so glad to have been of service. Won't you please call me David? May I call you Sarah?"

"Of course...David."

He seemed reluctant to release her hand. "Sarah, might I take you to dinner one night? I realize you and Captain Heinz fancy one another. My purpose in asking is not to compromise you in that regard, but there seems no reason for you to eat military fare all the time." When Sarah hesitated, he added, "I could keep my ear to the ground and pass along information about Captain Heinz that isn't classified."

Sarah pulled her hand from his. "I guess there wouldn't be any harm in it."

He drew a card from his inner breast coat pocket and wrote a number on it. "This is where you can leave a message for me. Is there one for you?"

"I'm afraid not. You can always come by the hospital. Leave a message if I'm not available, and I'll call you."

"Of course. May I see you back to the hospital?"

Sarah really didn't want or need the escort, but she couldn't think of a polite way to decline. "Sure, but I will have to go straight in." Phelps looked pleased, and taking her elbow, guided her along the pavement. He was the embodiment of the perfect English gentleman.

As they made their way back to the hospital in silence, it occurred to Sarah that she still didn't really understand why he had called on her. Cheering her up seemed an unlikely reason given their nearly nonexistent prior acquaintance and his coolness during their brief encounter. She glanced at his profile. Classic features, light brown hair, green eyes, rosy-cheeked complexion often found among the British upper classes. An inscrutable expression. Secrets? Definitely. Diffident? Perhaps. Self-effacing? It wouldn't be out of character for one of his background. Handsome enigma? Yes, that described him rather well.

Chapter 20

Kurt's mouth formed a tight smile as he watched his contact peering anxiously from beneath his Bedouin headgear. "Reggie, old man, I have no plans for being shot as a spy by either side, but thanks for the concern all the same."

Reggie nodded and lifted his hand. Pointing eastward, he said, "You'll find the road you want not far beyond that line of hills. Unless there is anything else, I best be on my way." One corner of his mouth turned up. "Wouldn't do for a Bedouin to be caught consorting with a spy."

"No, I guess not, but Bedouin? The new T.E. Lawrence, are you?"

"Not at all. I happen to be far more suited to working with the desert peoples than he ever was."

"How so?"

"I was born in Egypt. Arabic was my first language. I am what is unflatteringly called a half-caste, but my lineage is proving quite useful in this campaign. Rather like yours is soon to be."

"Impressive. I hope I blend in as seamlessly as I'm guessing you do."

"I'm sure you will from what I hear." Reggie extended his hand, which Kurt grasped. "Good luck. I don't suppose our paths will cross again. It has been a pleasure meeting you...even if for so brief a time."

"Same here. And don't worry about Hortensia. You're the only guy for her. You can take that to the bank."

Kurt watched Reggie mount his camel and give it encouragement to rise with his riding crop. At the top of the first hill, he stopped and turned in the saddle. With a brief salute, he tapped his mount again and disappeared down the other side, riding west toward the sand desert. Kurt was truly on his own. The success of the mission now rested on his shoulders alone.

A mission like this was something Kurt had trained for with a dedication driven by the need to prove his family's loyalty. As a boy during the Great War, he had secretly felt ashamed of his German heritage. Schoolmates called him and the other kids of German descent names like Kraut, Kaiser Kinder, Square Jaw, and the like. Even some of the teachers had made unkind comments. When Wild Bill Donovan recruited him, Kurt welcomed the opportunity to prove his patriotism, but now that it was at hand, an unnamed dread plagued him. It wasn't fear of dying. Like all military personnel, he had known from the beginning that he might be required to pay the ultimate price. This was something different and it felt an awful lot like fear of failure. So much rode on his confidence that he was man enough for the job—that he could do what was needed when the time came——that his skill and training would be enough to carry him through any situation he might face. The hesitation prompted by a single question now playing at the back of his mind with every action or decision had to be hammered down and eliminated. How Sarah felt about things could no longer be even a slight consideration. He had known from the beginning it was a mistake getting romantically involved at this point in his life, but he'd gone ahead and done it anyway.

Kurt ran a hand over his face. Compartmentalizing Sarah, locking her away in a deep mental recess was the only thing that made sense. It wouldn't do her, himself, or the mission any good if wondering about what she was doing, thinking, or feeling distracted him. His hands curled into fists. A deep need to hit something surged through Kurt, but he held himself in check. Sounds carried in the desert night like gunshots or explosions. Regardless of what it took, he would get back to her. No cost was too great. It was the only alternative he could live with.

Kurt drew a long breath, got in the *Kübelwagen*, and pressed the starter. It coughed and died. Cursing and pumping the accelerator, he tried again. This time, the engine spluttered before dying. He leaned back against the seat and hit the wheel with his palm. One more try before he started running after Reggie and his camel. Third time often being the charm, the engine started as though it had never given trouble. Before engaging the gears, Kurt rolled his head from side to side, his hands gripping the wheel until they began to tingle. Once he left this spot, there was no turning back. The pulse point in his throat throbbed ever so slightly. He searched the terrain for signs of other night travelers. Finding none, Kurt shifted into first.

Twenty minutes of slipping and sliding over sand on a barely discernible trail brought him to the road Reggie described. Kurt turned off his headlights and slowed to a stop. His gaze swept from horizon to horizon along the hard packed ribbon of sand winding east. No other humans appeared to be abroad. He reached out to flip the blackout headlamp switch and found nothing but smooth metal. Digging around in his pack, his hand lit on a box of matches. He withdrew it and struck one. The damned switch was on the opposite side of the dashboard from where he had been told it would be. SNAFU. Described the situation perfectly.

A sharp draft sent icy fingers crawling under Kurt's collar. He drew his tunic collar closer and slammed the gearshift into place. Releasing the clutch, he eased forward and the car bumped onto what passed for the main road. Winter rains had left it sloppy, but it was the ruts left by recent vehicular traffic that set Kurt's teeth on edge. With Rommel dug in hundreds of miles away in the Libyan desert at Wadi Zem Zem, there was no worry about running into the full Afrika Korps, but patrols and scouting parties were another matter. Less than forty-eight hours to reach Sfax, the port city one hundred seventy miles south of Tunis—it had to be sufficient. There was no other choice.

Chapter 21

"You got quite a stack today, Sarah. Looks like the mail's finally caught up with us."

Sarah smiled up at the young private who acted as the hospital mail boy and general gofer. "Thanks, Jimmy. Have you heard from your folks yet?"

"Yep. Got four letters all at once. Last one said they had got mine, too, and was mighty relieved to hear we was safe. Of course, the censors blacked out Casablanca and a lot of other stuff. Guess I should have known better, but sometimes they let stuff slip by. Mom really worries when she doesn't know where we are."

"I'm sure your parents understand. All of our families are in the same boat."

"Yeah, I know. Mom makes a big deal out of it, but with four sons in service, she's gotta know about the censors. Well, you have a good time with those letters."

"You bet."

Sarah thumbed through the stack starting at the bottom. The envelopes bore the expected Virginia postmarks and return addresses of parents, grandparents, and friends. She would sort them by date and start with the most recent, then go back to the oldest and work her way forward. Three letters down, an unexpected postmark surfaced. Sarah stopped flipping through the envelopes and drew this one from the stack. High Wycombe. Funny name. Now who would have written from England? She stared for several beats. The handwriting looked familiar, but surely it couldn't be, not after the way he had acted. The postmark was dated two weeks ago. Her heart beat a little faster. She turned it over and ran her finger under the flap.

Enclosed was a single page. She fingered the paper in hesitation and then drew it from the envelope. A glance at the sender's signature confirmed her suspicion. Bastard. Perfect timing as usual. Her mouth hardened to a thin line. How like him to write now that she had moved on with her life. Just who did he think he was? A bitter laugh bubbled up. He always knew exactly who he was and what he wanted. It was she who had been the unconfident, yielding partner in their tawdry little relationship. Now that her formerly dearest wish had been granted, how did she feel? Anger—dread—curiosity—foolish? Longing? Perhaps. Sarah drew a long breath and let it out in a rush. Against her better judgment, she smoothed the paper and read.

Dear Sarah,

I guess you are surprised to hear from me after the way I left things with you in Casablanca. Before you tear this letter up and throw it away without reading it, I hope you will hear me out. I've come to a realization. Leaving you without saying goodbye is the biggest mistake I've ever made. I didn't think I needed to be encumbered by someone waiting for me. I was a jackass too stupid to see what was right in front of me. I hope you can find a way to forgive me.

You are probably asking yourself why now? What has changed? It was watching the bomber next to mine blown from the sky and the crew fall into the hands of the Germans. That could just as easily have been my plane and my crew. All of us pilots know that this sort of thing will continue to happen with greater frequency as we increase the number of raids over Europe. When a guy comes face-to-face with his own mortality, it causes him to take a second look at the choices he has made and the people he wants in his life.

I know I hurt you. I was selfish and thoughtless, but I now realize I need you. I need to know there is a special someone I'm fighting for. I need to know someone is waiting for me at the end of this hellish war or who will mourn me if I don't come back. I am laying my heart at your feet and asking you to be that someone. I need you and I am hoping you still need me. Please write as soon as you get this and tell me you will forgive me.

All my love,
Bill

Surprise hardly described the emotions running through Sarah. She had once longed for this day, but now found it was the very definition of anticlimax. Sarah traced the letter's signature with her finger. She loved Kurt, but Bill's plea tugged at her heart nonetheless. She would always care about him because he had been her first. You didn't easily forget the guy who turned you from a girl into a woman which made his departing without a word all the more painful. Sarah had really thought he was the one. She had envisioned them raising a family together in a little Cape Cod surrounded by a white picket fence. Her naive hopes and dreams had been dashed against the realities of war and Bill's true nature. She had been so stupid. Well, not anymore. She had moved on, and Kurt was not Bill.

She found great comfort in the realization.

Sarah shoved Bill's letter into her pocket. The decision about whether to answer him could wait. Her patients needed their next round of meds and their bandages changed. She was halfway through her round when one of the recently arrived nurses appeared at her side. Sarah continued wrapping a wound with only a quick glance upward.

"Hey, Mandy. You're early."

"I'm not staying, just delivering a message. Again. That front desk corporal seems to think I'm his personal messenger service. You've got a caller. Again."

"Do you have a name? I'm not expecting anyone."

"Nope, but he's cute and too young for you. It's not fair. You've already got two guys on the string. How about sharing this one with me?"

"First, I've only got one guy. And second, as far as I'm concerned, you're welcome to every other man in North Africa."

"Gee, you don't have to get mad." Mandy's voice held a note of hurt feelings tinted with petulance.

Sarah stood and rubbed the small of her back. "I'm not angry, Mandy, just tired. Can you tell him I'll be there when I'm finished here?"

The young nurse grinned and called over her shoulder, "You betcha."

Now who on earth could it be this time? Sarah didn't know any men well enough for them to be calling on her. Whatever it was couldn't be important. She made no effort to rush finishing with her patients.

When Sarah neared the reception area, she saw Mandy leaning hipshot against the opposite wall with her head tilted to one side. In profile, her face appeared animated and her eyes sparkled. She was deep in conversation with a young man in flight gear. Sarah stopped in the doorway and watched the young couple. Mandy appeared to be making headway. Sarah gave them as much time as she could before calling, "Mandy, could you watch my ward?"

Mandy's head swiveled toward Sarah. She wrinkled her nose, but nodded. As she passed, Mandy whispered, "That's him. Thanks for taking your time. I got a date."

Sarah couldn't help smiling as she watched the young pilot's eyes following Mandy sashay down the hall. Sarah strode across the foyer to her visitor.

"I understand you wanted to see me. I don't think we've met."

"No, ma'am. I was asked to deliver a letter from a mutual friend."

"Who?"

"A friend who seemed pretty anxious to get word to you. Any more than that, I'm not at liberty to say."

Sarah frowned for a moment, and then her heart skipped a beat. It must be. It had to be. There was no other explanation.

"I see. May I have it?"

The young man reached into his flight jacket's inner breast pocket and withdrew one folded over sheet. "I hope the letter helps. Our friend was very concerned for you to get it as soon as possible. I came here straight from the airfield."

Without thinking, Sarah leaned forward and kissed the pilot's cheek. "It helps tremendously. Thank you so much for bringing it right away."

The young man smiled. "Anything for a friend.

Well, I've really got to be going."

"Thank you again."

The pilot turned half way before Sarah caught his arm. "Could you at least tell me if he is safe?"

"When I last saw our friend he was fine. I can't say more. Excuse me."

The boy rushed through the door before Sarah could ask another question. This was surreal. Two letters in one day. She unfolded the sheet of paper with trembling fingers.

My Darling,

I owe you an apology and I must beg your forgiveness. I still can't tell you where I'm going or what I will be doing, but I should have been honest with you about one thing. The chances of my coming back from this are not great. I should never have talked you into promising to wait for me. It was selfish and wrong. You are young and beautiful with your whole life ahead of you. You shouldn't spend months or years waiting and worrying, but even now, I cannot bring myself to tell you to forget me. A less selfish man would write those words and mean them.

If I don't make it, live life for both of us. Find a guy who will love you and take care of you. You deserve happiness, marriage, children, and that little cottage with the white picket fence you said you wanted. For now, I can't promise anything except that I love you with my whole heart and will cherish our time together as the most important and happiest of my life.

With All My Love,

Kurt

"Are you all right, Sarah?" The corporal at the reception desk rose from his chair. "You look like you're going to faint."

Sarah sat down on the floor and put her head between her knees. "I'll be okay in a minute. I've had something of a shock. That's all."

"How about a cup of water?"

"Have anything stronger?"

The private raised an eyebrow. "You know what happens to guys who get caught drinking on duty."

"You're not the one who is going to drink it, now are you?"

"Nope. I guess not. You wait right here."

When the corporal returned, he handed Sarah a metal hip flask. She unscrewed the top. The first fiery sip caught in her throat, producing a spasm of spluttering and coughing. The corporal looked alarmed and patted Sarah on the back with hands the size of hams. She returned the flask. "Thank you. Probably not the smartest thing I've ever done. Please don't tell anyone."

"Your secret's safe with me. You covered for me last week when I was late to my post. That makes us partners in crime." The corporal held out his hand and helped Sarah to stand. Somehow she made her way back to the ward without her knees buckling.

"Mandy, I'll take it now. Thanks for the help."

"Sure. See you at shift change."

Sarah slumped down onto the straight-backed chair and leaned her elbows on the desk. Dropping her chin into her upturned palms, she drew in several deep breaths. Knowing Kurt might be in grave danger had always hovered beneath Sarah's outward calm, but seeing it in writing was a punch to the solar plexus. They had only just found each other, and their time together had been so brief. Fate couldn't be so cruel as to take him from her. Even though they had known each other such a short time, life without him seemed unimaginable. But of course, there were couples like them all over the world praying the same prayers, burying the same fears, trying to be brave for each other and country. She had already seen enough of war to know that not all prayers were answered.

Agnes's face rushed unbidden to the forefront of her mind. Sarah blinked back tears and looked through the doorway toward the window across the hall. From this angle, if she ignored the bombed out gap in the exterior corner, the world looked peaceful and quiet. The low winter sun painted scudding clouds pink, blue, and gold. Dusk cast the single palm in the wrecked garden into shadow, making it appear whole and undamaged. A pleasant scene that tomorrow's sun would reveal to be nothing more than a dream. Sarah brushed her hand across her eyes. Her dreams and hopes were all wrapped up in Kurt now. Please, God, let him stay safe.

It wasn't fair to pray that they, above all the other couples caught up in this war, should come out of it together and unharmed, but she couldn't help it. She would pray the same prayer every day until Kurt was with her again, like every girl who waited for her guy to return. The guys with someone waiting for them surely had to be the luckiest ones.

So where did that leave Bill? Bill. What a jerk. His timing stank. A little over a month ago she would have rejoiced at receiving his letter. Her response would have flown to him as soon as the ink had dried on the paper. Dread now filled her at the idea of writing to him. It hurt to imagine him injured or taken as a POW believing that he had no one waiting for him, but she couldn't give him the answer he wanted. Sarah sighed. Poor Bill. Of course, he had brought this on himself. Unkind thought, but true nonetheless.

Oh, damn, damn, damn. There was no point to this mental going in circles. At this rate, she was destined to think herself into a deep depression, something that would help no one, least of all her patients. She must push both men completely from her mind. If she concentrated hard enough on her work, maybe it would sustain her until Kurt returned. Sarah got up and moved to the closest bed and examined its occupant. Lifting the patient chart, she began making notes.

The hours dragged to the end of the shift when Mandy appeared a little late as usual. She stood grinning in the doorway, one fist on her hip and wagging the index finger of the other hand.

"Good grief, woman. You have *got* to tell me your secret. That good-looking Brit is back asking for you. Like I said before, you've got more than your fair share of men."

Sarah tapped down the cap onto her fountain pen. Placing it in her chest pocket, she muttered, "Oh, lord, whatever can he want this time?"

Mandy shrugged. "No idea, but he seems kind of agitated. Kept shifting from one foot to the other until the corporal noticed him. Maybe you should go on and put him out of his misery."

Chapter 22

Kurt drove through the night after parting from the camel riding Reggie, erstwhile desert contact and devoted fiancé of Corporal Hortensia Linthwaite. The journey had thus far been uneventful. Though needing to secret himself behind some obliging hill for a few hours sleep, Kurt pressed on, taking advantage of darkness's cover for as long as possible. The fewer miles between him and Sfax, the better. Traveling during daylight, while necessary, was something he dreaded. Being a sitting target for anyone who cared to aim a weapon his way held no appeal, none at all. Some miles back, his route had made the turn to the north for the last short leg leading into Sfax. Kurt glanced to his right. Pale gray hovered on the eastern horizon. He shook his head to clear his mind and pressed down harder on the accelerator. The vehicle rumbled up and over the next hilltop, its wheels briefly leaving the road before plopping down in unexpectedly deep sand. When the vehicle fishtailed, Kurt took his foot off the accelerator. Yanking the wheel back under control, he swiped a hand over his eyes and stared into the distance. His heart rate picked up speed, but not due to the vehicle's careening. A slight speck of light, perhaps a struck match, flickered. It disappeared and then sparked again. Company somewhere up ahead.

Had they seen him? Hard to say. It could be

Tunisians traveling in their own country. Their lives went on despite the war swirling around and over them, but Kurt's money was on a German patrol. If he dodged behind the line of low hills to his left, he might avoid them altogether. Kurt searched the darkness up ahead. Nothing. No more flickering specks of light and no sounds, motorized or otherwise. Were the person or persons moving along the road or were they stationary? Impossible to tell. A break in the line of hills appeared. Kurt eyed it longingly and considered making a sharp left into its enfolding shadows, but if he were discovered in hiding by an Afrika Korps patrol, no explanation would satisfy hyper-suspicious Nazis. They would probably assume he was a spy or a deserter. Either way he would most likely be executed on the spot. Better to stay the course and try to bluff his way through it if he encountered trouble.

Several miles on, a line of shapes stretched themselves across Kurt's path. Courtesy of the early dawn, he could just make out white palm trees emblazoned on the doors of a *Hanomag*, the German half-track armored personnel workhorse, and a *Kübelwagen*. Two men sat smoking cigarettes in the back of the staff car. Beyond them on the eastern side of the road, a group of three men sitting on their heels huddled in a circle. One man leaned forward throwing flames at the ground. After several attempts, a fire flickered to life. Kurt would arrive in time for breakfast.

When Kurt came within a few yards, the more junior of the officers in the staff car unfolded himself and placed his jackboots on the road, crossing his arms over his chest. The men around the campfire glanced at their captain, who waved a hand. The men resumed their breakfast preparations. Kurt rolled to a stop in front of the troop carrier. The young lieutenant's eyes narrowed as he approached the car. He stopped beside Kurt's driver door, extended his arm, and clicked his heels.

"Heil Hitler. Papiere, bitte, Herr Hauptman."

Kurt returned the salute and drew his forged German orders from his inside breast pocket. He handed them over without speaking. The German read the documents and walked over to his superior. The major glanced through them and got out of the car.

Kurt's heart raced, but he willed himself to remain outwardly calm, fighting back a stupid grin that wanted to play across his face. It was a funny part of his job, but sometimes being a spy meant being a good actor. Kurt ran his gaze over the major and made a quick assessment. Adopting an appearance of casual boredom might be his best bet. The major came abreast his junior officer and gave a half-hearted salute, which Kurt returned in kind.

"Guten Morgan, Herr Hauptman." The major chewed on his lip and then continued, "What brings you into our midst on this glorious morning? We're supposed to be the only military on the road."

The story that Maitland had devised rushed from Kurt's memory. "My destination is Sfax." Kurt raised his arm and pointed toward the north. "By my calculations, it should lie a few miles beyond those hills. Am I correct?"

"You are. What brings you from the south? I'm not aware of troop movements in that particular area."

"Have you come from Sfax?"

"No. It is our destination also. Tell me why it is

yours. I'm afraid I must insist."

"I am meeting several of *Generalfeldmarschall* Rommel's staff officers in the city. I left Wadi Zem Zem later than expected. I'm overdue in Sfax as the others arrived there some days ago."

"And the cause of this unfortunate delay?"

"Information from Berlin did not arrive. I was required to wait for it."

"Even so, why did you drive over the desert instead of flying or coming by sea to the city?"

"I'm sure you understand that there are certain things an officer of the *Abwehr* is not at liberty to reveal even to a superior officer. We're a secretive lot, I'm afraid. And I should point out that we have been recently instructed to report the overly curious to our superiors in Berlin. The *Führer* himself has charged us with weeding out defeatists, conspirators, and double agents. He fears there are traitors among the Afrika Korps."

The major swallowed and cut his eyes at his men who were watching the conversation with interest.

"Get on with the food. We don't have all day." He turned back to Kurt. "Will you join us for a small repast? Surely hot food is a luxury even for one who travels with Rommel."

"I would be delighted, but alas I am already late as I mentioned."

"But it will take only a few minutes and we don't often have guests from Rommel's own camp. It would be a treat for my men. Please. I insist."

Kurt doubted the men gave a damn about sharing their breakfast with a member of Rommel's staff, but to refuse the offer might raise suspicions.

"I suppose a few minutes will not make any difference. Thank you. It will be my pleasure to join you. You are most kind."

"Excellent." The major turned to one of the privates. "Set up camp stools for us and serve our guest first."

Once they were seated, tin plates of fire roasted sausages and toasted bread were distributed. The conversation among the three officers progressed along lines of the banal until the major cocked his head to one side and quietly asked, "Tell me, *Herr Hauptman*, have you been in North Africa long?"

Kurt sensed disingenuousness in the question. He plastered a surprised smile on his face and stuck as closely to the truth as possible. "Not terribly long. Why do you ask?"

"You haven't the sunburned appearance that those of us who have been here for the duration. When did you arrive?"

"About three weeks ago. Straight from Berlin. Not much sun there in winter."

"No, of course. You must have been disappointed to leave the heart of the Third Reich, so near our beloved *Führer*."

"Knowing that I am doing the *Führer's* bidding is compensation enough for being away from Berlin."

"Your orders come directly from Hitler?"

"They do."

The major stood and stretched his arms over his head. He then walked over to the campfire and extended his hands as if to warm them. Over his shoulder, he said, "You must be well thought of in the high command."

"I like to think so."

The major appeared to adjust his tunic. When he turned back toward Kurt, he held a Luger. "Are you quite sure this is the story you wish to tell?"

Kurt smiled and raised his hands. "It is. Major, you will live to regret interfering with my mission."

"That may well be, but you see, I am well acquainted with *Hauptman* Helmut Heinz. He has been in North Africa far longer than you stated. In fact, when I was in Rommel's encampment recently, Helmut and I talked over old times as young officers about town in Berlin. He is presently in Sfax, but you knew that already, didn't you?" The major paused. His eyes traveled over Kurt from head to toe and back. "You could be his twin, I admit. There are subtle differences, however. You should not have bragged about orders directly from Hitler. Helmut would have shot me for asking him about his orders."

"I see. What exactly are you planning to do with me?" Kurt maintained a jovial tone that belied his heart's pounding.

"Contact my superiors and await their instructions." The major looked at one of the enlisted men. "Search him."

The young infantryman strolled over and bent forward, a *Schmeisser* MP 40 submachine gun swinging from his shoulder. His hands began fumbling with tunic buttons, but Kurt instinctively drew back at the man's touch. The private's mouth became a thin line. He grunted and jerked on the tunic. Kurt returned to his original position, after which, the man took his time opening tunic and shirt, jabbing his fingers into the flesh beneath as often as possible. Kurt's eyes narrowed. He glanced around the private to ascertain the position of the other men. With the private's eyes and attention on the last button, Kurt took the only chance he was likely to get. He put his hands on the German's shoulders and jammed his knee into the man's balls. An expression filled with pain flooded the private's face as he doubled over into Kurt's lap. Kurt caught the *Schmeisser* on its way to the ground. Grabbing the private by his tunic front, Kurt pulled the man close, using him as a shield against the bullets flying from the major's Luger. Kurt's finger clamped down on the *Schmeisser's* trigger. With the desert soaking up German blood, Kurt pushed the private from his lap and fired until the man's face was gone. The private couldn't have survived the major's shots, but adrenaline pumped through Kurt destroying conscious thought. The hail of bullets raged on until the gun's firing mechanism jammed.

The Schmeisser clattered on small rocks as it dropped to the ground. Kurt ran a hand over his face. He, surveyed the carnage, blinked a couple of times, then vomited his sausage breakfast. Although he had been through intensive training in the multiple ways that one might kill another human being, he had never actually committed the act until that moment. He wiped his mouth with the back of his hand and looked around him. Bodies littered the ground, some lying in the most appalling caricatures of the human form. Blood ran from beneath his victims, staining the sand all around. Kurt strode over to the campfire and picked up the rag the cook had been using as a potholder. Grabbing up the coffee pot, he doused the fire. With nothing else to be done, he went to his car. There was enough space on one side of the road where he could squeeze between the truck and a sand dune.

Praying the damned engine would start the first time and that no one was close enough to have heard the sounds of chaos he had created, Kurt shoved the clutch in and pressed the starter. The engine turned over once and died.

Chapter 23

Kurt boiled with impatience. He pressed the accelerator and jammed in the starter button for a third time. The damned car clicked and clacked, but the engine stubbornly refused to turn over. The fuel indicator sat at half-mast, certainly more than enough. Kurt slammed his open palm against the steering wheel. So much for German engineering. He ran his gaze over the truck and car blocking the road. No distinctive markings, no unusual flags or banners, nothing marked the staff car as out of the ordinary or easily distinguished from any other vehicle of its type. If time were on his side, hiding the corpses and truck in the hills would have made him feel more secure, but he needed to get to Sfax before Rommel recalled his officers to his headquarters at Wadi Zem Zem. There was no other choice. Climbing out of the captured *Kübelwagen*, he strode to the dead officers' car and stepped into the driver's seat. This time the engine rumbled to life and settled into the contented purr of a lap cat, but the fuel gage showed only a quarter tank. Wonderful time to realize his training had omitted information on the German staff car's fuel capacity. Kurt climbed out and rummaged through the back seat and storage compartment. Next he went to the truck and clambered over and through it. Odd. The Germans were supposedly the great organizers prepared for any

195

contingency, but there was no gas can, no rubber tubing, nothing he could use to syphon fuel from the other vehicles. Kurt looked to the east where the sky glowed red, gold, and pink in the first flush of dawn. It seemed walking at least part way to Sfax was probably in his future, hopefully later rather than sooner.

****

A bright sun shone high in a lapis sky by the time the car's fuel gage dropped below empty. The engine spluttered and the car crawled to a stop at the bottom of the only thing that might be called a hill for miles around. About an hour ago, the rolling hills had leveled out into the flat terrain of what Kurt hoped was coastal plain. His mouth thinned into a hard line as he scanned his surroundings. Rock-strewn sandy terrain stretched in all directions. Kurt's gaze fixed on the distance to the north. It could be wishful thinking, but if he shielded his eyes and cut his gaze just so, the faint outline of what appeared to be a line of buildings or dwellings hovered at the edge of the horizon. Digging binoculars from his pack, he trained them on a faint line that was darker than the intervening desert and adjusted the focus. A crenelated sand colored wall rose high above a few dusty palm trees with humbler structures scattered beneath their swaying fronds. He lowered the binoculars and climbed out of the car. Taking a couple of sightings, he did a quick calculation. If he remembered his geometry correctly, at his own height of 6'1", that line of civilization should be about three miles distant. Kurt removed the map of Sfax from his breast pocket and studied it. It wasn't a particularly large place, but the city served the Afrika Korps as a major port. It would be a miracle not to find the place crawling with Nazis who knew or at least recognized Helmut. Take the road he was presently on that lead through the heart of town or try to enter by another way so to avoid being recognized and perhaps drawn into conversation?

Kurt set out on foot for Route de Tunis, the coastal road leading into the town from the northeast. Helmut's hotel lay between Rue Thina and Rue Victor Hugo de France facing the old port. Coming in by the Tunis Road, he would have to cross the entire town below the medina, but that seemed a better plan than swinging far south and then back northeast to enter the city closer to the old port. Fifteen minutes fast march step brought him to the Tunis Road and a surprising amount of traffic. Dressed as he was in a captain's uniform, it wasn't long before he heard the squeal of brakes and tires grinding to a halt at his side.

"*Herr Hauptman.* What are you doing on foot so far from town?"

Kurt drew a long breath and turned toward the voice. It came from a pimple-faced boy in a corporal's uniform. Kurt raised his arm in stiff Nazi style. "*Heil* Hitler. My car broke down several miles back."

The boy flapped his arm in a parody of a salute and said, "Well, step in, friend, and ride with me." Kurt hesitated for a heartbeat. The young man's face reddened and he raised his arm in a perfect Nazi salute. "*Heil* Hitler. Forgive my familiarity, *Herr Hauptman.* May I offer you transport into the city?"

It was hard to tell whether or not this boy knew Helmut. He didn't greet him by name, but the corporal's initial informality made Kurt uneasy, leaving him in a quandary. Riding to Sfax would save shoe leather and give him time to reconnoiter before he began the real work of impersonating his cousin. Being detected as a fake by this kid might end his mission and would most likely prove fatal for one of them. Kurt calculated the distance to town and made a quick decision. "Thank you. I accept."

Kurt dropped his pack onto the back seat and settled himself beside the corporal, who shot him a quizzical look before putting the car in gear. Too late to climb into the back where officers usually ride.

From the corner of his eye, Kurt saw the boy sneaking glances at him as they traveled in silence. When they passed into Sfax's outskirts, the corporal drew a tentative breath and asked, "You don't remember me, do you, sir?"

Hell. Just his luck to accept a ride from someone who was acquainted with his cousin. Kurt plastered a smile on his face and turned toward his inquisitor. "I'm afraid you've the better of me there. I don't remember when we last met." Kurt paused and then launched a shot in the dark. "Was I drunk?"

The boy chuckled softly. "Perhaps a little worse for drink, but not so much to prevent kindness."

Kurt must have looked surprised, for the corporal continued in a rush, "Please permit me to explain. I mean no disrespect."

Kurt raised his brow. "Go on."

"It was last year after we learned about Stalingrad. My eldest brother was a sniper caught by the Russians. Rumors say that captured snipers were tortured before they were executed. My mother needed reassurance that I couldn't give. You gave me the right words to write to her. You said it was what your mother would want to be told if you were killed. I never got a chance to show you her reply. Would you like to read it?"

"You carry the letter on your person?"

The boy's gaze shifted to a spot in the distance. He nodded and replied, "It is a talisman of sort—my good luck charm for a safe return home. Perhaps you think me foolish?"

Foolish? Hardly. Anyone caught up in a war needed all the luck he could get. If his mother's letter served that purpose, then more power to him. Kurt eyed the boy while he guided the car around potholes and rubble. He couldn't be more than nineteen. War made it so easy to forget that the enemy was made up of living, breathing human beings. It seemed his cousin was capable of great kindness, something of a surprise considering his political affiliation. But why should it be? Helmut was not just the distant Nazi relative Kurt had never met. Helmut was a real person who surely must love his family and who had felt sympathy for a grieving subordinate, creating a sense of camaraderie between them that the differences in their ranks would make impossible. Still, the boy clearly felt comfortable with Helmut. A sensation similar to being kicked in the gut passed through Kurt. His orders didn't take Helmut's humanity into account. Far from it, in fact.

Kurt shook his head. "No, not foolish at all. I am honored that you want me to read your mother's letter."

Kurt scanned two heavily creased sheets of vellum covered in a neat hand, all the while thinking of his own mother. The last lines caused a lump to rise in his throat. Mothers were the same world over. They said the same things about eating right, staying warm, keeping safe. They wrote words of encouragement and love no matter how broken their hearts might be. Kurt folded the letter and returned it to its dirty, tattered envelope.

"She sounds like a wonderful woman. I'm glad she found some comfort in our words to her."

The boy nodded and put the envelope back in his inner jacket pocket. "Should I drop you at your hotel?"

The risk of coming face-to-face with Helmut on the street outside the hotel was too great. "No, drop me by the Protestant church. I feel the need to cleanse my soul with some prayer and meditation." Kurt had no idea whether Helmut was religious or not, but according to his map, the church was close to Helmut's hotel. It was the best hiding place he could think of on the spur of the moment.

The corporal glanced at Kurt with an expression of surprise, but did not remark on the request. Thirty minutes later, Kurt climbed out of the staff car and ducked into the church's dimly lit narthex. Finding himself alone, he entered the sanctuary and chose a pew in the darkest corner. The wooden seat was worn smooth, no doubt by the many bottoms that had sat on it over the years. In the rack on the back of the next pew in front of him, a Bible and hymnal leaned against one another. The odors of furniture polish, old books, and burning votives enveloped him. A sense of peace settled on Kurt, the same sensations he had felt as a boy during Sunday services at the little Lutheran church his family attended. It had been years since he prayed, but he fell to his knees and spoke to God with the fervor of the saints. He asked for wisdom to know what was right during the next few days and that he be given the strength to do it. His prayer completed, he sat once more on the pew to await nightfall. Only then would he venture out to the hotel and Helmut's room.

The sanctuary's warmth, darkness, and silence worked on Kurt until his eyes refused to stay open. He hadn't slept in almost 36 hours. Resting would be as good a way to pass the time as any. Stretching out on the pew, he put his pack under his head and instantly fell into a deep sleep.

Sarah filled his dreams. Her beautiful face floated on a pillow, smiling up at him, her hand caressing his cheek. He bent to kiss her. Her mouth melted into his as her arms and legs wrapped around his body. They were delirious with happiness, but then the scene changed. Her eyes widened. Her face suddenly contorted with fear, tears streaking its creamy surface. She became smaller, as though she was being dragged away by some unseen force. She screamed to him from a great distance, begging him to save her. Although he struggled with all his might, his feet remained glued in place as her face drifted farther away. When she became nothing but a shadow, she screamed one last banshee cry.

Kurt awoke with a start, heart pounding against his breastbone. He bolted upright, rubbing his eyes with the backs of his hands. So much for putting Sarah in a box and locking her out of his thoughts until the mission was completed. No matter how hard he tried, she floated at the back of his mind all the time, a constant unseen presence. She was woven into the very fabric of his soul.

The church's stained glass windows no longer cast their colorful patterns across the sanctuary pews and floor. Kurt stretched and headed for a door exiting the side of the building. He came out into a small walled garden with a gate opening onto Rue Victor Hugo. If his map was accurate, the hotel should be straight down Rue Charles Quint, halfway between Rue Victor Hugo and Rue Thina. Slipping through the garden gate, he strolled toward his destination with as much nonchalance as he could muster.

Five minutes proved both the map's and his desert contact's trustworthiness. Kurt stood at the corner of the hotel's walled garden. The place was just as Reggie had described it. With its garden nestled between the two sections of the building, the Hotel Sfax formed an "L". Helmut's room was supposed to be on the corner of the building next to the street. Kurt looked up at Helmut's purported second floor windows. A light shone through open French doors illuminating the promised balcony hanging over the garden wall, a perfect mounting block for anyone wanting unauthorized access to the room above. An ornamental iron gate set in the garden wall's end corner invited passersby to stop for a look inside. Kurt peered between the bars and tried the handle. The garden was deserted, but the handle wouldn't budge. He checked the street. No one strolled along its cobbles. Hoisting himself up and over the wall, he landed with a soft thud on the other side.

Water splashed in a central fountain surrounded by tile-covered benches. Palm trees swayed overhead, their feet grounded in a swath of grass running from wall to wall. Peace and quiet dominated the space. No wonder Rommel's staff officers had commandeered this place for their personal use. The hotel's garden was a lovely oasis amid the dust and traffic of the city.

Kurt checked his watch. Helmut would have to eat dinner at some point. Kurt prayed that room service was not one of the hotel's amenities. Spying a bench set in a dark corner, he went over and sat down to await his chance. Within half an hour, a figure came to the balcony's French doors and closed them, then the light in the second floor corner room went out. Patience rewarded.

Kurt gave it another five minutes and went to the area of the wall just below the balcony. Jumping to head height, he clung to the wall's lip and peered into the street. Somebody up there must be looking out for him: the street was empty. Once again, he hoisted himself atop the wall. Another glance up and down the street, then he leapt up and over the balcony's railing in one swift motion. The French doors gave way and swung inward at his touch. Odd that his cousin didn't lock them, but how was Helmut to know that a spy was hunting him? A couple quick strides and he stood in what he hoped was Helmut's room.

Kurt waited until his eyes adjusted to the gloom, then began a search. He wasn't sure what he might find, but he needed something to verify he was in the right place. Stuck between the bed's headboard and the wall, he found what he sought. With a little tugging, a satchel style briefcase tumbled to the floor, landing at his feet.

Kurt drew a small flashlight from his pack, knelt down, and undid the satchel's straps. Holding the light in his mouth, he thumbed through the case's contents. Inside lay documents bearing Nazi insignia and Helmut's name. His luck seemed to be holding. Large envelopes marked top secret sat in an enticing row behind a central divider. Kurt was on the verge of riffling through those envelopes when male voices sounded beyond the room's hallway door. He froze, his muscles quivering from the effort of remaining still and silent. The voices became louder, accompanied by the tread of hobnail boots. Kurt shoved the case back in place and eased upright. The sounds paused at Helmut's door.

"We won't wait all evening, Heinz. Be quick if you plan to dine with us." The voice held an edge of irritation.

"May I at least wash? I assure you it will make my company more pleasant."

"Take no more than fifteen minutes. I warn you. Horst here is hungry, and you know what that means."

"Of course. The bear must be fed posthaste to avoid destruction of all." A single voice sounded for all the world like it emitted a low growl. Several male voices chuckled. The voice Kurt assumed was his cousin's continued, "No need to demonstrate, Horst. I will meet you in the dining room in fifteen minutes."

Departing footsteps sounded as Kurt strode to the French doors. He was on the balcony in a heartbeat. Laughter drifted up from the street, making a return trip down to the ground via the garden wall out of the question. No choice but to flatten himself against the building in the shadow of the roof's eaves. From that vantage, he could see Helmut's shadow moving about the room and hear the muffled splash of running water. Ablutions complete, his cousin came to the French doors. One door swung out, nearly hitting Kurt in the face. A chair scraped back across the floor tiles. Next, the sound of a fountain pen scratching over paper drifted through the open door. Ten minutes later the

French door closed once again. Kurt let out a long slow breath. In another few seconds, the room's lights went out and the interior hallway door opened and slammed shut. Kurt was once again alone with access to Helmut's secrets.

Chapter 24

Mandy tapped her foot. "Go on. Go see what he wants before he has a coronary."

Sarah sighed and curled her upper lip. "How does he always manage to arrive right before I go off duty?"

"Oh, that's easy. He comes by and checks the shift roster. At least that's what the duty officer says. For a girl who claims to be engaged, you sure spend a lot of time with a guy who isn't your fiancé."

"He's just a friend and he's lonely. He's in love with a girl he can't have. I feel sorry for him. He also happens to be the one person who might be willing to tell me whether Kurt is okay. It's a win-win all round."

"I guess, if you say so. Well, get out of here. Taking five minutes of your shift isn't going to kill me. At least one of us will have a decent meal."

"Who says we're going to dinner?"

"Me. Because you always do."

"Don't say always. But if he asks, why don't you come with us?"

"Naw. I've already eaten at the mess. Shit on a shingle. Third time this week. If I never see cream gravy again it will be too soon."

"At least it's hot. And it beats K-rations."

"I suppose, but not by much. Anyway, I wouldn't want to be a third wheel in your little romance."

"It's not a romance, and you know it."

"Uh huh. Walks like a duck, quacks like a duck, so maybe it's a duck?"

"You're incorrigible."

Mandy laughed. "Yeah, but you love me."

Sarah took her time going to the front desk. What she had said to Mandy was true. She did feel sorry for David Phelps, but his checking the duty roster to know when she finished work, turning up unannounced, assuming she welcomed his company, giving others the impression that he pursued her romantically—all of it felt wrong and a little creepy. If it weren't for his association with Kurt and his working out of the same office, she would tell Phelps that she couldn't see him anymore. As she approached the reception area, she observed Phelps without calling out. Mandy was right. He looked like he was about to jump out of his skin. If he continued to pace like that he was going to wear a hole in the tile floor. Sarah hesitated, ready to slip away before he saw her. She would send Mandy back with an excuse.

Phelps turned in Sarah's direction and a big smile spread over his face. "There you are."

Sarah nodded, barely returning his greeting. "What brings you here tonight?"

"Well, that's not very friendly."

"I'm sorry, David. Long day. How are you?"

"Well enough thank you. Would you allow me to take you to dinner?"

Sarah paused, cocking her head to one side. "I don't know. It doesn't feel right with Kurt away. I'm not sure he would approve."

David chuckled. "Perhaps not, but if I were in his shoes, I would appreciate a chap looking in on my lady from time to time."

Kurt was unlikely to appreciate another man's attentions to her. When she failed to respond, Phelps continued, "What's more, I've heard something that will be of interest to you."

Sarah's heart rate kicked up a notch. "Can't you tell me here?"

"No. We might be overheard."

"Is it really important, or is that just an excuse?" His willingness to tell her something that was probably a secret made Sarah feel dirty.

He pursed his lips and raised an eyebrow. "You'll never know unless you have dinner with me."

"If it's not about Kurt, I don't want to hear."

"Is there any other reason I would have information to share specifically with you? And what will a little dinner hurt?"

Her need to know even the tiniest detail regarding Kurt's safety trumped common sense. Against her better judgment, she replied, "Oh, okay, but this really must be the last time you show up unannounced. It just doesn't look good."

"I would never compromise you, Sarah. Please believe that my intentions are only honorable."

That was what she feared. She didn't want him building up hope that they could ever be anything more than friends. They weren't actually friends in the traditional sense, but they were something more than mere acquaintances. They shared a bond of sorts, the bond of two people separated from the ones they loved. That was as far as their relationship could ever go.

Phelps took her to a little cafe tucked down a narrow side street not far from the Anfa Hotel. Sarah would never have found it on her own. The owner greeted them with a perfect Parisian accent, although he had the look of a native Moroccan. After showing them to a table in a private corner, he bowed from the waist and melted away, a knowing smile playing at the corners of his mouth.

"I believe our host thinks we are lovers," Phelps said with a smirk. "Rather a lovely thought, what?"

Sarah fixed Phelps with a glare. "Mind your manners, David."

Phelps had the good grace to turn pink about the ears. "Sorry. I meant no offense. You are lovely, you know."

She ignored the compliment. "Is the host a friend of yours? He seemed to know you."

"A friend? Perhaps, but only in the most commercial sense. I dine here often."

"Oh. So what do you recommend?"

"Whatever you wish. I am yours to command."

Sarah hadn't rolled her eyes at anyone since she was thirteen. The temptation here was almost too strong to resist, so she chose to ignore his attempt at gallantry, and conversation continued like a fencing match. Phelps lunged with flirtatious banter while Sarah parried with banal small talk. An uncomfortable thirty minutes passed during which Phelps seemed determined to set Sarah's teeth on edge despite her efforts to redirect his attention to mutually acceptable topics. When he turned to the subject of his lost love, Sarah saw an opening to ask about Kurt. Infuriatingly, Phelps waved away her request for information with the ploy of saving the best for last. Fearing he would refuse to reveal his information if she pressed too hard, she gave up and remained silent. Just when she was ready to scream with frustration, Phelps changed tactics.

"I must apologize. I have been a boor, talking and talking about myself without a thought to your wish to listen. You've not said a word in some time."

"You promised to tell me something about Kurt. What is it?"

"Only a small tidbit I'm afraid."

"Go on."

"It was reported to the office that he is on his way."

"On his way? That's what you brought me here to say?" Sarah had never thought she could happily strangle another human being until that moment. "Thank you for dinner. It will be our last. I'll find my own way back to the hospital."

Phelps grabbed Sarah's arm as she rose from her seat. "Please forgive me. I thought you would want to hear what our field agent reported. It means that Captain Heinz was well and alive when last seen by our side. The information is recent."

Some of the anger drained from Sarah. Burning for more information, she lowered herself onto the edge of her chair. "Is there anything else you can tell me?"

A studied sympathy rose in Phelps's eyes as he released her arm. "I'm afraid that's it. I take it you have heard nothing from the noble captain?"

Sarah shook her head. "He would never do anything that might compromise his mission."

Kurt's letter to her was too painful to think about and too private to share. She didn't want Phelps's sympathy or attention. The last thing she needed was to give him an additional reason to come around.

He reached across the table and took her hand.

"Please believe that I know what you must be feeling. I understand all too well the pain of not knowing what has become of a loved one. The hope, the fear, the longing for the slightest morsel of information. Even if the person were dead, it sometimes feels that it would be easier than the not knowing."

Fear-tinged anger bubbled up in Sarah. She jerked her hand from his grip. "Don't say that. Kurt is alive and well. You said so yourself."

"Forgive me. I am afraid I become maudlin at times."

Sarah gazed into the man's eyes and saw real sorrow reflected there. It was her turn to apologize. "I'm sorry I got angry. You're right. It hurts like crazy not knowing what is happening. Are you thinking about the girl you love?"

"I am."

"Does she live where there's been a lot of bombing?"

"I'm not sure. You see, I've lost track of her, and no one will tell me her whereabouts."

"That's so sad. Have you written to her family? Surely they will at least tell you whether she's all right or not."

"I'm afraid writing to them is not possible. Sometimes I fear the worst. But enough about me. Tell me what you have been doing, other than worrying about Captain Heinz, of course."

As uncomfortable as Phelps sometimes made her, Sarah's innate sympathy and desire to help the wounded kicked in. Perhaps she could distract him from his misery by seeking his advice and male perspective. She fumbled in her coat pocket and withdrew Bill's letter. Opening the crumpled page, she placed it on the table between them.

"I'm in something of a quandary. Maybe you can advise me."

"You wish me to read this?"

"Yes and to tell me how to let the guy down as gently as possible."

Phelps read Bill's letter. He placed the page on the table and tapped it with his index finger. "This is a former connection, I take it? Prior to Captain Heinz, that is?"

Sarah nodded and told him the story of what now felt like a tawdry little affair. Bill was a man she should have known better than to become involved with. He was the kind of guy her mother had warned her about, but the emotional roller coaster of war had blinded her to reality. All she had seen was a handsome pilot in a uniform. She had looked into the soulful eyes of a guy who might be killed at any time and had fallen for him like one of the bombs released from his B-17. Giving herself to him so quickly had seemed the right thing at the time, but the ensuing explosion had broken her heart.

Phelps tapped the letter with his index finger. "I assume this is another captain?"

Sarah nodded.

"What advice do you need, Sarah? It seems clear to me that *this* captain is beyond redemption." He leaned his head to one side and raised his brow. "Why bother to respond?"

"Yes. You're probably right, but I feel like I should give him an answer. He is in such danger with every bombing raid. I wish I could offer him some comfort. I will always care what happens to Bill, but I don't want to give him false hope that we can ever be more than friends now. I just don't know how to say it."

Phelps's lips thinned to a tight smile. He reached across the table and took her hand again. Gazing into her eyes, his expression became one of complete sincerity. "Write exactly that. If he is any kind of gentleman, he will appreciate your honesty and the continued concern for his welfare. In my opinion, that is the most the cad deserves. His treatment of you was beyond the pale. It is to your credit that you feel it necessary to respond at all."

"Thank you. I needed to hear someone else say it. You have been a friend tonight. I'm sorry I got angry earlier."

A strange, forlorn expression darkened his features, then a small smile flickered. His grip on her hand tightened. "I *am* your friend, Sarah. But if things were different, if I were a different man, we would be more than friends if you would allow it." He released a long slow breath. "Of course, Captain Heinz makes that impossible, but if you are ever in need, I hope you will come to me. Promise me that you will."

Sarah hardly knew how to respond without appearing harsh and ungrateful. There was only one man to whom she would turn in time of trouble, but now two others demanded promises that she couldn't...no, wouldn't give. Why was it that when a girl didn't want men pursuing her or vying for her attention, they buzzed around like bees drawn to the hive?

Chapter 25

Kurt stayed on the balcony for what seemed an eternity after Helmut's departure. Itching to get on with his search for information, he waited to ensure his cousin did not return for some forgotten article only to run headlong into his own mirror image. Coming face-to-face for the first time would probably be an electrifying experience for both of them. Kurt had no idea how much Helmut knew about his American relatives, but someone must surely have remarked upon their resemblance. Over the years, family photos had crossed the Atlantic in both directions. When Kurt was a little boy, Oma Heinz had taken out a photograph of the German relatives, pointing out a boy that Kurt had immediately insisted was himself. Despite Oma's efforts to explain, he loudly insisted that the boy in the Kodak snap could only be him. It made no difference that the photograph showed an older, taller boy. The face staring back at him was his own. He remembered how unsettling it had been to see his image placed among strangers in a location he knew he had never visited. Would Helmut have felt the same? Kurt would soon know the answer.

A light breeze drifted in from the sea, making Kurt shiver. He wore a winter uniform of gray wool, but would have welcomed the protection of a topcoat. Crossing his arms over his chest in order to rub his arms for increased warmth, he stepped to the railing and surveyed his surroundings. Helmut's room overlooked the old French designed port where an assortment of vessels in varying degrees of seaworthiness lay at anchor or were tied off to cleats embedded in the long rectangular bulkhead. Small buildings that could be boathouses or fishing shacks dotted the port side of the street opposite the hotel. A rock structure that looked sturdier than most of its neighbors lay directly across the street from Helmut's corner room. Apparently the owner didn't feel the need to lock up whatever was inside, for one side of the building's wide double doors stood slightly ajar.

Movement in the opening caught Kurt's attention. Instinctively, he flattened himself against the balcony wall in the shadow of the eaves, then silently laughed at himself. The light of the rising moon revealed a cat bearing its catch. The rat clamped firmly between the cat's jaws still had some life left for it squealed pitifully. Looking left and right, the cat trotted away, no doubt seeking a secluded spot in which to enjoy its evening meal. As Kurt watched the cat's hindquarters bounce out of sight, a sense of irony settled over him. The present state of human existence pretty much mirrored the little feline-rodent drama playing out on the wharf below. Predator and prey. In this war, you were one or the other, sometimes both.

Kurt glanced at the luminous hands on his watch. Enough time had passed to make it reasonably safe to reenter the bedroom without fear of an unexpected return. Kurt opened one side of the French doors and slipped into the darkened interior. Going to the bed, he felt behind the headboard and withdrew the briefcase.

Unbuckling the straps for a second time, he went straight to the three envelopes marked Top Secret, his small flashlight held firmly between his teeth. The first two held documents that he would save for a more leisurely perusal. The information contained therein had been intercepted and decoded by the Allies weeks ago. With the last envelope, his heart skipped a beat. He read the first paragraph and knew he had hit pay dirt. Scanning the document, a single name popped out at him several times—Raisa. Odd. Raisa was traditionally a Jewish girl's name meaning rose. He started at the top for an in-depth read through. Near the middle of the first page, the door's lock clicked. Kurt spat the flashlight from his mouth and dropped the document. Snatching his sidearm from its holster, he turned to face the intruder. The door swung back and a light switch clicked, flooding the room with electric light from the overhead fixture.

Helmut stopped just inside the door, a puzzled, disbelieving expression crawling across his features. Slowly, he raised his hands in surrender. He stared for another few seconds before saying, "*Goten Abend, Herr Hauptman*. I assume I have the pleasure of finally meeting my American cousin?"

Kurt couldn't help himself. His eyes searched every inch of his cousin before he responded in German, "You do." Then he fell dumb.

His tongue refused to form words. He couldn't tear his eyes from Helmut's face. The resemblance was even more uncanny in person than in the photographs. They were identical twins, carbon copies in all but birth. And it wasn't just their duplicate facial features and coloring that caused him to stare. They could have worn each other's clothes without difficulty, so alike in shape and size were they. Kurt drew a long breath and let it out. Finding his voice, he spoke in a near whisper. "I'm sorry about the circumstances."

"As am I." Helmut's eyes held what looked like real regret, even sadness. "It is unfortunate that this war has made enemies of us."

"Yeah, so it is." For reasons he could not explain, Kurt suddenly burned with rage. He would gladly have pounded something to dust. "You know, if your fucking *Führer* had kept his hands off his neighbors' property, we wouldn't be in this damned war."

"That is true." Helmut's lips thinned into a tight smile. "I hope you can believe that not all Germans are like Adolph Hitler."

Kurt didn't know what he had expected his cousin to say, but it certainly wasn't something treasonous. He opened his mouth, but words failed him once more.

Helmut shifted his weight from one foot to the other. Lifting his brow, he returned Kurt's gaze. They remained silent for several beats until Helmut cleared his throat. "Forgive me. I would wish to offer hospitality upon such a momentous occasion, but I am afraid you have me at something of a disadvantage."

Kurt waved his gun toward the ladder back wooden desk chair. "Lock the door and go sit over there."

One corner of Helmut's mouth lifted in a smirk, but he did as he was told. Once he was seated, he asked, "Now that you have found me, what are your plans? If I were your superiors, I believe that I would have you kill me and take my place in order to learn Germany's secrets." An involuntary gasp had Kurt nearly choking on his own saliva. "Well, it is what was discussed that I would do if the opportunity presented itself. Of course, my English is not as flawless as your German, so the plan was abandoned...for a...shall we say...a more pressing assignment."

A shudder ran down Kurt's spine. His own orders included several contingencies that would necessitate Helmut's demise at Kurt's hands. This knowledge was something that he had struggled with since the beginning of the mission. Being asked to murder his relative had caused him some distress, even though it was in the name of patriotism and the war effort. If he had any sense, Kurt would do the deed and get it over with, but he couldn't carry through, not at the moment. It would be sort of like killing a newly discovered part of himself. Maybe later, but not now. Besides, he might need to extract additional information from Helmut. On the other hand, Kurt couldn't leave his cousin tied up here in the room. One of the other officers was bound to catch on sooner or later. Kurt made a quick decision.

Without taking his eyes or his gun off Helmut, Kurt grabbed his flashlight, his pack, and stuffed the German documents inside his tunic. Next he shoved the briefcase under the bed. To Helmut, he said, "Go out on the balcony and keep your mouth shut. We're going to take a little trip."

Getting Helmut over the balcony rail and into the stone building across the street from the hotel went without incident. Kurt flicked his flashlight on. Its beam shone around the enclosure revealing a boathouse complete with tarp-covered skiff.

He inclined his head toward the boat. "Get in and lie down."

Searching through his pack, Kurt found a length of

sturdy, thin cord that should do the trick. He bound Helmut's hands and feet, then secured his arms to his upper body. With Helmut's own handkerchief, Kurt tied a gag over his mouth.

"Don't make me regret letting you live."

Helmut's only answer was a slight nod of the head. Kurt pulled the secret document from his tunic and began to read. The gist of the two pages was that something big was planned by the Allies, a conference to be attended by Churchill, FDR, de Gaulle, and Giraud. It was to take place sometime between January 10 and January 30. Moreover, their initial reports had been incorrect in one significant detail. The original translation of a waylaid Allied transmission placed the event at the White House in Washington, D.C. Recently, a more astute translator had given Berlin the correct location, Casablanca, Morocco. Raisa had been notified that the time for action was near. But what action? Kurt flipped the page over and looked on the back. Nothing.

Hellfire and damnation! There had to be at least one more page, one that he must have failed to gather up in his haste to get Helmut relocated. Kurt glanced at Helmut, who looked back at him with wide eyes. Grabbing the tarp, Kurt threw it over the skiff with a flick of his wrists. He was back inside the hotel room in less than a minute. After a rough start, his luck seemed to be holding. Peeking out from under the bed were two more pages. He snatched them up.

What he read made his blood run cold. A decoded enigma message from someone named Raisa outlined the proposed policy of unconditional German surrender. There would be no chance for negotiated peace if

Roosevelt got his way. The message went on to reveal where and when President Roosevelt and Prime Minister Churchill would be most vulnerable. Getting word to Maitland and MacFadyen was imperative. He searched through his pack for the radio frequency he was to use to communicate with headquarters in case of extreme emergency. He found the envelope at the bottom of the bag and tucked it under his shirt. The next big problem would be locating the Krauts' radio room. Kurt slumped down on the desk chair. It was no doubt manned night and day. He would do his best to send a message, but orders or no, he saw only one choice after that. Getting back to Casablanca was the only sure chance of preventing disaster. Even then, it might be a long shot, but one he was willing to die trying to make.

Kurt shuffled the papers to the second page and couldn't believe his eyes. He wanted to laugh out loud. Travel orders. Damned beautiful travel orders, complicated and detailed as only the Germans could make them. Helmut's travel documents had simply dropped into his lap. They commanded Helmut to be airdropped into Morocco in the desert west of Casablanca and to connect with the agent named Raisa with the greatest possible speed. Kurt noted the date and time of departure. The flight left at 0100 tomorrow. Kurt's watch showed 2100. A smile lifted one corner of his mouth. In four short hours, it looked like he would be impersonating his cousin in a way unanticipated by London.

Kurt folded the pages and put them back in his tunic. Consulting his map, he found that the airstrip lay not too far from his present location. He could walk it in a half hour if his luck held. He rose and began gathering his own possessions, then rifled through Helmut's drawers and closet looking for anything that could be of use. Finding a topcoat and a civilian suit, he donned the topcoat and stuffed the latter into his pack. He wouldn't be a faux Nazi forever. Civilian clothes might become useful. As he threw the coat's hanger on the bed, the sound of hurrying boots rang in the hall. Kurt turned off the lights and went at the balcony doors. The boots stopped outside Helmut's door followed by a sharp rap on the door's wooden panel.

"What's keeping you, Heinz?" Kurt froze, his hand on the balcony door's knob. The knocking started again with greater vigor. "Come on. We know you're in there. We saw your light. The colonel will not be pleased if we're late."

Kurt made a quick decision. He drew a deep breath and tried to remember how Helmut's voice sounded in the few words that he had spoken. "Sorry. I've just puked my guts up, and I think I have a fever. I was just going to have a lie down. Tell the colonel I'm indisposed."

"You really are sick if you think a tummy ache will get you out of this meeting. Don't make us come in there and drag you out, you unsociable bastard."

With his heart rate soaring, Kurt took off the topcoat and turned toward the door to the hallway.

Chapter 26

The next few minutes, maybe hours, would test Kurt's training, his ability to mimic Helmut's habits and personality. He hesitated at the door to the hallway and drew a long breath, then let it out slowly. Grasping the knob, he yanked the door open. His heart lurched into his throat as he looked into the eyes of four Nazi officers ranging in rank from lieutenant to major.

The major tilted his head to one side and gave Kurt the once over. The blood drained from his face, leaving him a little lightheaded. At this point, there was no way out if they caught onto the deception.

"You look awful, Heinz, white as a ghost. I'd keep quiet about being sick. It boggles the mind. The colonel orders armies on the battlefield without turning a hair, but gets squeamish as a little girl at the mention of a germ."

Kurt nodded. He closed the door and waited to follow the others to wherever the meeting was to take place.

"Aren't you going to lock it?"

Kurt hesitated, then smiled sheepishly. "Afraid I've misplaced the key. I will stop by the front desk for another."

The major frowned. "Very careless. Not like you at all. You really are sick, aren't you?"

Despite the coolness of the hallway, a bead of

sweat formed on Kurt's upper lip. He nodded and ran a hand over his mouth. The less he actually said, the better for the success of his performance.

The major turned to the very large lieutenant on his right. "Horst, get the captain another key, lock his door, then join us in the colonel's suite."

Horst clicked his heals, bent slightly from the waist, and strode off in the direction of a staircase farther down the hall.

The trip to the colonel's suite wound up and down a couple of staircases and through dim halls until they must have been on the other end of the building. The hotel was much larger than it appeared from the street. It seemed to take up most of a square city block. Kurt did his best to memorize the route, but there were more turns and staircases than he knew a place with only four floors could have. Several minutes after leaving Helmut's room, they stood in front of a large door emblazoned with a fake coat of arms replete with nonsense motto and gold leaf flaking from fleur-de-lis and shield.

The major glanced at the others and then knocked once.

"Kommen Sie herein."

A corporal opened the door and ushered them into a sitting room with a large table standing in its center. The table held stacks of papers and an assortment of light refreshments. The sight of food reminded Kurt that he had not eaten since the deadly encounter on the road early that morning. His stomach growled loudly.

The one called Horst sidled up to Kurt, placing a key in his hand. "You must be out of sorts. By the sound of your stomach, I'd say you are in for a long night."

"Perhaps it will pass quickly."

A throat cleared and four pairs of boot heels clicked, catching Kurt off guard. It was too late to follow suit. His gaze followed that of the others. Their attention was fixed upon an officer of the old school standing on the threshold to the next room, a large double bed just visible beyond him. An indention on the bed indicated that the colonel had been resting yet not a hair was out of place. Kurt studied the old boy from his squared shoulders to his patrician features. The colonel's valet had outdone himself.

Kurt suppressed an untimely grin. *You could probably see your face in his boots.*

The spotless uniform must have been professionally tailored, but the perfect fit somehow didn't seem to suit its wearer. He possessed a full head of steel gray hair upon which the spiked iron helmet of the last war had surely rested with greater ease than the Nazi cap. The old man was every inch the Prussian Junker, but one transported into a less agreeable era of German military endeavor. No doubt he hid his humiliation under an armor of determined forbearance and sense of duty.

The colonel's salt and pepper gray mustache quivered ever so slightly as though he detected a disagreeable odor that he was much too well bred to mention. "You are precisely seven minutes late."

His companions' eyes all turned to Kurt. He cleared his throat and took a shallow breath. "I must apologize. Our tardiness should be laid at my door."

The colonel's brow rose. His gaze traveled over Kurt. With a frown, he said, "That is not like you,

Heinz. See that it does not happen again."

Kurt snapped to attention, clicked his heels, and inclined his head. "*Mein Oberst*."

The colonel's gaze swept the others. "Sit. Enough time has been wasted."

Horst chose a chair next to Kurt, shooting him a sideways glance as they all pulled up around the table.

The meeting proceeded like military staff meetings in any army. Information was discussed, reports were made by each member present, nothing unexpected or of particular interest occurred until the corporal brought a message addressed to Helmut and placed it on the table before Kurt.

"This has just come over the wire from Berlin, sir. It is marked urgent."

Kurt picked up the folded over paper. "May I?"

"Of course." Kurt hesitated and glanced at the others. The colonel stood. "That will be all. Horst, as *Hauptman* Heinz's adjunct you may stay. Corporal, see that we are not disturbed."

When the others had gone, the colonel nodded. "Read it aloud. We need to be prepared for all contingencies."

Kurt opened the page and read. "Proceed Casablanca greatest speed. Allied leaders to be eliminated first opportunity. Girl Rosa dead one month. Typhus. Control Raisa." He looked up to see if the others understood the cryptic message.

The colonel pursed his lips, then fixed Kurt with a cold stare. "Under no circumstances must Raisa be told about the girl. He would refuse to cooperate."

Grasping at straws, Kurt spoke slowly. "Of course. And his cooperation is vital."

"Heinz, you are really not yourself tonight. You are not usually given to stating the obvious, but yes, his cooperation is vital. At the risk of my stating the obvious, without him, the assignment is doomed. But you will see that his continued cooperation is guaranteed, won't you." It wasn't a question, but rather a command.

"Naturally."

"With the success of this mission, your little contretemps over the woman may well be forgotten. You may be back in Berlin soon, my boy."

"It is what I hope."

The colonel glanced at his watch. "It grows late. Let us partake of the refreshments before you must leave for your flight."

Kurt gladly took sandwiches, pastries, and beer. The beer was room temperature, but being German, was smooth and satisfying. The corporal cleared the table of the light supper and replaced it with schnapps and cigars.

Food wasn't the only thing Kurt had gone without since leaving Casablanca. He hadn't smoked a cigarette in some time and would welcome an influx of nicotine. Reaching for the humidor, he extracted a plump Havana and clipped it with the wrist flourish Phelps had drilled into him. The colonel's eyes widened.

Horst looked at Kurt like he had lost his mind. "Sir, when did you take up tobacco? Everyone knows you can't abide breathing in the smoke."

Kurt choked on his puff from the cigar. He tensed the muscles in his arm to prevent his hand shaking. "You are right. I thought to be sociable as the major admonished, but clearly it was a mistake." Hopefully, the other men thought his choking was due to his being a nonsmoker instead of the terror that Horst's comment had elicited.

Kurt rose and inclined his head toward the colonel. "*Mein Oberst,* I beg your indulgence, but I must prepare for departure. May I be dismissed?"

The colonel squinted at Kurt through the blue plume of his own exhaled smoke. "By all means. Go and make ready."

Kurt clicked his heels and walked to the suite's door with all the calm he had left. Just before he reached it, the colonel called, "*Hauptman* Heinz, it occurs to me that you have not addressed me by name this evening. Quite odd. You really are not yourself tonight. And aren't you forgetting something else?"

Kurt's heart jumped in his chest. He turned to face the table. The second page of his orders from MacFadyen floated before his mind's eye. He searched it until he found the item he needed.

"Forgive me, *Oberst* von Schlieben." Kurt raised his right arm in the stiff Nazi salute. "*Heil* Hitler."

The colonel held Kurt's gaze for several beats and replied, "You are dismissed."

With his pulse pounding against his eardrums, Kurt exercised extreme self-control by not running back to Helmut's room. The colonel and Horst, Helmut's subordinate, might be on to him. It was difficult to know until they made a move against him, but as worrisome as that was, an even greater concern loomed. As he stalked the hotel's corridors, his last minutes with the colonel and Horst played on a continuous loop. *It simply couldn't be. There must be another explanation.*

His pace slowed ever so slightly while his hands

clenched until the nails dug into the flesh of his palms. *Fool. There is only one logical interpretation of the facts. The real question is why?* Kurt's stride lengthened as he looked down the hallway getting his bearings and trying to remember the way back to Helmut's room.

Kurt only made two wrong turns before finding the correct passageway. Once inside the room, he leaned his back against the door and let out a long slow breath. His watch showed midnight. All he had to do was survive for one more hour and then he could board the plane for Casablanca.

Chapter 27

Sarah stepped through the cafe entrance, her eyes scanning the handful of tables scattered about the dim interior. Irritation and self-recrimination tap danced in rhythm with her rising pulse rate. She must be nuts. After she had told David Phelps she wouldn't see him again, she had agreed to have coffee with him. What had she been thinking? Of course, thinking, or rather the lack thereof, was the issue. His forlorn expression and pleading eyes had touched her desire to nurture. Feeling sorry for him overrode common sense bringing her to this present dilemma. Something about David put her teeth on edge, like fingernails on a chalkboard. Despite a veneer of outward calm and good manners, each time they met he appeared more high-strung, more uncomfortable in his own skin. That he truly suffered, she had no doubt, but she was not the person to help him with his problems. On top of all that, he was not anywhere in sight even though she was ten minutes late. Good excuse to leave and be done with him.

Turning on her heel, she bumped headlong into Phelps, who grabbed her arm to steady them both and smiled broadly. "So sorry. Got held up at the office. Shall we?" Without relinquishing her arm, he propelled them to a table in the back corner.

Irritation boiled into anger. "Look, I can't stay long. What is it you wanted to talk about?" Inwardly,

Sarah winced at her tone. What a witch she was becoming.

David's smile became brittle. "Can't a man be desirous of a beautiful woman's company?"

"Oh, please. Don't start that."

The ever-present English schoolboy swaths of pink gracing Phelps's cheeks deepened to crimson. "Forgive my crude attempt at charm. I'm afraid I'm out of practice."

"Hmmm. Yes, I can believe that." Ouch. That was downright nasty. To make amends, Sarah plastered as sincere an expression as she could muster on her face and changed the subject. "The way you looked when you came by the hospital earlier today, I thought you might need a shoulder to cry on."

Phelps's gaze dropped to the floor. "I suppose I must seem rather pathetic to you." When Sarah didn't respond, he looked up into her eyes. "Won't you at least sit and have one coffee with me? It would be a kindness."

He looked so sad. A pin pricked the bubble of her irritation. "Okay, but only one."

Once coffee had been placed on their table, an uncomfortable silence descended. It was as though the effort required in persuading her to stay had robbed him of the power of speech. Sarah studied the little whirlpool created by her spoon while she added sugar and milk. How to best get this over with? Encouraging him to talk really held no appeal, but the silence only prolonged the encounter. Perhaps head on was the best approach.

Sarah placed her spoon on the saucer with more force than she intended. The resulting clatter made both of them jump. "David, why did you ask me to meet you?"

Phelps's head snapped up, an expression of anxiety in his eyes. "How embarrassing. I hope you will forgive me. My neediness has made me boorish. I apologize for insisting that you stay." His gaze shifted to the left. He let out a long breath before looking directly at Sarah. "Perhaps we could start again?

Sarah didn't respond at first, then nodded. "Why don't you begin by telling me what this is really about?"

Phelps smiled. "I've been wondering if you ever wrote to the other pilot, the one you wanted to let down." His face looked like an actor's wearing a mask, but his tone was light, like he was making conversation with a good friend.

Sarah's eyes narrowed. "I took your advice and wrote to him saying that we could only be friends."

"Have you heard from him again?"

"No." Her impatience came through in her tone. As long as she was to be subjected to an inane inquisition from a man who likely arranged this meeting under false pretenses, she had a question of her own. It was the only reason she kept agreeing to spend time with David Phelps. "Have you heard from Captain Heinz?"

"We do not expect to. He is in a phase of communication black out."

He fell silent once more. His shoulders slumped, an expression of misery creasing his features. The glib man about town, the socially adept butterfly had devolved into a caterpillar.

After what seemed an eternity, Sarah felt compelled to ask, "Are you okay? You look like you're in another world."

Phelps smiled ruefully. "Beg pardon. I drifted away, I'm afraid. Something has me rather in a spin."

Sarah inwardly sighed. "Go ahead. Tell me what's on your mind."

Phelps's eyes took on a distant expression, like there was a presence only he could see. "It is that which never leaves me." He stopped and searched Sarah's face. "I suppose it would be a relief to speak to someone about her."

Sarah's compassion for the suffering kicked in. The corners of her mouth lifted in an encouraging smile. "Then I am ready to listen."

"Thank you. I feel a strong connection with you, Sarah. I have for some time now. I suppose it comes from knowing we both suffer the pain of loss and worry for a loved one. That is the real reason I needed to see you. That connection. Being in the company of a fellow traveler, if you will."

"Oh, my. You poor man. What's your girl's name?"

Phelps's eyes became unnaturally bright for a moment, then his sense of manliness must have taken over, for his expression hardened. "Rosa. She is as beautiful as her namesake. Like you in some ways, but her coloring is different. Sweet disposition. Caring and loving, like you. Dark hair and eyes. Creamy skin. I loved her from the moment I first saw her. She was sitting with another girl at a sidewalk cafe in Leipzig. It was a sunny spring day. A light breeze lifted the stray curls from around her face. She was the loveliest thing I had ever seen."

Without warning, Phelps dropped his head onto his

upturned palms. He shook with silent sobs. Sarah had never seen a man cry like that. Her father had allowed only a single tear to roll down his cheek when his own mother had died. The depth of Phelps's emotion disconcerted Sarah, but it brought home to her the extent of his pain. Instinctively, she patted his shoulder. He grasped her hand like a drowning man grips a life ring.

Sarah cast about for the right thing to say. She decided to ask what first came to mind. "Is Rosa still in Germany?"

"I don't know. I last saw her in 1935."

"Does she love you in return?"

"Yes. She loved me as I love her."

Easing her hand from his, she said, "Forgive my asking, but why didn't you bring her to England? Wouldn't it have been safer given how things were in Germany? Even in 1935 being in love with a foreigner couldn't have been looked on with favor by the Nazis."

Bitter laughter erupted. "Of course it would have been safer, but I could not get her out of Germany. She is a Jewess, not practicing, but a Jew nonetheless in the eyes of *Der Führer*. The Germans wouldn't let us marry. Take a dim view of what they deem racial intermarriage, do our fine National Socialists. Without a marriage license, England wouldn't let her in. My own nation wouldn't bend an unjust rule to save the woman I love. It boggles the mind. Then I was ejected from Germany. Officials discovered we had been intimate. It became illegal in Germany for Jews and non-Jews to have relations. Did you know?"

Sarah nodded. "Such stupid laws. How did they learn about you? Was there a child?"

"I don't know really. We thought she might be expecting. Just before they put me on the ship for England, she had a medical examination. I suspect the doctor to whom we went reported us. After that, I could learn no more about Rosa or our child. She...they simply vanished."

"How heartbreaking."

"Yes. There have been times when I thought I could not go on. But then the war came and everything changed."

"How? Did you get word from Rosa?"

Phelps looked startled as though he had forgotten Sarah's presence. The color drained from his face. His mouth opened with an audible intake of breath followed by coughing. When the choking eased, he looked as though someone had walked over his grave.

"I've said too much. I don't know what I was thinking." Phelps grabbed her hand in a vise grip. "Promise you will not tell anyone what I have told you." Sarah nodded. "Say it. I need to hear you promise."

Startled, Sarah wrenched her hand from Phelps's grasp. "My simple agreement should be enough, but if it means so much to you, I promise not to repeat what you've said. Now I really must go. Goodnight." She rose from the table and turned for the door before he could react. Her empathy for suffering souls had its limits. A shudder passed down her spine. There was something decidedly wrong with David Phelps.

When she heard the cafe door click closed behind her, Sarah breathed a sigh of relief and said a silent prayer. Oh God, please send Kurt back to me safe and soon.

Chapter 28

Fifty minutes till flight time. But before Kurt could set out for the airfield, there were things he had to do. If he succeeded in one of them, whether he lived to see Casablanca again would become inconsequential. The most important task assigned to him, or ever likely to be, would be accomplished. Icy bands tightened around his heart as Sarah's face came into focus before his mind's eye. To never see her again, to leave her ignorant of his fate, possibly doubting him, seared his heart like nothing he had ever experienced. Kurt drew a long breath, then exhaled slowly. He tightened his mouth into a thin, hard line. He had always thought he was psychologically and emotionally prepared to make the supreme sacrifice if it became necessary, but now the thought was almost unendurable. Becoming involved with Sarah had been a mistake for both of them. If he survived this mission, maybe the kindest, most loving thing he could do would be to set her free. His work with the OSS would prevent his giving her the security she needed. Kurt ran a hand over his face. Stupid thought. In war, there was no security. Nothing was guaranteed. Kurt shook his head. Decisions about Sarah needed to wait until he was able to think clearly about her and the future.

Kurt fingered the scrap of teletype paper in his tunic pocket. Von Schlieben and his staff had been in

Sfax long enough to set up a communication system that could communicate directly with Berlin. Impressive. It also meant a sizable communications room must be somewhere in the hotel. Kurt reviewed the route they had taken to the colonel's suite. He remembered seeing an enlisted man with a rifle across his knees sitting outside a room several doors beyond the colonel's. Grabbing his pack, he gave Helmut's room a once over. It was as his cousin had left it. The hallway was empty, the hotel quiet and settled for the night. Retracing his steps to the colonel's wing brought Kurt to where the young private still sat, his head lolling to one side as he dozed. Kurt glanced at a sign on the room's door. With typical German efficiency, it announced *Kummunikationsraum*. Kurt could hear the clicking of the radio key beyond the closed door. He reached out and tried the knob. Locked. Of course.

Kurt kicked the private's boots. The boy's eyes flew open as he leapt to his feet.

"*Heil* Hitler."

Kurt threw up his hand in the half-hearted Nazi salute he had seen the colonel use. "*Heil* Hitler. Is the radio free?"

"No one other than the operator is in the room, *mein Hauptman*."

"Unlock the door for me."

A quizzical look from the guard sent a chill down Kurt's spine. The private leaned over and knocked. "Karl. Come to the door. *Herr Hauptman* Heinz wishes you to send a message."

Hobnail boots clicked on the wooden floor within and a key turned in the lock. A corporal opened the door, but did not stand aside to admit Kurt. "If you will be so good as to pass me your message, *Herr Hauptman*, I will put it in the queue with the others."

Kurt's stomach turned over, but he only missed a single beat. "My communication is for Berlin's eyes only. I must insist that you give me privacy."

An expression of surprise crossed the corporal's face, then suspicion filled his eyes. "That is most unusual, *Herr Hauptman*. I must get clearance from my superior."

Kurt didn't have time to wrangle. His jaw hardened and his eyes narrowed. He spoke barely above a whisper through gritted teeth. "You will allow me entrance at once and voluntarily exit the room. Do not detain me further or when I leave, it will be with your balls in my hip pocket. Do I make myself clear?"

"But my orders—"

"Your orders are to do what a superior officer tells you to do. Get out and do not come back until I am gone."

The private and corporal exchanged glances. After a moment's hesitation, the corporal swung the door wide and stepped into the hall. "May I wait here, sir?"

Even though Kurt's message would be encoded, anyone standing outside the door could hear the clacking of the radio key. Good radio operators dreamed in Morse Code. Kurt couldn't take the chance this operator would recognize the tapping as non-German code. "Give me ten minutes and you may return. Do not loiter in the hall."

The two young men exchanged a further glance, then the corporal answered. "*Sieg Heil, mein Hauptman*." An edge of sarcasm tinged his voice.

Kurt watched until the two enlisted men were out

of sight around the corner. He closed the door and locked it. Radio equipment covered the wall next to a single window. He opened his pack and removed the envelope containing the emergency frequency. Sitting in the corporal's chair, he studied the knobs and dials before selecting one and setting the frequency. His message would be brief, the code developed for special situations like this and committed to memory. The code was so deeply engrained it had become as much a part of Kurt as breathing. He picked up the corporal's earphones, flipped a switch and hesitated. Did he dare mention his concern regarding Phelps? He had no proof, only his dislike of the man and the incident with the cigar. If Kurt named Phelps and was wrong, there would be hell to pay. If he was right, but not believed, then he ran the risk of Phelps being forewarned. Kurt sighed heavily and began tapping the radio key.

Conference compromised. Churchill Roosevelt grave danger. Assassin code name Raisa. K Heinz returning Casablanca Luftwaffe flight departing 0100.

He sent the message a second time. Glancing at his wrist, he swore under his breath. The hands on his watch were more advanced than he expected. Was there time to wait for a reply or to be sure that his message had gotten through? Kurt caught his lower lip between his teeth and considered. Grabbing the frequency dial, he gave it a twist. Time was running out and he had one more assignment before he left Sfax.

The thing that had loomed over him since he opened his orders was at hand. No one in London or Washington bothered to ask how it might affect him. They said it was paramount his infiltration of Rommel's staff go undetected. It would be vital to the war effort, but what wasn't? Every damned detail, every decision or action no matter how small was or could be a matter of life and death, winning and losing, democracy and National Socialism. Shoving the chair back, he rose and went to the door. Slipping the lock, he peered into the hall. The private and the corporal sauntered toward him, chuckling over some matter of concern to only them. Kurt strode past them without stopping. He felt their eyes following him as he went around the corner.

Within five minutes, Kurt walked through the hotel's entrance and across the street. He paused at the boat-shed door and looked over his shoulder. Empty and dark. He glanced left, then right. No one. Nary a soul to watch him do what in any other circumstance would be unthinkable. Do it in the name of duty. Kurt leaned his forehead against the door's rough boards, his hand on the latch. During training, he never once doubted he could do any task set before him. It all came so naturally to him—the code breaking, the subterfuge, the acting, the physical demands, the skill with weapons. It was like he was wired to be a spy, but what was required of him next fell beyond anything he could have imagined. His pulse pounded in his ears while his stomach churned in rhythm. Kurt wiped a bead of sweat from his upper lip. He had to get a grip on himself. Losing perspective got spies like him killed. Breathing deeply, he straightened his shoulders. No amount of handwringing was going to make the situation better. Besides, Nazi dogs deserved what they got. Best get on with it.

Sounds of struggle and muffled cries came from under the tarp covering the skiff. Helmut had heard his return. Kurt dropped his pack and squatted beside it, rummaging for his flashlight. Grabbing it, he went to the boat, threw the cover off, and shined a light in Helmut's face. His cousin blinked and squinted.

Kurt turned the light toward his own face and back to Helmut. Apprehension followed by understanding dawned in his cousin's eyes. Looking into the face of a family member he was about to kill became unbearable. Kurt shifted his gaze toward the back of the shed where a small window allowed a limited view of the harbor. As he watched a boat's lights bobbing past, it occurred to Kurt that this would be his only chance to learn who he was killing. The urge to know became irresistible. He removed the gag, then could think of nothing to say.

Helmut watched Kurt for a moment before speaking. "You have come to kill me, haven't you, Cousin? I can see it in your face. I suppose I should be grateful, really. A bullet to the head is surely far less painful than starving or being eaten by the rats."

"Yeah, I guess you're right. Tell me something."

"Why should I?"

"Because I ask. Because we are relatives. Because I can make your death slow and painful or quick and pain free. Take your pick."

"Ask your question."

"Tell me why you became a Nazi. Was it worth it?"

The corners of Helmut's mouth turned up in a twisted parody of a smile. "You would want to know that." Anger and disgust oozed from Helmut. "If my grandfather, instead of yours, had chosen to emigrate, our positions would be quite reversed. Ironic, isn't it? As a boy after the last war when we were starving, I dreamed of going to America. Everything comes so easily to you Americans. You decide to do something and it is accomplished. You determine your own destiny. Unlike us Europeans, you have no history, no obligation that hangs about your neck like an anvil. I became a Nazi because my father told me to do so. It was my duty to my father and to my country. I have paid a greater price for being dutiful than you can possibly understand."

Surprise curled through Kurt. Was his Nazi cousin human after all? "Try me."

Helmut stared at him for several beats, then an expression of utter misery settled over his features. "I loved a girl once. A beautiful girl. We were to marry, but the laws were passed that forbade it."

"She's Jewish?"

Helmut nodded. "Was Jewish. Rachel's dead now."

"How did you meet her?"

"At university. Being from a highborn Berlin family, she was several steps higher on the social ladder than I. I didn't think I had a chance, but she loved me nonetheless. When her home was confiscated and her parents and sister deported to Auschwitz, I hid her." Helmut's features froze and his eyes glittered. "I never knew who reported us. One day I went to deliver food and an SS officer greeted me at the door. She was sent to Dachau and I to North Africa."

Kurt blinked several times. It was a sad story. One he hadn't expected. Had MacFadyen known these details and purposely omitted them? Sarah leapt into his thoughts. Sickness filled his gut at the thought of her being sent to such a place. "Seems a high price for doing your duty."

Helmut broke eye contact and looked toward the

ceiling. "Use your pistol to blow my brains out. You might be doing me a kindness."

Kurt put his hand on the flap of his holster and undid the snap. He fingered his pistol. The crosshatched grip fit so easily in his hand. The gun's balance was perfect as only a German made weapon could be. The sound of the shot could be muffled with the folded tarp. It would be over in a heartbeat. Kurt watched as Helmut closed his eyes and his body visibly relax, the stress of living easing away. He really seemed prepared to die. Kurt swallowed hard and tilted his head to one side, considering this second cousin whom he met for the first time less than twenty-four hours ago. His hand dropped to his side.

Helmut may welcome death, but he would have to leave this world by a different man's hand or by his own. Kurt shoved the pistol back in place and snapped the flap.

To hell with duty. Killing his own cousin in cold blood. No reason was good enough.

At the sound of the holster snap, Helmut opened his eyes and peered at Kurt. "What are you waiting for? I didn't take you for the kind who likes to prolong the agony of his victims."

"I'm not. I don't kill members of my family either."

"Then what do you plan to do?"

"This." Picking up an oar lying nearby, he slammed it against Helmut's forehead.

After retying the gag, Kurt lifted the unconscious Helmut out of the skiff and placed him slumped against the wall. Next, Kurt took a knife out of his pack and placed it near Helmut's hands. If his cousin was half as good as he had been told, cutting through a little rope wouldn't take him too long. Helmut would wake up with a terrific headache, but alive. What he would choose to do after that was anyone's guess.

Chapter 29

Kurt eased the boat shed's door open an inch and peered through the crack. Fog creeping in from the sea now shrouded the whole area, making it appear ghostly and out of focus. The glow of hotel lights created fuzzy pools on the sidewalk below the windows. The sound of an engine idling came from somewhere nearby. It took a moment for Kurt's eyes to adjust to the haze, then his heart skipped a beat. The street was no longer empty. A momentary swirl lifted the fog revealing a staff car purring beside the hotel's entrance. The figure behind the wheel looked over his shoulder at the hotel door as though he expected his passenger or passengers to exit the building at any moment. Kurt turned his wrist so that the luminescent hands of his watch glowed upward. He had to start now if he was going to get to the airfield on time. Breathing in and out in a slow rhythm that helped maintain calm, he visualized the street, trying to remember possibilities for cover when he left the shed. Damn it to hell. Nothing. The garden wall and the hotel took up the entire opposite side of the street. The shed was the end structure on the harbor side, leaving an empty stretch of street without cover in the direction he needed to go. Making his move would have to be in the open. The muffled wail of a boat's foghorn somewhere out in the harbor sent a chill down his spine. The answering call must have come from right behind the shed because its volume rang in Kurt's ears and made him jump. It would be funny if the situation weren't so dire. Leaning against the doorjamb, Kurt drew a deep breath, but it caught in his throat. The odor of decaying fish and rotting wood filled his nose and mouth. He stifled a cough and exhaled slowly. Perhaps the car would move on soon.

Against the wall, Helmut moaned under the gag. Kurt glanced over his shoulder. Helmut's legs and arms strained under their restraints despite his still closed eyes and semi-conscious state. Shit. Time and luck had run out. Kurt glanced at the knife he had placed beside his cousin. Should he take it and leave Helmut to get free as best he could? Common sense said yes, but a feeling that this would doom his cousin kept Kurt pinned hard by the shed door. If he wasn't willing to kill by his own hand, he certainly wasn't going to leave Helmut to a possible slow, isolated death. Kurt's mouth went dry. Nothing for it but to bluff his way if he ran into any of the Germans. Kurt watched the staff car's driver until he looked back over his shoulder at the hotel's front steps, then picked up his pack. Slipping through the shed doorway, Kurt put his free hand in his pocket and sauntered along the harbor side of the street back toward the church where he had napped a lifetime ago. Fog left a veil of water droplets on his face. The damp slid under his collar and slithered beneath his tunic, sending a shiver down his spine. He flinched at the crunch of his own boots beating against the pavement. Would the driver of the car notice? Behind him, the staff car's engine suddenly growled as gears were engaged. The sound of tires rolling over cobblestones grew nearer. Kurt swallowed hard, but did not look over his shoulder at the vehicle rolling up behind him. Brakes squealed. The hair on the back of Kurt's neck rose in response. Out of the corner of his eye, Kurt could see the car's front bumper. He let out the breath he had unconsciously been holding as his stomach turned over.

"*Herr Hauptman*?" Kurt froze and inclined his ear toward the voice. "I nearly missed you in the fog. I was told to wait by the hotel entrance. Please come now. Your flight must take off within the next fifteen minutes to stay on schedule."

Kurt heard tension in the driver's voice. Perhaps the man feared bearing the blame if Helmut missed his flight. His cousin seemed to create a certain wariness among his fellow soldiers, but that would not be Kurt's concern for much longer. He adjusted his features to an expression of military authority and turned to face a very handsome, very young private who leapt from his seat and raced around to open the car's passenger side door. In Kurt's experience, the most attractive enlisted men serving as drivers in the Allied Armies usually drove the higher up brass. He doubted the German army would be any different. This boy must be the colonel's personal driver.

Kurt dropped down onto the seat and watched the young man as he came around into the sliver of light cast by the shuttered blackout headlamp. Not as young as he appeared at first glance or maybe he was just war worn and deeply sunburned. Kurt gave the boy a half smile. "Sorry to have kept you waiting. I needed to clear my head, so I went for a little evening stroll."

The private's eyes grew a little rounder, but he didn't respond. Damn, another misstep. It seemed he was changing his cousin's personality or character to the collective surprise, perhaps consternation, of Helmut's Nazi comrades. He prayed they didn't catch on to his deception until he was on the ground in the desert outside Casablanca. His stomach clinched at the thought of what might happen if he failed. The outcome of the war could depend on his reaching the Anfa Hotel before dawn. Raisa must be stopped, no matter the cost.

Ten minutes later, Kurt was climbing out of the staff car onto the airfield tarmac. "Well, thank you for ferrying me out here." He almost gave an American style salute, but switched to the stiff armed Nazi style at the last moment. Lack of sleep was a bitch. It made a guy careless.

An airman ran to Kurt's side. Pointing through the fog toward the middle of the runway, he said, "*Herr* Heinz? You must board at once. The schedule is tight."

Kurt nearly choked on his own spit when he found the craft to which the airman pointed. It bore the star and stripes insignia of a US Army Air Corps plane. Kurt wondered how the German pilot would handle it if they were intercepted since Allied pilots would surely recognize the body design of the single engine Fi 156 Storch. Kurt did a quick search through the glass canopy that covered the upper half of the entire cabin. No machine gun or gunner. Unwelcome company could make for a bumpy ride.

Kurt followed the airman and climbed in through the hatch. The portal slammed shut and the sound of the lock engaging filled the tiny two-seater cabin. Kurt settled himself in the seat directly in line behind the cockpit and watched the pilot flip switches and adjust knobs. The prop began to spin as the engine roared to life. They taxied and were airborne in a matter of seconds. The sky became ever clearer the higher they went. Once they reached cruising altitude, stars filled a cloudless sky, but there was no moon. Perfect jumping weather.

The pilot half turned and spoke over his shoulder to Kurt. "You should be at your destination before dawn as per schedule. You will have a good view of the desert from up here. It's quite beautiful at night."

"I'm sure it is, but I believe I'll get some sleep. It's been a long day, and tomorrow—or I should say today—will be eventful if all goes as planned."

"Of course. I will wake you when it is time to prepare for your jump."

Kurt pulled his cap down over his eyes and folded his arms across his chest. He had no idea how long he had drifted between light dozing and partial wakefulness when the sound of the plane's radio crackling brought him fully alert. After the first words, the pilot clapped his earphones down, listened, and then cut his eyes back over his shoulder. Kurt couldn't be sure, but it sounded for all the world like the operator on the other end had told the pilot to turn back.

Chapter 30

Mandy stood in the doorway to Sarah's ward and called, "That English guy is at the front desk again asking for you. You going to see him this time?"

Sarah looked up from a report on the desk before her and frowned. "No, I'm not going to see him. I've already told him not to come around anymore." Irritation gave her voice a sharp edge. Seeing Mandy's pained expression, Sarah softened her tone. "Please be a sweetheart. Go tell him you can't find me and that you have no idea what my schedule is. I'll owe you a big one."

"Well, if you're sure. Okay." Mandy half turned and stopped. "I have a better idea. You may not want him, but he's cute. How about coming with me and telling him you aren't interested so I can stay and console him." Mandy giggled like a little girl, setting Sarah's teeth on edge.

"I know you think he's a catch, but you don't know him. There's something off about him."

"Like what? He seems pretty normal to me."

An unsettled sensation tightened Sarah's throat. What was it she sensed in David Phelps? He hadn't really done anything wrong except be a pest, and yet….Sarah swallowed and shook her head. "I don't know. It's hard to explain. I'd stay away from him if I were you." Sarah cocked her head to one side. Looking for anything to change the subject, she snapped, "Who's with your patients? We aren't supposed to leave them unattended. You know that." Sarah disliked her schoolmarmish tone, but she was tired beyond exhaustion and it was making her cranky.

Mandy's lower lip protruded a little. "I only stepped out for a little fresh air. I haven't been gone long. The guys are all asleep anyway." The girl added a frown to her pout. "You sound just like our fearless leader, Bossy Beatrice. And you have all the luck to boot. You've got a guy who loves you and another one who can't stay away from you. It's not fair."

Mandy's silliness tried Sarah's patience sometimes. She spoke before she thought. "Mandy, don't be such a child! Being with the wrong man is much worse than having no man. It's past time you understood that." Her words cut through the quiet of the ward.

The younger nurse's face fell and her eyes grew unnaturally bright. "Gosh, you don't have to bite my head off. I've run plenty of interference for you with this guy already." The girl turned on her heel and flounced away.

Sarah massaged the back of her neck to ease the tension building there. To heck with David Phelps. He could wait all night for all she cared, but poor Mandy didn't deserve to be spoken to that way. She was very young and a long way from home. After the nice young pilot she dated a few times was killed, the girl had latched onto Sarah, looking to her for advice and support. Their relationship was developing in much the same way that Sarah and Agnes's had. Guilt and grief stabbed Sarah to the core. It was her turn to be the older sister figure. Agnes would have expected no less. Sarah would try to make it up to Mandy, but wasn't sure how. It would take some thought and creativity. Offering to take one of Mandy's shifts would probably have worked, but Sarah was already dead on her feet. She glanced at her watch. 0400. Only three hours to go before bed and the blessed oblivion of sleep.

About twenty minutes later, determined steps echoed from the hallway, slowed, and stopped at the ward entrance. Sensing eyes on her, Sarah looked up from administering medication to see the head nurse, Beatrice, with a fist on each hip and a scowl that matched the disheveled appearance of her nightgown. Sarah had a sinking feeling she was the focus of her boss's anger. She liked the recently promoted head nurse well enough, but the woman was overbearing at times. And she would never be Agnes. Not her fault, but it put a wedge between them, one that Sarah worked to overcome.

"Go get rid of that man. Right now," Beatrice barked. "He refuses to leave until he's spoken to you."

"I'm so sorry they bothered you." Bewildered, Sarah continued, "Why didn't the duty officer turn him away?"

"Because the man flashed his credentials and threatened us with his boss. Get out there. Now!"

Sarah dug her nails into her palms to keep from snapping at her boss. She opened her mouth to apologize again, but Beatrice turned and stormed off. So much for making peace with her co-workers. So far, she was two for two on the wrong side of the scoreboard. Sarah bit down on the inside of her lower lip to keep from screaming in frustration. Why wouldn't David Phelps get the picture? Showing up in the middle of the night was really beyond the pale. What an arrogant S.O.B. he had turned out to be. Boxing his ears when she got to the front entrance would feel really good. He deserved a good dressing down, as well. And to think she had felt sorry for him because of the lost girlfriend. At this point, it looked like his Rosa had had a lucky escape.

Oh, God, what a terrible thing to say. That poor girl was probably suffering unknown horrors in a concentration camp. Sarah didn't like herself very much when her temper turned nasty. Besides, unkind thoughts wouldn't solve the problem of getting rid of David. Damned if she did and damned if she didn't. She wasn't supposed to leave her post until someone arrived to relieve her, but Beatrice wanted Sarah to deal with David in the reception area now. She looked over the ward. The round of pain meds she had just administered seemed to be taking effect. All of her patients were asleep or at least resting quietly. She straightened her uniform and turned toward the hallway.

The single utility lamp on the duty officer's desk illuminated two male figures, one in uniform, the other in a rumpled civilian suit of brown tweed. The corporal behind the desk caught Sarah's attention and rolled his eyes, then inclined his head toward Phelps who leaned on the desk with both fists.

Phelps looked up and smiled. "Oh, there you are. I apologize for the hour, but I have wonderful news."

Sarah tossed her head as anger boiled to the surface. She didn't care what he had. "Really. Couldn't it have waited until daylight?"

"No, it couldn't." Phelps looked down at the

corporal. "My news is of a highly confidential nature. Could you give us some privacy, please?"

The duty officer looked up at Sarah who hesitated, then nodded. Once the corporal had disappeared, Sarah looked at Phelps through narrowed eyes. "So what is so important that you had to come out in the middle of the night? I told you the last time we met not to come around again. This had better be good."

"Oh, I promise you will not be disappointed." Phelps paused and raised his brow. "I have a message from Captain Heinz. He has returned to Casablanca and sent me to fetch you. He is waiting for you at our offices in the Anfa."

Sarah's heart lurched. Kurt. Back in Casablanca. Thank you, Lord. But fear stopped her cold. Kurt would have come for her himself unless he couldn't. Her hand flew to her mouth. "Oh, God. He's not hurt is he?" Her voice rang in the cavernous space.

Phelps gripped her upper arm. "Don't be alarmed." His gaze darted around the area, then settled back on Sarah's upturned face. Phelps ran his tongue over his lips and smiled. "Captain Heinz is being debriefed. He was most concerned that you be told of his return. He wants to see you immediately."

Something in Phelps's sickly sweet words made the hair at the nape of Sarah's neck stand on end. Her eyes narrowed as she gave him the once over. His face was ghostly. Sweat beaded his upper lip. The hospital's central heating, never reliable, was always turned off at night. It couldn't be above sixty degrees where they were standing. Something wasn't right.

Sarah pulled out of his grasp. "I'm not off until 0700. I'll go to the Anfa as soon as my shift ends."

Anger or fear momentarily shone in Phelps's eyes. It was difficult to know which. There for a moment, it disappeared in an instant. He frowned as he reached out with a finger toward her cheek. Sarah jerked her head back before he could touch her. Phelps's mouth turned up in a tight smile. "But my dear. The captain is desperate that you go to him now. Don't you want to see him?"

Sarah stepped back. Something in his expression made her skin crawl. She paused for a beat, then her heart rate surged. "If he's being debriefed, he won't be able to see me now. I'll go when I get off work. There's no need for you to hang around until 0700."

Phelps grabbed her arm. Bending close to her ear, his voice dropped to a harsh whisper. "Sarah, I really must insist. Captain Heinz was most explicit in his desire that you be brought to the Anfa immediately."

He tried to pull her toward the door, but she remained rooted in place. Struggling against his grasp, Sarah tore at Phelps's fingers where they pressed into her upper arm. "You're lying. I'm not going anywhere with you. Now let go or I'll call the duty officer."

Clamping down harder on her arm, Phelps slipped his free hand into his coat pocket. "I see. If that is your position…"

A slight flick of his coat hem drew Sarah's gaze. The pocket's fabric strained over an object too perfectly round to be his finger. She froze as her eyes rose to meet his.

"That's right, my dear. I have a pistol aimed at your heart. Move to the door quietly. I have a motorcar waiting at the curb."

Chapter 31

Feigning sleep, Kurt observed his companion of the air from beneath his cap brim. The pilot adjusted his earphones and listened to the radio transmission with growing intensity, his shoulders tense with the effort. When the radio stopped squawking, the pilot answered with a single "*ja.*" The pilot cut his eyes back at Kurt, then turned his attention to his flight instruments. The plane tilted to the left ever so gently.

Kurt glanced at the luminescent hands of his watch and did a quick calculation. They had been in the air for sufficient time to be over the Moroccan desert. How close to Casablanca they were was anyone's guess. They hadn't encountered any other aircraft, so they could be a long way from civilization. Despite the chill of altitude, a bead of sweat broke out under Kurt's cap brim as his heart rate kicked up a notch. Returning to Sfax was not a viable option. Kurt took a silent, deep breath. It was now or never.

Slipping his pistol from its holster, Kurt leaned forward and jabbed the barrel against the back of the pilot's head. "Don't even think about turning back. Keep on course."

The young German's shoulders and back stiffened. His head swiveled to look behind, but Kurt bumped his head with the gun. Eyes wide, Adam's apple bobbing up and down with a hard swallow, the pilot faced forward once more. With the next heartbeat, the plane plunged toward the desert floor. Kurt lurched forward, his seat harness catching him before he slipped headlong into the back of the pilot's seat. Bracing himself against the plane's frame with his free hand, he stiffened the arm extending the pistol. Somehow he managed to keep his weapon against the pilot's head.

"Pull up now," Kurt shouted above the roar of rapid decent.

The stupid boy ignored the warning. Perhaps his heart was pounding so hard he hadn't heard the words. Whatever the reason, the plane continued its dive. Kurt moved the pistol forward, shoving the barrel's end into the pilot's temple until the flesh rose around it.

"Pull up if you want to live."

If the pilot refused to follow the order, Kurt would have no choice but to splatter the German's brains all over the windscreen. Kurt glanced around the pilot at the instrument panel. He ran his tongue over his lips as he studied the dials, some with labels, others without. His training at Bethesda had included rudimentary flight instruction, but he did not want to put his limited flight skills to the test. Making matters tougher, getting a dead weight out of the pilot's seat and himself into it would require a feat of gymnastics beyond what the cramped space of the little cabin would probably allow. To give his demand added emphasis, Kurt bumped the pilot hard with the pistol's barrel. The boy did not look at Kurt, but he eased back on the stick and the plane leveled out.

Helmut was supposed to bail out over the desert near Casablanca and rendezvous with Nazi agents in a safe house on the outskirts of the city. Kurt briefly considered keeping with the plan, but impersonating his cousin was wearing thin. He had no guarantee his luck would hold. Most likely the agents had already been notified of his deception, meaning all would be lost. The conference would be doomed. The war effort would be severely damaged. But worse than that, he wouldn't live to see Sarah again. Her beautiful face floated before his mind's eye. A tight smile played across his lips. He might be proven a fool in the end, but in a moment of lightning clarity, he saw letting her go would be beyond what he could endure. A better plan—well maybe not better but at least one with a greater chance for success—presented itself.

"We're going directly to the American Air Base at Casablanca." Kurt withdrew a scrap of paper from his tunic pocket and scribbled some numbers. "Here are the coordinates." Kurt could almost hear the German's heart beating faster. His arms trembled, momentarily breaking his grip on the yoke. This time, the boy turned so that he could look at his passenger. Kurt eyed the pilot's profile. Firm jawline. Clear skin except for a couple of pimples near the hairline. He really was very young, probably not more than nineteen or twenty. Stamping down a tinge of compassion, Kurt shouted, "Good news for you, my man. You'll be out of the action. And we treat POWs a lot better than you Nazis treat our guys. Now fly us to Casablanca."

Kurt didn't say, but the boy surely understood, that once they entered Allied airspace, it would be a craps shoot as to whether they were blown from the air or gunned down on the spot once they landed.

Chapter 32

Sarah stared at David Phelps and saw someone she didn't recognize. The mild mannered, diffident English gentleman had disappeared. In his place stood a stranger with a wildness in his eyes that might be blossoming insanity. Or perhaps it was simply a ruthless desire to force his will on her. Whatever it was, it made Sarah's muscles jerk and tremble. She wanted to cry out, but her leaden tongue was glued to the roof of the dust bowl her mouth had become. Heart rate soaring, she struggled against the vise grip he had on her arm. He couldn't. Surely he wouldn't shoot her there in the hospital lobby.

With greater strength than his wiry frame should possess, Phelps yanked Sarah toward the door, lifting her sideways off her feet. She suddenly found her voice.

"Why are you doing this? What have I ever done to you?"

Phelps paused and looked into her upturned face. "Poor, dear, sweet Sarah. Of course you don't understand. How could you?"

Her chest felt like it might explode. "Help me to understand. Tell me what has come over you. Maybe I can help you. Maybe the doctors can help." Desperation rang in every syllable.

A small, tight smile crept across Phelps's face. "So,

you believe I've gone off my head? I wish I could say it was so, but alas, I am in complete possession of my faculties. More's the pity. Come along nicely, my dear. We really must be going."

Sarah regained her balance and planted her feet spread apart, knees bent. "No." Her voice was low, quiet, but firm.

"Oh, really, Sarah. Don't force me to shoot you right here."

Her eyes narrowed. "I don't believe you'll do it. The noise would bring too many people."

He heaved a sigh, then spoke, his voice barely above a whisper. "I suppose you are right. And so you give me no choice."

Phelps's hand left his pocket. Metal glinted in the light of the desk lamp and everything went black.

****

A cool, damp wind circulated around Sarah, sending a chill through her body and compounding the ache in her head. Lifting her lids, she looked into an early morning sky still filled with stars winking from black velvet. Pins and needles ran through her hands and feet. When she tried to move, she discovered she was trussed up much like a calf ready for branding, hands bound to feet. A gag of what felt like muslin split her lips and spread her teeth wide. It tasted of cleaning fluid and made her mouth dry. She lay on her side, face pressed against gritty concrete. The ocean's salty tang drifted with the breeze, and something rattled just beyond the white barricade in front of her. Palm fronds. That was it. Palm fronds rattling in the wind coming in off the Atlantic. But where?

"I see you have returned to the land of the living."

259

Phelps's voice came to her as though through a soggy blanket. Sarah looked up, struggling to bring his face into focus. She blinked several times before his double image melded into one. The odor of sulfur filled the air. He held a match cupped behind his hand to light a cigarette.

He took a drag, squinting through the smoke. After watching Sarah for a few moments, he removed the cigarette from his between his lips and exhaled through the corner of his mouth so that the smoke blew away from her. "I apologize for the condition in which you find yourself, but I did warn you. You really should have come along when I asked. If I remove the gag, do you promise not to cry out? I can shoot you here and no one would hear, so calling for help will be unwise."

Sarah nodded. Phelps untied the rag. "There. That's better. Would you like water?"

"Yes." Sarah's voice was barely above a whisper.

Cradling her head so that she could sip from a canteen, he continued, "I don't want to hurt you, but I hope it is clear now that I will do what I must. Is that understood?"

Sarah met his gaze and nodded. With more water, her ability to speak clearly returned. "Where am I?"

"The uppermost deck of the Anfa Hotel."

Searching his face for some sign of the man she thought she knew, Sarah spoke softly. "David, why are you doing this? What possible reason could you have?"

He did not reply immediately, but turned toward the Atlantic and inhaled deeply. "I love the sea. The salt air is so cleansing." He took another deep breath and let it out slowly. Turning to Sarah, he said, "I believe you and Captain Heinz have formed an attachment, have you not?"

"You know we have. What does that have to do with kidnapping me?"

Again his gaze shifted away from Sarah. "What do you suppose he might do to save your life? Would he do anything, commit any act, no matter how repugnant, to save you from certain death?"

Taken completely off guard, Sarah's breath caught in her throat. She blinked as the question whirled through her mind. What would Kurt do? No answer came. It was a matter she had never considered, not once. Still, its implications sent a chill down her spine.

Keeping her voice as even as she could, she asked, "What kind of act are you talking about?"

"One that would cause deaths, perhaps many deaths. An act that would prevent one's ever returning home. Let's turn this around. What would you do to save the captain? To what lengths would you go? Would you, say, kill another person? Or betray all that you hold dear?"

Sarah's heart banged against her breastbone. "Are you talking about…treason?"

Phelps didn't answer, but looked at some point out to sea. "You may remember my telling you about a girl I loved once?"

"You said she was dead."

"No, I said I didn't know her whereabouts, but I hope you can forgive that small prevarication. In point of fact, I have known where she is for some little while now."

"And that would be?"

"*Theresienstadt*. Have you heard of it?"

"It's a concentration camp. Isn't it supposed to be

the good one?"

Bitter laughter erupted from Phelps. When the laughter died, his voice came in a low growl. "I suppose you could call it that. The Nazis use the place for show when the Red Cross makes too much noise. They send artists, writers, musicians, composers—anyone of culture—to that hell in a chocolate box, and they call it a resettlement community." Sarah heard fury boiling beneath his quiet words. "But I suppose it beats the gas chambers of Auschwitz. My Rosa will remain in *Theresienstadt* as long as I do what I am told."

"And what have you been told to do?" Terror and desperation fought for control of Sarah's mind and heart.

Phelps took a final drag on his cigarette and ground it out on the balcony's concrete floor. His mouth became a thin line, then the corners lifted in a parody of a smile. "That, my dear, will be revealed, all in good time. For now, we wait."

Chapter 33

Kurt rubbed his eyes and searched the night for signs of civilization. Stars above them, desert below them, but only darkness ahead to the west. Had he gotten the coordinates wrong? His memory for figures was usually reliable. Perhaps they hadn't traveled as far as he had estimated. Or maybe his mind was too exhausted to function properly. He glanced at the instrument panel's clock and compass. Two hours until the sunrise. At least they flew in the correct direction. He ran his hand over his face and leaned his head against the frigid glass of the canopy. If he could only get some fresh air on his face, he might think more clearly.

He blinked and squinted. Was that a glow on the horizon? The speck was there and then it disappeared. Oh God, please don't let my eyes be playing tricks. The future of the world could depend on whether we arrive in time to prevent disaster. Kurt searched the west where the sky met the earth. There it was again, only brighter and more permanent. Another five minutes and the lights of the metropolis glimmered in the west. The plane's clock showed one hour thirty minutes until Raisa made his move. Dear Lord, let us make it in time.

Kurt felt in his pockets for the slip of paper bearing the emergency channels and grabbed the headset from the pilot. Leaning around the German, he twisted the radio dials into position and began calling.

"Papa Alpha November. I repeat. Papa Alpha November. Casablanca tower, this is Captain Kurt Heinz, U.S. Army, service number 18 011 546. Do you read?"

The radio popped and crackled, but remained devoid of human sounds. He called again, this time with better response.

"Casablanca tower reads you. We have you on radar. You have entered American airspace. Identify your aircraft."

"Luftwaffe Fi 156 Storch. Markings U.S. Army Air Corps. Notify Colonel Alister MacFadyen, British Intelligence, Anfa Hotel."

The radio went silent for several minutes, then crackled to life again. "You have clearance to land, Captain. Are you in need of assistance?"

"No. We are good to land."

"Estimate your ETA at 0730. Maintain present course. Over and out."

Kurt's stomach turned over. That was too easy. He glanced at the pilot. The boy's eyes were wide with fear, but he stared straight ahead. Better fill him in on what to expect. Switching to German, Kurt translated the airfield tower's instructions, ending with a warning. "This is not the time or place to try to be a hero of the Fatherland. Do as you are told and you won't be harmed."

The German eyed Kurt and nodded, but his knuckles turned white where he gripped the yoke. They flew on in silence. At about 0720, the lights of the airfield blazed before them. The buzz of fighters sounded behind them to their left and right. Kurt peered over his shoulder. At least two, maybe three planes tailed them. In a couple of seconds, two planes came up, one on either side of them. Kurt looked directly into the eyes of the American pilot who stared at him in return. Could the guy see the Nazi uniform? Hard to tell, but they would know soon enough what kind of reception they would get. The planes began their descent in perfect formation, as though this was a flight exercise for entertaining the public. The little Storch touched down in a perfect three-point landing and rolled to a stop near the first hangar. Immediately, they were surrounded by backlit figures who must be MPs, weapons drawn and aimed at the plane.

Blinded by spotlights shining through the glass canopy, Kurt ducked his head a little to fend off the worst of the glare and raised his hands. When the German failed to follow suit, Kurt growled, "Get those hands up. And don't make any sudden moves."

Kurt grabbed his pack and opened the hatch door. With the barrel of his pistol, he bumped the pilot in the back so that the boy climbed down first. Tossing his pistol onto the ground below, Kurt climbed down onto the tarmac where he was greeted by a Midwestern accent.

"Search 'em and cuff 'em, boys." The voice came from a figure of medium height and build holding a rifle aimed squarely at Kurt's heart. Hands poked, prodded, and patted up and down the length of his body, turning out pockets and scattering his scraps of info filled paper in the process.

The private who knelt beside him turning out the contents of his pack let out a low whistle. "Hey Sarge, look at this. My German's not great, but I'm pretty sure this says top secret. It's a whole file of stuff."

The sergeant gave Kurt the once over. "Take these two to the colonel on the double."

Hands secured behind their backs, Kurt and the German marched between burly MPs to offices in a Quonset hut beside the tower. A colonel and a major in Army Air Corps uniforms bent over papers on the desk before them. The major stood up and came forward to meet the private carrying Kurt's pack. When the private whispered in the major's ear, his eyes grew larger. He grabbed the folder held out to him and took it to his superior. The colonel flipped through Helmut's orders, pausing at the scrap of teletype paper, then turned to a private hunched over a typewriter in a corner of the room. "Find the translator."

Smoke curled from an ashtray close by the colonel's hand. He lifted the smoldering cigarette to his lips as he studied Kurt. He took a drag and exhaled. "Do you speak English?" Kurt nodded. "Sit here." The colonel waved toward a straight-backed chair opposite his own.

Kurt did as he was told. He doubted the wisdom of speaking until spoken to, but time was not on his side. He had to get to the Anfa before it was too late. Clearing his throat, Kurt asked, "Sir, if I may?" The colonel's eyes narrowed, but he nodded, so Kurt continued, "I'm an American OSS officer returning from assignment. The mission was a joint operation between OSS and British Intelligence. If you will contact Colonel Alister MacFadyen at British Intelligence at the Anfa, he will verify my identity. Sir, forgive me, but time is of the essence. You must speak to my superiors. I have vital information that can only be delivered to them."

"And what would that be?"

"I beg your pardon?"

"Your...assignment. The one you're returning from."

"The eyes only kind, sir. More than that, I'm not at liberty to say."

"Then we will wait for the translator to have a look-see at the documents you carried. That will enlighten us, I'm sure."

"But, sir. You don't understand. This is a matter of life or death."

"So help me to understand."

Kurt glanced at the wall clock. Thirty minutes until dawn. He made a decision, one that could cost him his commission and possibly send him to Leavenworth, but time to argue had just run out. Kurt outlined for the colonel the barest details of his mission into Rommel's command and then shared the contents of the coded teletype sent the previous evening from Berlin. The colonel blanched and picked up the telephone handset. After a lot of barking on the colonel's end and several transfers, Kurt thought he heard Hortensia's dulcet voice, followed by Maitland's cry.

The colonel dropped the receiver in its cradle and shouted, "Get an MP vehicle here immediately." Turning to Kurt, he said more quietly, "You are to meet Lieutenant Commander Maitland at the hotel entrance. Colonel MacFadyen is already engaged with conference business and can't be reached."

The drive to the Anfa took fifteen minutes, rather than the usual twenty-five. When the crossbar at the gate came into view, it lifted as if by magic. The MP jeep slid to a halt by the front entrance where Jeremy Maitland waited, shifting from one foot to the other.

Kurt leapt from the jeep and he and the commander hit the lobby at a run. Maitland glanced at Kurt as they sped across the floor tiles.

"Heinz, you are unarmed."

"Yeah. Something about a guy in a Nazi uniform having a weapon gave them pause out at the airfield."

Maitland looked around the lobby. Spying a grizzled noncom with the obligatory handlebar mustache, he shouted, "Sergeant Major, follow us and bring an extra side arm."

Slowing at the elevators, Kurt banged on the up button. No sound of movement came from the elevator shaft. He turned to Maitland. "Let's take the stairs."

"To where?"

"The top deck. Somewhere up there, the German agent Raisa is waiting for the president and Mr. Churchill."

Maitland's intake of breath was audible. "How is that possible? No one is allowed up there except authorized personnel."

"Because I believe he is one of us."

"But who?"

"I'm not totally sure, but I have a good idea. Where is David Phelps right now?"

"I couldn't really say. He was due in at the office early this morning to go over his duties regarding today's conference meeting, but he never showed. MacFadyen is furious."

"Not as furious as he's going to be. I believe David Phelps is the agent Raisa."

"Impossible. He came here directly from Bletchley.

What possible reason could he have for such treason?"

Kurt shrugged. "I think the Nazis may be blackmailing him over a girl. What I know for sure is that Raisa has been ordered to assassinate the president and the prime minister. Information only someone inside the conference would know was in decoded enigma messages from Raisa to his Nazi handler on Rommel's staff. Would Phelps know the president and prime minister's habit of watching the sun rise together on the top deck?"

"Not many do, but he is one who would. He has a high clearance."

Pounding up the final flight of steps, the duo came to a halt beside the closed door that led out onto the top deck of the hotel.

"Do you think he would be hiding in the restaurant up here?" Maitland gasped as he bent double with his hands on his knees, chest heaving.

"Is that where FDR and Churchill will be?"

"No. They enjoy taking the air. Say it clears their minds. They find the morning chill a bracing relief from the stuffiness of the conference rooms."

"Then my guess is Raisa, Phelps, will be hidden outside as well."

Kurt reached for the doorknob, but Maitland stopped him, laying a hand on his outstretched arm. "Did you know that Mr. Churchill carries Mr. Roosevelt onto the deck in his arms? They have really become good friends as well as allies."

Kurt sighed. "Let me guess. They refuse all security for these little outings?"

"Afraid so. They get so little peace and quiet, you see."

"Which leaves them completely defenseless. My God, what a mess."

Taking a pistol from the sergeant major, Kurt eased the door open a crack and peered around it toward the east. The deck was empty. Hearing footsteps pounding behind him, he released the door and wheeled around. Philippe Badouri, sometime restaurant *maître d'* and bouncer, bounded toward them, pistol in hand.

Chapter 34

"What the hell are you doing here, Badouri? You were told never to come here." Maitland hissed.

"Haven't you heard? A German agent has an appointment at dawn with your prime minister and president. If he succeeds, it will mean disaster for all. He must be stopped."

Kurt grabbed Badouri by the front of his flowing white tunic. "How do you know that, and who the hell let you into this compound?"

Badouri shoved Kurt's hand away and shook his jacket back into place. "Deliverymen are allowed in with fresh vegetables and fruit each morning. Today, my cousin gave me his place. To you Europeans, we all look alike. And it so happens that the resistance may be better at information gathering than your official network."

"Would you recognize David Phelps?"

"Phelps? No. I do not know a Phelps."

"Okay. Follow our lead."

Kurt eased the door open again, this time slipping out onto the deck. Maitland, the sergeant major, and Badouri followed as the call to morning prayers rang from a nearby minaret. Kurt held out his arm as a signal for the other three to stop. Then he inclined his head toward two figures emerging from the restaurant. A portly English gentleman with a face like a bulldog carried in his arms an aristocratic appearing American with braces on his legs and a cigarette holder clamped firmly between his teeth. The men upon whose shoulders rested the future of democracy and human decency had come to take the dawn air. Catching sight of four armed men, one still in a Nazi uniform, the Allied leaders froze in position.

Without awaiting permission to approach, Kurt went to them and whispered, "Sirs, it would be best if you returned to the restaurant and allowed one of my men to accompany you to safety." Kurt motioned for Badouri. "Go with this man. He will not let anything happen to you. We are on the trail of an assassin."

The two heads of state glanced at one another, then Churchill asked, "How do we know you aren't the assassin? Considering how you are dressed, one might take you for a Gerry."

Kurt jerked his head toward Maitland and the others. "Despite the uniform, please believe me. I'm OSS and I'm sure you can see two of your own over there. The commander is British Intelligence. We don't have time to explain further. Please sirs, believe that we are here to save your lives."

FDR took the cigarette holder from his mouth and blew out a puff of smoke. "I think we can trust this young man, Mr. Prime Minister. After all, no German has surely ever developed a Western drawl quite like his. Texas, is it?"

Kurt answered, "Yes sir. Hill Country."

"Yes, I thought as much. Winston, let's go back the way we came, shall we? And take this fine fellow with us." FDR nodded toward Badouri, and the three disappeared into the darkened restaurant.

Maitland slipped up beside Kurt, leaned in, and whispered, "Look over your shoulder to the cooling tower. Do you see a shadow that shouldn't be there?"

"Yeah, I believe I do."

"Heinz, we must take him alive. He knows a great deal about the German spy network."

****

Sarah watched Phelps's face. The glittering confidence in his eyes had devolved to uncertainty and fear. Something had gone wrong for him. Just before sunrise, he had unbound her feet and moved her to a corner of the deck where the cooling tower for the building's air handling system stood. Mechanical whirring made conversation difficult, but the tower provided cover behind which he knelt after pushing Sarah into the corner next to the outside railing. Water splashed over the tower's wooden slats, sending droplets onto her face and into her eyes. She wiped her face across her shoulder and searched the portion of the deck that she could see, trying to discern what had thrown Phelps into such a tailspin. Figures appeared, backs plastered against the restaurant's glass walls. Her heart leapt to her throat. Two men in British uniforms edged toward the cooling tower.

Phelps cocked his pistol and took aim. The percussive explosion of a bullet leaving its barrel pierced the morning. The two Brits ran to a place where Sarah could no longer see them and returned fire. Movement at the corner of her field of vision sent a chill down her spine. She cut her eyes toward it and blinked, then blinked again. Phelps' blow to her head must have done more damage than she realized. Her eyes were playing tricks. A man who could be Kurt, except for his Nazi uniform, stood with pistol aimed at Phelps. Surprise followed by fear played across his face. He smiled encouragingly and put his finger to his lips. Sarah choked back a cry. No matter the uniform, she would know that face anywhere.

The noise coming from the cooling tower covered Kurt's approach. When he was between Phelps and Sarah, Kurt shouted, "Drop your weapon. It's over, Phelps."

Phelps wheeled around, searching for Sarah. He took aim and yelled in reply, "I will shoot her. Never think I won't do it. She's here because I was warned you had escaped Sfax."

"You'll have to go through me first. Besides, I never took you for a killer of innocent women. Is that what your girl would have wanted?"

An expression of anguish spread over Phelps's face. His gun hand trembled. "Do not speak of Rosa. You can't possibly understand."

"I understand a lot more than you know."

"How could you? Don't force me. Take Sarah and leave. I must complete my mission."

"No you don't. Your Rosa is dead. She died of typhus about a month ago. Drop your gun and let's end this."

"You lie. I would have known. Rosa is alive. They promised she would live if I did as they said."

Kurt drew the teletype message from his tunic and threw it to Phelps. "Read it. It came in last night just before I left Sfax."

The two Brits appeared behind Phelps, though several feet of deck still separated them from the trio at the cooling tower. At a slight shake of Kurt's head, they stopped short of the tower.

Sarah could stay quiet no longer. Struggling to make herself heard, she shouted, "David. Please. Listen to Kurt. You have no reason to do this now."

"Shut up. Shut up!" Phelps's scream rang over the tower's noise. The scrap of yellow paper fell from his hand. His eyes darted from Kurt to Sarah and then back. Slowly, a peaceful expression played across his face and he smiled. "You are right. I don't have to complete the mission now. Unfortunately, I can never again be a proper Englishman." The barrel of his gun flew to his temple.

Kurt lurched forward, but did not touch Phelps. "No. Don't! You can still help the war effort with what you know."

"And then what? A lifetime in a prison cell to regret the past and long for death? I think not."

Phelps's trigger finger pressed down. The explosion echoed through the dawn as bits of gray matter and blood splattered the white deck railing and flew onto the gardens below. Phelps slumped to his knees and keeled over onto the deck floor. Kurt knelt beside the body and placed his fingers against Phelps's throat. Looking up at the Brits, he shook his head.

Sarah heard someone screaming, but she wasn't sure who it was. Odd how close the voice seemed, yet she couldn't find its source. Someone gathered her in strong arms and held her tightly. With the world edging toward darkness, she looked up at Kurt. He kissed her forehead.

"Let's get you away from all this." Cutting her bindings, he took her stiff hands in his and rubbed life back into them. Sarah tried to stand, but her knees buckled. Kurt grabbed her shoulders and lifted her in his arms. He carried her past David's body, past the two Englishmen, out of shadow, and into the glow of the rising sun. Stopping just short of the restaurant entrance, his lips found hers. Sarah's heart beat in rhythm with the pounding she felt coming through Kurt's tunic.

She pulled back and looked up into his eyes, terror gripping her. "You put yourself between David and me."

A smile played across his face. His lips brushed her cheek, stopping at her ear. He leaned his forehead against her hair and whispered hoarsely, "I would die for you."

Chapter 35

Sarah glanced at the wall clock and wondered how much longer she would be kept waiting. As soon as they had descended from the top deck, Kurt had taken her deep within the hotel. They were met by a colonel, who whisked Kurt away with him. Commander Maitland had taken her statement and then left her alone. Now she reclined on a sofa in a well-appointed room that had been pressed into service as an office. With two interior doors, one on either side of a bank of windows overlooking the hotel's front gardens, Sarah assumed she was in the former sitting room of a rather large suite. A bulky metal desk, military issue, stood with its back to a row of metal shelving perpendicular to the windows. A nameplate announced this to be the domain of one Colonel Alister MacFadyen. The woman Sarah had heretofore known only as a faceless voice over the telephone opened the outer office door.

"Sarah, would you care for another cup of tea or a sandwich? The hotel will send up a tray. You must be famished."

"Thank you, but I don't think I could keep food down."

Sympathy filled the girl's eyes. "I understand completely. How about a blanket? You could try to get some sleep while you wait."

Sarah shook her head. "Couldn't sleep either, but a

blanket would be welcome. I can't seem to stop shivering."

The corporal left and returned with a wool blanket of red paisley design. Definitely not military issue. "Thank you, Corporal Linthwaite."

"You are welcome. And please. It's Hortensia."

Sarah smiled. "Thank you, Hortensia." Sarah paused and then rushed on. "I know you may not be allowed to tell me, but is Kurt all right? It's just that they took him away so quickly. We didn't really have time to talk."

"Captain Heinz is being debriefed. He has done something rather important, as I'm sure you know."

"But that's just it. I don't know, not really."

Hortensia hesitated before smiling again. "I'll let you know something as soon as possible. Now do try to rest." She turned to the door, then stopped and turned back. Leaning her head to one side, Hortensia eyed Sarah thoughtfully. "I don't suppose this little bit will hurt. Jakob and Rebekah Maimaran said to tell you hello and that you and Kurt must visit them again when all of this is over." The corporal winked as an impish grin spread over her face. "Rebekah also said to tell you that El Jadida is a lovely place for a honeymoon."

Sarah couldn't help giggling. Corporal Hortensia Linthwaite was a pearl beyond price. Something in the way she said Kurt's name let Sarah know that they were good friends.

At some point, Sarah drifted off, because she awoke with a start as the western sun slanted through the window blinds. The clock indicated she had slept through the morning and into the late afternoon. Sitting up, she stretched and yawned. The rest had done some good after all.

Raised voices came from the other side of the closed office door. That must be what woke her. Sarah tiptoed to the door and opened it a crack. Hortensia stood behind her desk with her hands on her hips.

"Madame Ahmed, I must ask that you lower your voice and resume your seat. Shouting at me will accomplish nothing. The colonel will be with you when he arrives and not a moment sooner."

The woman to whom Hortensia spoke turned toward the open door. It was Laila, the woman with the beautiful house whom she and Kurt had visited before their midnight trip to El Jadida.

Spying Sarah, Laila's eyes narrowed and her mouth became a hardened sneer. "You again. I suppose it is you whom I should thank for getting my husband killed?"

Sarah swallowed hard. "I'm so sorry about your husband, but Kurt and I only wanted to talk to him about my missing friend. He must have been followed to El Jadida by whoever killed him."

"Perhaps. I really do thank you, you know. Jalal was becoming a nuisance and a liability. You saved me the trouble of killing him myself."

"But we didn't…" Stunned by the woman's harsh revelation, Sarah's words trailed away. "What will you do now that your husband is gone? Will you be safe?"

"Me? I will be…What is the English expression? Safe as houses? Yes, that's it. I will be safe as houses. In London. Our flight leaves in one hour."

"That's more than enough, Laila." Hortensia came from behind the desk, planting herself between Sarah and the Moroccan woman. "Colonel MacFadyen will be none too pleased to hear that you have developed loose lips at this stage in the game."

"What?" Laila leaned out and peered at Sarah. "Oh, I see. You have not told the girl. As you wish. I will say no more."

Hortensia turned around. "Sarah, dear, please go back into the office and close the door."

"But…Tell me what? What does she mean? What are you not telling me?"

Chapter 36

Kurt looked up as the door opened. Hortensia came into the room, pausing a moment before walking to where he sat at a metal table. She tapped him on the arm and handed him a small stack of loose pages held together by a paperclip. "I've just finished typing up your statement. Please look it over and sign if all is in order."

Kurt smiled up at her. "Knowing you, I'm sure every word is correct."

"Thank you, Captain. Your Sarah is lovely, by the way."

"She is, isn't she? How is she doing?"

"Rather well. Getting a bit of sleep at the moment."

"Good. She's had a rough day." Kurt caught Hortensia's hand as she turned to go. "I have a bit of news for you. Reggie misses you a lot."

Hortensia's intake of breath was audible. "You saw him? Is he well?"

"I did. He looked like an Arab. Other than that, he seemed fine."

"Did he say anything about me?"

"Let me see. If memory serves me correctly, his exact words were, 'Tell her she is the dearest person on earth and that I love her more than words can express.' Something like that. Does that sound about right?"

"Oh, yes." Hortensia threw her arms around Kurt's

neck as tears streamed down her cheeks.

The door to the hallway opened again and MacFadyen strode into the room. "That will be enough, Corporal Linthwaite. Captain Heinz has work to do before he leaves for London. Run along now. There's a good girl." He waited until the door clicked closed behind her, then glanced at his watch. "Ten minutes to go over that document. That should give you just enough time to make it to your flight."

"Five. I need to see Sarah before we go."

"Ten and you will be seeing no one before you go. Other than Maitland and myself, of course."

"But, sir. I can't leave without saying goodbye. What will she think?"

"I am not given to understanding the workings of young women's minds. You will leave without seeing her."

"Can I at least write her a note?"

"No communication. London's orders."

Chapter 37

The office door clicked open. Sarah opened her eyes. Despite all intentions, she had fallen asleep again. Hortensia bumped the door wide with her hip and entered bearing a loaded tray.

"Suppertime. I will brook no arguments. You've eaten nothing since you arrived at dawn." Hortensia placed the tray on the low table beside the sofa and removed the covers from a plate and a clay pot topped by a dome shaped lid. The fragrance of a spicy *tagine* of lamb with dates wafted from the clay pot. Sarah was suddenly ravenous. Taking bread, she tore off a piece and dipped it in the stew. The perfect combination of sweet and savory. She ate several more bites before looking sheepishly at Hortensia.

"Oh, I'm sorry. Here I am eating like a pig and I haven't offered you any. It's delicious. Won't you have some?"

"Thank you. No. I ate earlier in the dining room." An expression of discomfort or uncertainty passed over Hortensia's features. She cleared her throat. "Sarah, there is something that I must tell you. I'm not really supposed to talk about it, but I feel that you have a right to know after all you've been through."

Sarah dropped her *tagine* soaked bread on the edge of the pot. "You're scaring me. What is it? Is Kurt in trouble?"

"No, he's being hailed as quite the hero. It's that he was ordered to leave Casablanca."

"Was? Do you mean he's already left? Without even saying goodbye?"

"I'm sure he would have seen you if he had been allowed."

"When will I hear from him?" Voice high with emotion, Sarah grabbed Hortensia's arm.

Hortensia looked startled, then patted Sarah's hand. "Oh, poor you. I'm afraid I really couldn't say. I didn't know he was being sent away until after his flight departed." Hortensia's cheeks turned a rosy hue. "I really am sorry. He quite fancies you, you know. Now I must get back to the bloody typing or His Nibs will have my head. Finish your supper while I arrange for you to be given a ride to the hospital. That is where you're billeted now, isn't it?"

Numb, Sarah could only nod in reply.

By dusk, her bruises and abrasions had been attended by one of the military doctors, who tut-tutted over her not having been seen earlier in the day. With an ice bag for the bump on her head, a hot water bottle for a strained muscle in her back, and more than the recommended dose of analgesic tablets, Sarah crawled into bed just after sunset, but sleep didn't come immediately as she had thought it would. She lay on her back staring at the ceiling, tracing the crack patterns in the plaster with her eyes. Tears seeped down her cheeks and into her ears. Rolling onto her stomach, she buried her face in her pillow, shoulders heaving with muffled sobs. Why did the men in her life always fly away without a word? Damn, damn, damn it all to hell!

Chapter 38

Beatrice entered the ward with a frown on her face, waving a handful of papers. She marched straight toward Sarah. "If you wanted to be reassigned, young lady, you could have at least had the courtesy to say something to me first. Really, Sarah, I wouldn't have expected you, of all people, to be so underhanded." Beatrice came to rest beside a wounded soldier's bed.

Sarah put the final touches on a change of dressing and turned toward her boss. "What are you talking about? I haven't asked to be reassigned."

"Well, you have been." Beatrice threw the orders at Sarah. "Why on earth do they think they need experienced field nurses in England? Last I heard, the Germans hadn't landed there. Not yet, anyway."

Sarah scanned the documents, then looked at Beatrice in bewilderment. "I have no idea. I didn't ask for this. I wouldn't without telling you."

Beatrice's expression softened. "You really didn't know, did you, kiddo?"

Sarah shook her head. The older woman wrapped an arm around Sarah and hugged her. "That's okay, I guess. I can live with losing one of my best. Don't like it, but I can live with it. Start packing. You ship out at the end of the week."

****

On a blustery February morning, Sarah leaned

elbows on a troop carrier's railing watching gray-green swells smash their whitecaps against the ship's steel hull. Queasiness accompanied Sarah no matter where she went, but being up top in the fresh air beat the stuffy, dank atmosphere below deck. They had been at sea for nearly two weeks, the temperature dropping steadily the farther north they sailed. Pulling her coat tighter around her shoulders, she looked out at a gray world—gray water, gray sky, gray ship, gray mood.

She and Kurt had shared so little time together before he went away to God only knew where on the mission for Colonel MacFadyen. He had reappeared long enough to save her from the tormented David Phelps and to tell her he would die for her, then he disappeared from her life again without a word of goodbye or promise of return. That brief period felt unreal, as though the days had never been. Even the events on the Anfa Hotel's top deck had taken on a dreamlike quality. Sarah placed her forehead in upturned palms. *Oh, Kurt, where are you? Why haven't I heard from you? Did you really love me, or was I simply a means to an end? Lord, will I ever know the answers?* Sarah straightened and wiped tears from the corners of her eyes. Crying and feeling sorry for herself wasn't going to change anything or get her patients cared for. England couldn't be more than a day away.

Being assigned to England really made no sense. There were other nurses with greater seniority who would give their right arms for this gig. Who selected her for special favor and why were a mystery. Whatever the source of her luck, maybe the change of scenery would be good for her. She knew it would be good for the seriously wounded men she accompanied. They would get better care in England than the field and evacuation hospitals in North Africa could provide.

A flight of seagulls drifted into view. They swooped down toward kitchen scraps being thrown from the stern, screaming at one another. They were said to be messengers of nearing land. Sarah squinted toward the north where a dark line appeared at the horizon. She should return to her post, but for once she neglected duty. She couldn't bear to go below to the humid, claustrophobic space set aside for the makeshift hospital ward. Something she couldn't put a name to demanded she maintain her vigil at the railing. As the ship sped on, the dark line grew in size until walls of red brown rock appeared beneath a swath of brownish vegetation. Cornwall's Land's End reared up from the sea. The Portsmouth docks and her new assignment would soon be in sight.

****

Sarah shifted her kitbag for better balance as she walked beside a stretcher being carried by two burly sailors down the gangway toward the dock. She held the hand of a boy who faced months, maybe years, of rehabilitation from a crushed pelvis and broken legs, the result of a plane that didn't make the runway before running out of fuel. During the voyage from Casablanca, he cried out at night, keeping the other patients awake. Sarah's presence by his bed seemed to calm his terrors. She had assured him she would go with him to his new hospital.

Icy droplets began falling from the steel gray evening sky. Only 1600 hours and dusk was already settling a misty darkness over everything. The line of disembarking crew picked up the pace. Stretcher bearers reaching the end of the gangway made a dash for waiting ambulances. Half way down, Sarah heard footsteps pounding behind her and her name shouted over the general roar of disembarkation. Turning back, she saw a sailor running toward her.

"This just came for you." The sailor shoved a scrap of message paper into her hand.

Sarah Barrett, US Army Stop Orders amended Stop Proceed with Commander Fraser, British Admiralty Stop

Sarah read the message twice. It didn't make sense. What would the British Admiralty want with a lowly American army nurse? A voice came from the bottom of the gangway.

"Miss Barrett? Commander Fraser, Aide to First Sea Lord, Sir Alfred Pound. You are to come with me, please."

"What's this all about? I can't leave my patients." She pointed toward a stretcher being loaded into a van. "I promised that boy I wouldn't leave him alone with strangers."

"I assure you he will be given the best of care." He glanced at his watch. "We really must be going. The car is this way."

"Where are we going?"

"London."

"But why?"

"I'm really not at liberty to say. Please. We must be underway." He took her arm and guided her to a staff car humming in the lee of a warehouse.

Between the rain and the blackout regulation headlights, the ride through the English countryside might as well have been through a coalmine for all that

Sarah could see through the car windows. It didn't matter anyway because she would have had no idea where she was even if she could see something. All of the road and directional signs had been removed from the south of England in preparation of the dreaded day when the Germans might actually invade the island homeland. Even when they entered the outskirts of London, the streets were eerily dark and deserted. As they neared the city center, vehicular and foot traffic increased significantly. At one corner, Sarah caught a few letters on a shop sign as they turned into the street. King Ch...

The car slowed and stopped by a set of steps with an equestrian statue set halfway to the top. The steps sat between two large ornate buildings that looked as though they contained offices.

The commander came around to Sarah's door, opened it, and held out his hand.

She peered into the night. "Where are we?"

"King Charles Street. The Clive Steps." Nodding toward a building, he continued, "Treasury on the right, Foreign and Commonwealth Offices on the left."

Once on the sidewalk, he led her to a rather insignificant looking door under one side of the steps. It was simple, made of solid steel with large rivets running around the outer edges. He pressed an intercom button. A voice crackled through the speaker on their side of the door. After the commander spoke the pass code, the door swung back and they entered a long tunnel with electric light bulbs strung along the ceiling. The door clanged shut. Sarah glanced over her shoulder to see a soldier, holstering his sidearm, resume his seat by the door.

The farther they walked along the corridor, the louder the noise of human activity became. The tunnel ended, and they were suddenly in the thick of it. Telephones rang. People rushed by carrying papers and folders. Voices shouted. No one seemed in the least concerned that a strange woman had mysteriously appeared in their midst.

The commander led her along the corridor and around a bend. He stopped beside a door and rapped once. A voice from the other side called, "Come in."

The commander turned to Sarah and bowed slightly from the waist. "This is where I leave you, Miss Barrett. The door is unlocked. You may go in." He smiled reassuringly, then turned on his heel. Sarah had no choice but to follow his instructions. Grasping the knob, she twisted it and pushed the door inward.

A figure behind a large wooden desk rose to his feet. "This must be the young woman. Welcome to the War Cabinet Rooms, such as they are. This is my private chamber. Please come in, Miss Barrett." Sarah froze. She blinked rapidly, but couldn't seem to make her feet move. The man chuckled and beckoned her forward. "My dear, despite rumors to the contrary, I do not bite. Won't you please come in and close the door?" The voice came from a smallish man tending toward fat. His bulldog's face smiled at her from around a smoldering cigar clamped firmly in his mouth. He removed the cigar and placed it on the desk ashtray. Gesturing toward the other side of his desk, he continued, "I believe you may know this officer? He has certainly been anxiously awaiting your arrival." From the other end of the desk, Kurt stepped forward and smiled. He looked tired. Sarah pushed the door closed behind her as the blood drained from her head.

"Oh my, do go to her, Captain Heinz. It would not do to have her fall over in this crowded space."

Kurt's arms enfolded her and led her to a chair. Sarah wanted to speak, but she couldn't make her tongue move.

"Water, my dear?" A carafe clinked against a glass.

Taking a sip, Sarah finally found her voice. "Thank you, Mr. Prime Minister." She searched Kurt's face. "How?—Why?—I don't understand."

"Perhaps we should get on with the ceremony. I believe all will be made clear." Churchill picked up the handset of his desk telephone and barked into it, "We can begin."

The door opened and a British officer entered bearing a velvet pillow. He came to rest beside the prime minister. "If you will be so kind, Captain Heinz, I need you over here."

Kurt looked into Sarah's eyes and whispered, "It'll be all right. I love you." He then rose and went to stand before Churchill.

"For acts of most conspicuous bravery and daring valor, I award this, the Victoria Cross, Britain's highest honor, to Kurt Johann Heinz, Captain, United States Army. May you wear it in the full knowledge that it carries with it my personal gratitude and that of the entire nation."

Churchill took the medal from its cushion, leaned toward Kurt, and pinned it above the chest pocket of his tunic. He smiled and extended his hand. "There. Looks quite well, don't you think? Congratulations, and you do have my and Mrs. Churchill's deepest gratitude." The prime minister chuckled. "Without your timely intervention, our conference would have ended before it started. Your president is a most persuasive man. Our sources tell us that Mr. Roosevelt's insistence on a policy of unconditional Axis surrender has many of Adolph's henchmen in something of an uproar." He extended his hand, which Kurt took.

Kurt inclined his head. "Thank you, sir."

"Well done, Captain. Mr. Roosevelt personally approved your receiving this award, you know. I believe he may have a little something for you as well." Churchill turned to the officer still bearing the velvet pillow. "Let us depart for the map room so these young people might have a moment of privacy. I believe Miss Barrett deserves an explanation."

The prime minister and his aide disappeared as the door clicked shut behind them. Kurt came to Sarah and knelt beside her. Taking her hands, he said, "I'm sorry you weren't told. Orders sent me here straight from Casablanca. Please say you forgive me."

Pain, fear, and uncertainty filled Kurt's eyes. Sarah laid her fingers against his cheek. "I'll forgive you only if you tell me the whole story, or is that another secret that you must keep?"

His arms slipped around her, pulling her to him in a gentle but firm embrace. His lips brushed her forehead, her cheeks, her hair, finally settling onto her lips. Sarah's lips and arms developed minds of their own. She returned his kiss and caresses with an intensity matching his.

He broke their kiss and pulled back, searching her face. "I love you. You do know that, don't you?" When she nodded, his eager mouth found hers once more. Sarah would have gladly stayed just as they were, but

Kurt broke their embrace once more.

"It's time you understood all that has happened since I left you after we returned from El Jadida."

Kurt then told her about Raisa, Helmut, the impersonation, Sfax, his return flight to Casablanca, and being ordered to London under strictest secrecy. When he stopped speaking, she remained quiet for nearly two full minutes. Finally, he asked, "Do you forgive me for leaving without saying goodbye?"

Sarah nodded and tilted her head to one side. "Of course I forgive you. I love you. And if that wasn't enough, you saved my life and the lives of the two most important men in the world." She drew a long breath, still struggling to absorb everything Kurt had said. "But there are things I still can't work out. Who killed Jalal in Jadida?"

"We're not sure, but most likely it was Phelps. I suspect he followed us there."

Sarah nodded. "Yes, that makes sense with what we now know. Poor man. He really was a tormented soul, you know."

"Yeah. I guess, but it doesn't excuse betraying his country and putting so many lives at risk. The man was a traitor, sad story or not."

Sarah mulled over the harsh words. Kurt was right about David, but even so, part of her ached for him and his Rosa. She wondered if she might not have acted as he did if she found herself in the same situation. Thank God she would never have to find out. Frowning slightly, she said, "What about Helmut and David? They were both in trouble with the Nazis over girls. Was that just coincidence?"

"I left out an important detail, didn't I?" Kurt

brought her hand to his lips, then his mouth thinned into a tight smile. "It all started when they were university students at Leipzig. My cousin and David Phelps were friends and roommates who fell in love with a pair of Jewish sisters. Rachel and Rosa Birnbaum were from a prominent Berlin family that sent their daughters to the university. Although I doubt either man knew it, both of them were manipulated by the Nazis because of the women they loved."

"Do you know if Helmut's Rachel is still alive?"

The frown lines between Kurt's eyes deepened. "She died in Dachau not long after the Germans invaded France. I got the feeling from Helmut that he wasn't all that dedicated to German victory because of what happened to Rachel, but maybe that's just wishful thinking. Then again, the *Abwehr,* German Army Intelligence, is made up of old guard *Wehrmacht.* It's no secret inside Germany or out that there's little love lost between the *Abwehr* and the SS."

Sarah made a bridge with her fingers and leaned them against her chin. Something Kurt had told her about David rang a distant bell. "David's German code name was Raisa. That's German for Rose or Rosa, isn't it? How cruel."

Kurt's eyes hardened. "Yeah. The Nazis have a twisted sense of humor. I'm sure they enjoyed the irony."

"Such a tragic story. It's hard to fathom. Four people whose only crime was they loved the wrong person and now three of them are dead because of it. Has our side been able to find out if Helmut is still alive?"

Kurt shook his head. "When this is over, maybe I

can find Helmut and get to know him. He is family, no matter what side he's on."

"I can't stop thinking about those poor girls. How can people be so horrible?"

"When I was a child in Sunday school, I was taught that evil is an external force lurking to entrap the unwary, but I'm no longer given to that superstition. Evil is something much more frightening than an invisible bogeyman. It exists because it lives in the human heart. Take a wrong turn and anyone can become just like the Nazis." Rage tinged Kurt's voice.

Sarah pulled back and studied Kurt's angry face. She had one more question, but she couldn't see the answer. Heart rate rising and fearing what he would say, she asked, "So where does this leave us? Where do we go from here?"

Kurt's anger disappeared as his eyes softened. He pulled her close with one arm while using his free hand to tilt her face so he looked directly into her eyes. "What would you say about the magistrate's office and a marriage license?"

Sarah's heart leapt in her chest, but her joy was quickly dampened by common sense. "With your job, how will we ever make it work? Are OSS officers even allowed to marry?"

Kurt kissed her hand and grinned. "That's my smart girl. Always putting your finger directly on the crux of an issue. You're right. We would have to get permission to marry, but I've already taken care of that pesky detail."

Kurt drew a letter from his pocket and flashed it before Sarah's eyes. She couldn't read the body of the letter, but two things stood out clearly—White House letterhead at the top and Franklin Delano Roosevelt's signature at the bottom.

"So, what do you say, Miss Barrett? Are you willing to change it to Mrs. Heinz?"

Sarah sighed and caressed Kurt's cheek with her fingers. "You still haven't answered my question. How will it ever work with you doing what you do?"

Kurt's gleeful smile disappeared. He answered in all seriousness, "I think that if we can survive an assassination plot, we can make one little marriage work, don't you?"

Sarah's common sense screamed that the two issues were completely unrelated, but her heart told common sense to shut up and stand down. She gazed into the eyes of the man with whom she knew she wanted to spend whatever time they were allotted, be it only a few months or be it a lifetime. "Yes, Captain Heinz, I will marry you."